Owen O'Shea

Stay-At-Home Dad, Wannabe Detective

Also by C. McGee

Exteriors and Interiors ISBN: 978-1-78535-516-5
Feral Chickens ISBN: 978-1-78535-790-9

Owen O'Shea

Stay-At-Home Dad, Wannabe Detective

C. McGee

ROUNDFIRE
BOOKS

Winchester, UK
Washington, USA

JOHN HUNT PUBLISHING

First published by Roundfire Books, 2024
Roundfire Books is an imprint of John Hunt Publishing Ltd., No. 3 East St., Alresford,
Hampshire SO24 9EE, UK
office@jhpbooks.com
www.johnhuntpublishing.com
www.roundfire-books.com

For distributor details and how to order please visit the 'Ordering' section on our website.

Text copyright: C. McGee 2021

ISBN: 978 1 80341 452 2
978 1 80341 453 9 (ebook)
Library of Congress Control Number: 2022921507

A CIP catalogue record for this book is available from the British Library.

Design: Lapiz Digital Services

UK: Printed and bound by CPI Group (UK) Ltd, Croydon, CR0 4YY
Printed in North America by CPI GPS partners

We operate a distinctive and ethical publishing philosophy in
all areas of our business, from our global network of authors to
production and worldwide distribution.

For Momma K, because she loves herself a mystery.
And for Bethy K, because everything is for Bethy K.

Prologue

Lola screamed in my ear, but it barely registered. She would be fine. At least that's what I assumed based on past experience. Unfortunately, I couldn't say the same for myself. Things weren't looking great. I'm a fairly optimistic guy, but it's hard to put a positive spin on a big fork in your leg and a homicidal maniac on your back. On a scale of one-to-completely-screwed, I was somewhere around completely-screwe—

Grunting like a hog with septum issues, I stumbled forward, trying my best to carry the killer on my back out into the cul-de-sac. Our neighborhood street lamps are faux old-timey affairs, cozy but weak. There was no guarantee that making it into their amber haze would result in my being seen and saved, but it was worth a shot. Certainly better than going down in the backyard where nothing but the stars could shine light on my demise.

Just a few more yards, Owen. Don't be a sack. Get there. Move your feet.

I spurred myself onward. It felt like I was coaching again, but with way higher stakes. I wasn't pushing college soccer players to finish off stoppage time, I was pushing myself to avoid death by chokehold.

Whatever. Same difference. Potato, tomato. Right? No. Tomato, potato. No. Fuck.

My cognition was dulling, the pain in my leg sharpening. It was twelve more yards to the street lamp. It seemed like twelve hundred.

Move. Push. Grit.

Coaching buzzwords popped in my head. Trite yet effective, they prodded me on. One labored shuffle followed another and another until the streetlamp was within reach.

Good work. Now what?

Harnessing the dregs of energy that remained, I turned and launched backward into the pole, a last-ditch effort at freedom. The maneuver failed. The grip around my neck was unaltered. The sound of my assailant's back crashing into the streetlamp drew no attention.

Shit. This is it.

I expected thoughts of my wife and daughter to appear in my head. I wish they had. I'm ashamed they didn't. What I got instead were trivial frustrations:

These lamps are useless.

Stupid Homeowners Association.

Why are these pants so tight?

I should have worked out more.

What the hell is in my pocket?

Oh crap, I'm gonna puke.

Please don't puke.

Please don't —

Then came a crackle of static. The voice of my dead mother. "How did this happen?" she asked.

It's a long story...

Some Weeks Earlier

Chapter 1

"Owen, babe, wake up."

"Huh?"

"Wake up. RPS me for it."

"What's that?

"She's awake. Rock-paper-scissors."

"Right. Yeah."

I sat up in bed. Eyes heavy. Mind slow. Still half asleep, I defaulted to rock. Per usual I lost. Having decided the next sixty minutes of my life, I delivered a swift kiss to Izzy's cheek and got out of bed.

"Love you, babe," she muttered, while turning onto her side. "Wake me up if you need any help."

"Love you too, Iz," I replied.

It's true, I love Isobel Bang, she's the wife of my dreams, but goddamn I hate how good she is at rock-paper-scissors. People say it's luck, but it's not. My losses are too frequent for it to be chance.

Best of one and you throw rock right out of the gate? C'mon, O'Shea.

I critiqued my RPS performance while shuffling down the hall in my slippers. My steps were noisy, but I didn't care. Lola was already up, and she would continue to be up for at least another hour no matter how soft my tread.

"Hey, baby girl!" I picked our daughter up and greeted her with an effortful smile. No one is actually excited to see anyone at three thirty in the morning. "That's quite the saggy ass you have there, what you got going on in that diaper?"

Lola cried with indeterminate meaning.

"Alright, you don't want to tell me, don't tell me."

I laid her down on the changing table, undid the excessive number of snaps on her pajamas with a single rip, opened her

1

diaper, and smiled. No poop. Sweet. A quick wipe, a new dipe, and three-out-of-ten snaps later we were out the door and headed to the kitchen. I crossed my fingers on the way. I didn't recall making any bottles, but I hoped that my sleep-deprived memory was off. It wasn't. I had to make one and I did a bad job. A quarter of the formula spilled on the counter, and the straw-like contraption that reduces burbs got left out. I realized the latter mistake before walking away, but didn't fix it. Instead, I convinced myself that the straw is a gimmick, then brought Lola over to the wingback, and plopped down for another night of bottle holding and staring out the window at the cul-de-sac.

Ten minutes later Lola spit up everything.

"Eff."

I got up and remade the bottle *with* the non-gimmicky straw-thing inside.

"Alright, girl, we're good now," I said. "Set for the night. No more mistakes, no more drama."

Man, was I wrong.

Chapter 2

We'd been in the cozy wingback for twenty minutes when I saw it out the window. I'm not sure what *it* was, but it was something. I mean who gets boxes delivered by an unmarked van at four-something in the morning? Well, the Stoneciphers do, obviously. It was happening right in front of my eyes. What I really wanted to know was why?

"Why are the Stoneciphers getting boxes delivered at four in the morning?" I asked Lola.

Lola didn't answer. Mainly because she's zero, but also because she was sleeping.

Wait. Sleeping! Yes!!!

I celebrated my daughter's unexpected slumber in my head, then calmly carried her upstairs to the nursery. I wanted to hustle so I could get back to spying, but hustling with a sleeping baby in your arms is a fool's game. Instead, I laid her in her crib as if I were a gentle sloth parent, then backed out of the room, eased the door shut, and tiptoed back to the study.

As soon as I arrived I turned the lights from dim to off, then got down on all fours and crawled from the door to the picture window. The crawling was unnecessary, but I did it anyway. It seemed to up the stakes in a fun way, like when you're a kid and you commit to the idea that the playground wood chips are real lava.

This time I'm a real detective, I thought.

After settling in on the floor next to the corner of the window, I peeked outside to see if the Stoneciphers were still unloading the van. They were. I was pumped.

I got you, you bastards, I thought.

In reality I didn't have them. Not even close. I didn't even know what they were up to. I was just assuming that it was shady business because it was transpiring at an odd time and

3

because the Stoneciphers suck. It was entirely possible that they were doing something benign, maybe even something good, but my gut told me otherwise, and my gut needed to be heeded. That's what detectives do.

You have to document this, I thought, already feeling like a hard-boiled gumshoe. *Get some evidence on the perps.*

Instinctively, I reached for my phone. No luck. It was upstairs in our bedroom serving as a sound machine. There was no way to get it quickly and quietly without waking Izzy.

What else?

I scanned the study for inspiration. Within seconds my eyes landed on an unopened package on the bottom bookshelf. It contained an action camera—one of those plastic cubes that suburbanites use when they want to feel like extreme athletes.

I crawled over, grabbed it, then swore.

The unopened package was of the thick-plastic, heat-sealed, clamshell variety. The sort of container that requires an acetylene torch and a chainsaw to open. I didn't have a shot in hell of getting that camera out in time.

I tried anyway, grabbing a pair of nearby scissors and getting to work.

As expected, my initial attempt failed. The fortress of plastic squirted out from between the scissor's blades and onto the ground.

I swore, then picked up the package and tried again.

Again, it ended up on the ground.

Another try.

Another failure.

"Grrrr."

I had devolved past profanities, driven to primal expressions of frustration by the impenetrable container, yet I didn't relent. Acting on impulse and anger I went for it one last time. I picked the package up, jammed it into the blades as far as it would go, and squeezed the scissors decisively. As to what happened next, I'm not entirely sure. There was a violent crack, a sudden absence of resistance, and then pain.

"Mmm Fuu Ghh!" I exclaimed in the way you exclaim when you can't exclaim — serious and intense but muffled by gritted teeth and tight lips.

I looked down. The package had fallen to the floor, a line of blood was blooming from my index finger, the blades of the scissors were smeared with red. Not good.

Looking to move quickly and avoid staining the rug, I stood up and made my way across the study toward the tissue box. En route, I did my best to keep a level head both literally and figuratively. Blood and I do not get along. Another glimpse of my own wound and I was liable to go down in a heap.

Once I arrived at the tissue box, I pulled out one after another adding each to the pile I was gripping on my cut. Eventually the stack grew thick enough to prevent the blood from seeping through and I calmed.

No longer on the verge of passing out, I made my way over to the wingback, sat down, and took slow and deliberate breaths. After a minute I felt confident enough to open my eyes.

The first thing I saw was Chip Stonecipher. He was carrying the last of the boxes through the side door of their garage. The next thing I saw was his wife, Alexandra. She was closing and locking the door behind her husband. The opportunity to catch their misdeeds on film had passed.

"Damn it."

Grumbling, I stomped over to the impregnable container, eager to throw it angrily into the trash. Reaching out with my uninjured hand, I leaned over to pick it up. A sharp pain suddenly blazed across my fingers.

"Mmm Fuu Ghh!"

I looked down. The mangled package shined red. A wound like a thick paper cut ran diagonally across all of my digits. Each finger issued blood with abandon. As I processed the visual, my spine and triceps began to prickle, then my mouth grew salty, my legs soft, and my head light.

All at once, I went down in a heap.

Chapter 3

"Holy shit, are you okay?" Izzy shook my shoulder. "Owen, babe, you okay?"

"Huh? What? Yeah, I got her. I got Lola. You stay in bed and get some rest."

Izzy laughed, she was amused now that she saw I was alright.

"We're not in bed," she explained. "You're on the floor of the study."

"I am?"

"Yes, and it looks like you had a rough night."

I sat up, rubbed my eyes, then looked down at my hands. They were caked in blood but none of it looked fresh. The bleeding must have stopped on its own.

"So, what happened here?" Izzy inquired.

"That stupid package happened." I gestured at my plastic foe. "I cut the shit out of myself trying to open it."

"Those things are the worst. Come here, let me see your hands."

I stood and turned my palms up. Izzy looked at them. I looked away.

"Damn, babe, these are bad. You need stitches."

"Sounds good," I replied with forced nonchalance.

Izzy smiled. It was silly of me to feign machismo. She knows I hate stitches.

"Alright then, tough guy, let's go to the kitchen. I'll fix you up while you tell me what inspired you to open that camera in the middle of the night."

I did as instructed. Izzy returned a minute later with the requisite gear.

"So go on then," she prompted while getting to work on my hands. "Explain yourself."

"I was trying to record the Stoneciphers," I replied.

"Oh yeah, what were they up to?"

"No good."

"Of course not, they're terrible people. What were they doing? Was it hard drugs? I bet it was hard drugs."

"No, it wasn't drugs. At least I don't think so. But I didn't see what was in the boxes they were unloading, so I can't say for sure. Definitely something shifty though."

"Okay, but there's a big difference between seeing something suspicious and seeing something that's unequivocally bad. Suspicious isn't that out of the ordinary. Think about it, that entire half of the cul-de-sac is suspicious: the Stoneciphers, the Russians, the Peabodys."

"False," I countered. "Tanner lives on that side and he's awesome."

"Yeah, he's the exception though, everyone else is shady. And even Tanner has his flaws."

"Like what?"

"Like he's kind of slutty."

"Of course he is. He's single, cool, good looking, and bisexual. His opportunities to hook up are infinite. You can't blame the man for capitalizing."

"Fair enough. But, also, he shaves his legs. I don't know why, but I don't like that."

"He has to tape his ankle for adult league soccer."

"So, use pre-wrap like a normal person," Izzy retorted while tying off the last suture in my right hand. "Good, now give me the other one," she instructed.

I lowered my right, raised my left.

"The Russians though, you're right about them," I conceded. "They are a little off. I mean they've been here for three years and we don't even know their names. There's been ample opportunities too, we have those cul-de-sac parties all the time and they've been to like one."

"I know their names," Izzy countered, her eyes still fixed on her work.

"Serious? You've been holding out on me, Izzy Bang. Come on, out with it, what are they?"

"Boris and Natasha."

"Okay, good one."

"What? That's their names. Ryan told me."

"Boris and Natasha?"

"Yeah. Why are you skeptical? Those are the exact kind of names I would have guessed. We know they're Russian and those are Russian names."

"Yeah, *too* Russian. Those are literally cartoon names for Russians."

"Sure they are," Izzy nodded sarcastically. "From the *Boris and Natasha* cartoon."

I opened my mouth to counter but Izzy had already moved on.

"Alright, babe," she said, standing up and putting her suture kit away. "You're good to go. Just keep these bandaged and dry today, alright?"

"No prob."

"Well, maybe a little prob. You do have to change poopy diapers and stuff."

"Shit, I didn't think of that."

Izzy pulled out her phone. "You want me to call a babysitter?"

"No, I got it. And if I don't, I'll just get Riddhi or Elle to help."

"You sure?"

"One hundred percent. Don't worry about me, babe. You have an OR day today, you focus on that."

"Alright, if you're certain."

"I'm certain," I smiled. "Now get that sexy ass upstairs and get ready, those bones aren't going to weld themselves together."

9

Izzy laughed. "Nine years with me and you still don't know anything about orthopedics, do you?"

"Not one thing. My ignorance is part of my charm, right?"

"Yeah, it kind of is."

Amused, Izzy gave me a kiss then headed upstairs with a smile on her face. I checked out her butt as she departed. It did look sexy. The fact that she birthed a child a few months ago seemed crazy. She was already fit and back at work. I, on the other hand, hadn't left the cul-de-sac in two weeks and hadn't seen my abs in two months. I used to look like the "after" picture on a diet commercial, now I look like the "before." Ugh.

It's a good thing I'm charming, I thought.

Then I thought, *What the hell were those Stoneciphers up to?*

Then I thought, *How the fuck am I going to change Lola's diapers?*

Chapter 4

"What's up, my bitches? I brought you all coffee. A small soy latte for Elle, and a large red eye for Owen."

Riddhi laid out the drinks on the table in front of us, talking as she went. The words spilled out of her mouth at a ridiculous clip. It was as if she had already downed a pitcher of espresso with a bit of cocaine thrown in for taste. She hadn't. That's just Riddhi. Based on the velocity of her speech, you would think she was auctioning cattle not having a conversation.

"Thanks," Elle and I said in chorus.

"No worries. Oh my God, Owen, I never knew what was in a red eye, and now that I do, I'm confused as to how your stomach still exists. Why would you do that to yourself?"

"Necessity. If I didn't consume this much caffeine then this girl"—I nodded my head down toward Lola, she was in a baby carrier strapped to my chest, gnawing savagely on her overpriced giraffe toy—"would already have put me in the grave."

Riddhi and Elle nodded sympathetically.

"I don't know how moms that give them the boobies can do it," I went on. "Breastfeeding, and not sleeping, and not getting any caffeine. That shit is a nightmare."

"Eh, I just drank caffeine anyway," Riddhi said with a shrug of her shoulders. "Maybe that's why my boys are such terrors, they've been amped up since birth."—A brief pause and a contemplative look at her Americano—"Fuck it. It was worth it."

Smiling at Riddhi's cavalier remarks on parenting, I reached for my drink, exposing my bandaged hands to the girls for the first time in the process. A parade of questions immediately followed. In response I detailed the previous night's events in their entirety. Riddhi and Elle were a good audience. The former provided theatrical reactions at all the appropriate moments, the latter listened intently, coffee cup perched on her bottom lip, eyes wide.

"Those fucking Stoneciphers," Riddhi said, the instant the story concluded. "We should call the cops. No, we have to call the cops. It's like our civic responsibility to call the cops. Look at what they've already done to your hands. They have to be stopped."

Riddhi's response made me smile. She sounded like my mother both literally and figuratively. The similarity of their voices is striking, and the tenor of their support even more so. Once Riddhi's in your corner, she's in your corner—infinity percent, no exceptions, for life. I love that. It's one of the things I miss most about Mom.

"I'm loving the enthusiasm, Riddhi, but I think a call to the cops might be premature."

"Very premature," Elle added. "Don't get me wrong, I would love to have dirt on the Stoneciphers, nail their pretentious asses to the wall, but there's just not enough evidence. In fact, there's no real evidence."

"There is too enough evidence," Riddhi contended. It was half-hearted. She knew we were right, she just objected on principle.

Elle offered nothing more than a look in response—half a smile, eyebrows raised, head tilted to the side. *I love you, girl, but come on,* that's what the look said.

"Yeah, yeah, I know you're right," Riddhi conceded. "It's just Alexandra Stonecipher is such a bitch. Why isn't that a crime? Can that be a crime? Can we report her for that?"

"Oh, for sure," Elle replied, sarcasm heavy in her voice.

"Absolutely," I added. "Just yesterday the news had a story about a guy that got convicted on three counts of bitch."

"Ha, ha, laugh it up, ya turds," Riddhi answered, taking the ribbing in stride. "Obviously, I know bitchiness isn't a crime. If it were you two would already be locked up."

"And your sassy ass wouldn't be?"

"Of course I would be, but that's beside the point."

"And what's the point again?"

"The point is that we may not have enough to report the Stoneciphers right now, but that doesn't mean we can't get enough to report them in the future."

"Interesting," Elle said.

"Very," I agreed. "You have an idea?"

Chapter 5

"I know you wouldn't dream of having an epidural, but that's not the only way you can ruin the birthing process. For instance, some mommies-to-be think that it's okay to use things like nitrous oxide or Pitocin during labor. They think that those kinds of drugs are gentler and therefore acceptable, but that's simply not the case. A proper, low intervention, natural birth does not allow for anything that hinders your ability to be fully present. Baby can sense that sort of thing. Baby knows if Mommy is not completely there when it enters the world. That's why I gave birth to both of my children completely drug free."

The second I heard this sanctimonious bullshit leave Alexandra Stonecipher's mouth I realized that Riddhi and Elle had been right all along. Truth be told I used to think that their disdain for her was a bit overblown. That all changed when Izzy got pregnant. Alexandra Stonecipher, that judgmental taint, didn't even offer us a congratulations. The moment she found out about the pregnancy she just jumped right in and started preaching and disapproving. I remember her words verbatim because I couldn't believe she said them. I just stood there slack jawed as they spewed out of her thin-lipped butthole of a mouth. When I looked over at Izzy, I assumed I would find a similar expression on her face, but I didn't. She wasn't stunned at all, and when it came time to respond, she did so calmly and simply with just a hint of attitude.

"That's not quite what I learned in med school," she said.

It was an amazing reply, brief and biting.

I had some choice words to add, but Izzy gave my arm a squeeze that indicated she preferred I refrain, so I kept my mouth shut.

"Oh, so you don't have a natural birthing plan?" Alexandra condescended.

"Well, I have a plan," Izzy replied, picking up an hors d'oeuvre. "I plan on going to the hospital and doing what the OB tells me to."

"I see, well I suppose a natural birth isn't for everyone."

"True, at least not anymore. I mean back before modern medicine I think it was all the rage."

Alexandra responded to Izzy's words as if they'd been a slap, first stunned then furious. She stomped off without a peep, suddenly eager to join her husband in a conversation about investments I didn't understand with the Russian neighbors I barely see.

Impressed as usual with my bad ass wife, I laid a smooch on her cheek. She gave me one back, then casually returned her attention to the hors d'oeuvres table, declining to give the hostile exchange another thought. I didn't let it go quite as easily. I scowled at the Stoneciphers at least six more times before the night concluded, and I've watched them like a hawk every day since.

***

For some reason this story, the origin of my disdain for the Stoneciphers, was running through my head while Riddhi laid out the plan. As a consequence, I missed the entire thing. I had no idea how we were going to snoop on the Stoneciphers.

"Sorry, can you repeat that?" I asked.

"What part?"

"All of it. The whole plan."

Riddhi shook her head and exhaled in frustration.

"Yeah," I nodded. "Sometimes I feel like that about me."

Riddhi smiled despite herself then repeated everything. It didn't take long. The basics of the plan were as follows: One, wait until the Stoneciphers leave. Two, grab the leash for Riddhi's dog, Diva. Three, go outside holding the leash and randomly call Diva's name so that it looks like we're searching for her. Four, under the auspices of searching for the not-missing dog, snoop around the outside of the Stoneciphers' house and see what we can find out. Five, arrive back at Riddhi's with a bunch of dirt on the Stoneciphers.

It was a simple plan, but most good plans are.

Of course, good plans don't always lead to good outcomes.

Chapter 6

We didn't walk directly to the Stoneciphers'. That would have been too conspicuous. Three grown-ass adults making a beeline across a cul-de-sac draws attention—or at least we worried it would. Instead, we traced the perimeter: a right at the end of Riddhi and Ryan's driveway, then past Izzy and my place, past Elle and Sota's, past the Russians', and past Tanner's. We randomly called for Diva as we went—not loudly, but not softly either. The volume was key. So was the amount of concern in our voices. We had to find the right balance, evince enough distress to support our cover story, but not so much that it would result in a gaggle of neighbors coming outside to help us look. I think we succeeded. Evidently, Riddhi did as well. As soon as we arrived at the Stoneciphers', she turned around and flashed a thumbs up, a goofy, childlike grin of success on her face.

I laughed.

Elle looked like she wanted to admonish both of us, but offered instructions instead: "Alright let's split up, walk around the house and see if anything is visible through the windows."

"Got it."

"And make sure to call out for Diva every once and a while."

"Diva!" Riddhi yelled.

"You don't have to do it immediately." Elle said, her eyes closed in frustration, her thumb and index finger pinching the bridge of her nose.

"Oh, right. Got it." Riddhi replied, flashing me a wink. She took two more steps and then called out Diva's name again. "Was that better?"

"Yes, so much better," Elle answered through a begrudging laugh.

17

A smile on my face, I headed off toward the right side of the house. Riddhi went to the left. Elle went straight toward the front door.

I tried my best to proceed at a normal pace, but it was difficult. My strides just naturally quickened. We were about to acquire evidence of the Stoneciphers' wrongdoings and that had me excited.

After I arrived at the side door to the garage, I called out for Diva then looked back to check on the progress of my co-conspirators. Both Riddhi and Elle were still a few steps from the house. I must have been moving even quicker than I realized.

Calm your shit, Owen.

I took a deep breath, then another, then tried the side door to the garage. Half the neighborhood leaves their doors open like its Mayberry, so I figured there was a decent chance of success.

No dice. It was locked tight—the handle and two deadbolts.

Two deadbolts?

It was seriously fishy.

What are you up to, Stoneciphers?

I desperately wanted to know, but I wasn't going to find out via that door, so I moved on. Proceeding through the side yard, I split the difference between the Stoneciphers' house and Tanner's in an effort to not look shifty. If I was honestly looking for a dog, I reasoned, then I wouldn't be hugging one side or the other I'd be walking down the center. It was probably an unnecessary precaution, but whatever.

I kept my gaze fixed on the side of the Stoneciphers' house as I went. It was fieldstone from top to bottom—gorgeous but odd. Something about it just hit the eye wrong, like looking at a poorly photoshopped picture.

"What's weird about you, Wall?" I muttered quietly to myself as I walked.

"…" Wall replied.

Four steps later I muttered, "Shit."

My right foot was soaked. I'd stepped into a low point of the yard, the area between houses where drainage gathers. It was cold and dirty and my sneakers had let it all soak through. Gross. I was tempted to take my shoe off on the spot, but I refrained.

You need your shoes on. Stay focused. Find the evidence.

I moved around the corner to the back of the house. Riddhi was already there.

"Anything?" I asked, while visually scanning the place.

"Nope. You?"

"Not really...Well... Maybe. I mean nothing concrete, but there is some stuff that seems off. Come here, check this out."

I walked Riddhi back the way I had come.

"Does anything about this wall seem odd?"

"Yeah, it's the sidewall of a garage and it's made out of fieldstone—real fieldstone, not just a façade. You know how expensive that is? What an insane use of money."

"That's definitely correct, but that's not it—at least not totally. There's something else that's off about it."

"Sure, there's no windows."

"Yes! That's it. Wait, no it's not. Lots of garages don't have windows."

"True, but the Stonecipers' garage used to. They covered them up a few months back. Didn't you notice when it happened?"

"No, but that's around the time Lola was born. Those first six weeks I didn't notice anything, I just survived."

"I don't miss that age."

"Nope. Brutal." I shook off the memory and plowed on. "Anyway, the solid wall isn't the only weird thing, come over here and check this out." I walked Riddhi to the side door. "Two deadbolts. What the hell is that about?"

"That is weird," Riddhi said, with clear enthusiasm. "Like super weird. No one around here has the side door to their garage locked down like that?"

"Exactly."

"They are *so* up to something. I knew it. I totally knew it. Do you think Izzy's right, you think it's drugs? I mean I can see it. And it lines up with what you saw last night. But I could also see it being something else. What if it's like money laundering, or stolen goods, or—" Riddhi cut herself off with a gasp. Her face lit up with a mixture of excitement and fear. "Murder! Oh my God, Owen, what if it's murder. You know what, now that I think about it, they seem super murder-y."

I laughed. Then I stopped.

Shit, I thought, *they do seem kind of murder-y.*

Chapter 7

The idea went from laughable to plausible in the span of a breath. Maybe the Stoneciphers *were* homicidal maniacs. Why not? I mean homicidal maniacs *are* people, and the Stoneciphers *are* people. That's not nothing.

Oh my God, yes, it is nothing. It is literally nothing. Keep it together, Owen. You're losing it, man. Rein this in.

"The homicide hypothesis seems a bit rash," I said to Riddhi. "I think we should try and avoid being impetuous."

I didn't mean to sound like an asshole, it just came out that way.

Riddhi was having none of it.

"Alright, three things," she replied swiftly, her voice filled with a cartoonish amount of attitude. "One, don't be a dick. B, a hypothesis is supposed to be a possible explanation based on the evidence you've got, so I don't think it's crazy of me to throw the idea of murder out there. And three, or C, or whatever, don't use words like *rash* and *impetuous*. That's Elle's job. She's supposed to be the smart, obnoxiously level-headed one. We can't have two of those, it will throw off the whole group dynamic."

"Yeah, I could hear the arrogant twat-iness in my voice as I said it."

"I'd be surprised if you couldn't. It was—"

A crash cut Riddhi off mid-sentence.

"What the fuck was that?!"

"Dunno."

"It was close, huh? Not real close, but close."

"Yeah."

We paused and listened.

"Holy shit did you hear that?" A mixture of fear and uncertainty took hold of Riddhi's face.

"Uh-uh."

"It sounded like a scream. A muffled scream, but a scream."

We waited for more.

Nothing.

Riddhi shook her head. "Maybe I'm just hearing things."

"Yeah," I said, with more confidence than I felt. "Probably."

Looking for composure, Riddhi returned her attention to the Stoneciphers' side door. "I'm not imagining this sound though. Listen."

I moved closer to the door as suggested.

"You hear that?"

"What?"

"That loud fan noise."

My eyes widened as the sound came to the fore.

"Yeah, I missed it at first too," Riddhi said, reading the dawning comprehension on my face. "It just blended in."

"What do you think it is?"

"Not sure. It sounds like some sort of industrial fan or something."

"Maybe a massive AC unit?"

"Could be, but if it is, it's a crappy one. It's way too noisy."

"Yeah, and the Stoneciphers would never purchase a low-quality version of anything," I reasoned aloud. "So, if it is a fan, or AC, or whatever, it must be cooling off something serious, keeping things super cold."

Riddhi gasped for the second time in five minutes.

"What?" I asked, confused.

"Think about it, Owen. Why would the Stoneciphers need some sort of massive cooling unit?"

"I don't know." I shrugged my shoulders. "Why?"

"To keep the dead bodies cold. Obv."

Chapter 8

Riddhi's suggestion was ridiculous, wildly speculative, irresponsible even. But I couldn't quite laugh it off. I put my ear directly against the side door in the hope that a closer listen might provide some insight into the origin of the noise. It didn't. All I learned by smashing my cheek up against that metal door was that metal doors are hard.

"Owen," Riddhi chided. "That's not looking-for-the-dog behavior."

"Alright, alright."

I pulled my ear away from the door and stepped out into the side yard. Riddhi moved in the same direction.

"Diva," she called out with appropriately moderate intensity.

"Diva," I echoed.

Then came a different call, one that stood in stark contrast to the restrained efforts of Riddhi and I, one that was laden with legitimate concern for a lost pet.

"Diva, girl! Where are you? Come on out!"

Riddhi looked over at me, an oh-shit expression on her face. Within a second she was calling out to her husband, running in his direction, waving her hands over her head.

"Ryan! Babe! Ryan, over here," she cried out.

Ryan took no notice. It wasn't malicious, he wasn't intentionally ignoring his wife, he was just focused on finding Diva. Ryan loves that little dog. He doesn't like to admit it, but he does. He wanted a large, stoic, masculine creature—a Great Dane, a Wolfhound, a Newfoundland. What Riddhi brought home was Diva: a throw pillow magicked into a canine. I was there when the puppy arrived. Ryan tried to act disappointed, but you could tell his heart wasn't in it. That fluffy, smashed-face, little monster won him over the second it came in the door. He will do anything for that dog. If Riddhi didn't get to him quickly there would be trouble. He'd have the entire neighborhood out looking.

"Ryan! Ryan! Hold up. Let me talk to—" Riddhi gave up mid-sentence. The opportunity for intervention had passed. Ryan was already speaking with the Peabodys, Tanner, and a couple I didn't recognize. Even the Russians were headed over, Boris's stride uneven, Natasha's long and graceful. It turns out we live in a nice area where authentic cries for a missing pet result in numerous offers of assistance.

Stupid neighborliness. Sometimes helpfulness is so unhelpful.

Riddhi slowed once she realized it was too late. I caught up with her before she got to the group.

Riddhi, this is bad, I thought but didn't say. What good would it have done? She could see that it was bad. Helen Keller could see that it was bad. I took a beat to come up with something constructive.

"We need a distraction," I said.

"Good idea. I'll lead them away. You go get Diva out of the house then track us down and act like you found her."

"Sounds good...Wait. No. It's your house you shou—"

"Ryan, hey, babe." Riddhi cut me off. She had to. We were within a couple of yards of the group. "I didn't think you were getting home until late."

"The meeting got canceled," Ryan explained succinctly, his mind plainly preoccupied with finding the dog. "I heard you guys calling for Diva when I got out of the car. What happened? How did she get out?"

"You know it was the weirdest thing, I opened the door to go get the mail and she saw a vole and she just took off after it."

A vole. Seriously? Come on, Riddhi.

"Okay, which way did she run?" Ryan asked, his face as earnest as ever.

"Her collar, did she have this on?" Natasha followed up, the tone of her heavily accented voice even more grave than Ryan's.

"Yeah, I'm pretty sure she had her collar on, and she went that way." Riddhi pointed vaguely into the middle distance. The entire search party traced the trajectory of her finger with their eyes, peering off into the dusk in the hope of spotting the lost animal. A couple of seconds later, their visual inspection having yielded no results, the group started to walk in the indicated direction.

Riddhi hung back from the group to boast. "Oh my God, I'm so good. What was that, thirty seconds? Thirty seconds to divert the entire search party. I'm operating on an entirely different level right now."

"Yes, your vole ruse was a real winner."

"Thank you." Riddhi smiled, ignoring my sarcasm.

"Babe, come on." Ryan interrupted from thirty yards ahead, urging us to catch up. "Owen, you too."

"I'm on my way, hon. Owen has to stay here though. He's watching Lola and he has to stay within the baby monitor's range, so he can't leave the area."

"Of course. That works well actually, he'll be here if Diva comes back."

"Yeah," I said, flashing a thumbs up. "I'll keep looking around here and I'll give you a call if I find her."

Ryan nodded then turned and continued with the search. Riddhi jogged off to catch up with him. I headed toward their house, feeling better about the current state of affairs with each step.

We're almost in the clear, I thought. *All I have to do is pop in, grab the dog, pop back out, and then make a call. This investigating business is cake. Maybe I really should be a detective.*

I took a few more steps and thought some more.

Well... Maybe not. I mean this first snooping effort has had a hiccup or two. I am sneaking into a friend's house to grab a dog that's not missing, so we can pretend that it was missing, while that same friend is out leading the neighborhood on a fake search. Meanwhile my other friend is… My other friend is… Wait. Where the fuck is Elle?

Chapter 9

"Where the fuck is Elle?"

I said it out loud the second time. No one was around to hear, but I did it anyway. The childish part of me was hoping that if I gave voice to the query it might spontaneously resolve itself—you know, a puff of smoke, and, voila, there she is.

It didn't work.

Debating how to proceed, I stood frozen on Riddhi and Ryan's porch, my hand resting on the handle of their front door, my eyes gazing across the street at the Stonecipher's place.

I should get the dog, right? Get problem one under control before addressing problem two. But what if Elle is in serious trouble? Maybe she got hurt, or trapped, or locked in a freezer full of dead bodies, or—

No, that's crazy talk. Just get the dog, Owen.

Having decided on a course of action, I turned the handle on Riddhi and Ryan's front door, opened it up, and stepped inside. I was almost done closing the door behind me when a pair of headlights caught my eye. They were obnoxiously bright with a blue tint. There's only one household in the cul-de-sac with cars that possess such lights: the Stoneciphers. They were back early.

Shit.

Diva instantly moved down my priority list. There was no debate this time around. If someone found Riddhi's dog in Riddhi's house there would be questions, but those questions had plausible answers. Elle not so much. If she got caught, she was screwed. We were screwed. At best, she would make up some bullshit excuse that the Stoneciphers would accept, but doubt; as a result, their awareness level would go up; as a result of that, our investigation would become borderline impossible. At worst, the Stoneciphers would catch Elle snooping outside their house, murder her, chop her into cubes, and make her into a nice bourguignon.

Since I didn't want my friend to get eaten, I hustled across the street. I tried to be casual about it, but hustling and nonchalance are mutually exclusive, so I failed. The Stoneciphers could tell something was up the second they stepped out of their oversized, overpriced vehicle. I could see it on Chip's face. The way he looked down his nose at me was different than normal, still haughty, but with an added note of distrust.

"Hey Stoneciphers!" I said, as peppy as I could muster.

Chip frowned.

Alexandra smiled.

I looked for their kids then remembered they were at boarding school.

"Sorry to bombard you the second you get home," I continued, "but I wanted to let you know that Riddhi and Ryan's dog is lost and that there's a search party out looking for her."

"Oh no," Alexandra said, squeezing my arm. "They have that little mixed-breed right? Dilly?"

"Diva."

"Right, Diva. Oh, that's terrible. Of course we'll come help you."

"Awesome!" I steered Alexandra away from her house. "Come on, most people headed out this way. Riddhi saw Diva run—"

"Why aren't you out looking?" Chip interrupted, halting our departure.

I turned around to reply. He was scowling, but I kept my tone friendly.

"I have to stay close to our house. Lola's napping and the range on the baby monitor is limited."

"I don't see a monitor."

I turned my head and pointed to the tiny earbud in my right ear.

"That's not a baby monitor."

"You're right, it's better. The world's smallest long-range earbuds connected to an old tablet in Lola's room."

Chip grunted, unimpressed.

"Don't be so disagreeable, Chip." Alexandra chided. "Let's just go and help."

"Fine, just let me change first. I don't want to traipse around in a five thousand dollar suit."

"Oh yes, I should change as well," Alexandra agreed. She turned toward me and gave my arm another squeeze. "We'll just bring our stuff in from the car, then put on appropriate attire and come right back out."

As the Stoneciphers returned to their vehicle, I looked around for Elle, hoping to confirm that she was no longer snooping around the outside of their house before they headed toward the door. I spotted her almost immediately. She wasn't outside though. She was inside, staring through their living room window and into my eyes.

Chapter 10

I immediately met Elle's gaze and mouthed the words "What the fuck?"

She mouthed back something unintelligible.

I shrugged and shook my head.

She mouthed the words again.

I shook my head again and waved at her to exit.

She held up her index finger and crawled out of view.

Trying my best not to freak out, I looked back at the Stoneciphers. Chip was closing the driver's side door, Alexandra the trunk. Elle had thirty seconds max.

Frantic, I looked back toward the picture window. Elle had returned. She was holding up a sign that said: STALL.

I mouthed the word "no," but Elle didn't see. She'd already disappeared back into the house.

Crap.

Seeing no other option, I decided to do as Elle requested, or, at least a poor approximation of what she requested, blurting out the first lie that came to mind.

"We-were-thinking-of-giving-Lola-all-her-vaccinations-at-once-what-do-you-think?!"

Alexandra stopped in her tracks. "What did you say?"

"I said that we were thinking of getting all of Lola's vaccinations done at once."

The discordant nature of my words should have given Alexandra pause. The fact that I was soliciting medical advice from a neighbor with no medical background despite having a wife that's a physician, should have made her downright suspicious. But nope, Alexandra was so confident in her own internet-researched expertise that she didn't give it a second thought.

"Owen, that is positively unthinkable," she scolded. "Giving your child all of those vaccinations at once is tantamount to child abuse. Indeed, giving your child *any* of those vaccinations is tantamount to child abuse. You might as well shoot a syringe full of autism directly into her veins. I mean to think..."

Blah, blah, blah. Yadda, yadda, yadda. I gave zero shits about Alexandra's stance on the measles-mumps-rubella vaccine, but the longer she talked, the more time Elle had to get out of the house, so I let her blather.

How the hell does Chip endure this shit?

I did a quick glance in his direction, expecting him to be fully checked out, but the opposite was true. Chip was alert, present, listening, assessing. And he wasn't just listening and assessing what his wife was saying, he was assessing me as well.

Wait, why is he assessing me? Shit. He knows something's up. It's okay, just stay calm, and whatever you do don't look toward that big picture window. He'll see you look, then he'll look, then Elle will get spotted, then everything will go to shit. But everything will be fine so long as you don't look. Just don't look.

Do.

Not.

Look.

Obviously, I looked. After that, I freaked out about looking. After that, I freaked out about the possibility that Chip saw me looking. Then I reined in the crazy, calmed my ass down, and attempted to properly gauge the situation.

Another glimpse in Chip's direction provided little information. His face was as inscrutable as I wanted mine to be. Maybe he saw me steal a glance or maybe he didn't. Maybe he didn't care either way. I couldn't tell, and in all likelihood it didn't matter. Elle flashed out of sight the second I moved my eyes toward the window. I saw nothing more than a momentary flicker of her sweater, which means Chip saw nothing more than nothing.

"...so you see, better hygiene, better sanitation, better refrigeration, these are the breakthroughs that actually eliminated diseases such as measles, meningitis, and polio. Vaccines played absolutely no role. Indeed, it's quite possible they exacerbated the problem," Alexandra concluded.

"That makes so much sense," I lied.

"I'm so glad to hear you're coming around. You know the last time we talked..."

Alright, Elle, get your ass out here. If I have to hear another five minutes of this garbage, I'm going to tear out my earballs. Not to mention the Diva business that still has to be dealt with. Riddhi is probably wondering what the hell's —

A bark interrupted my torrent of thoughts. It was followed by another and another.

Fuck.

They were loud and close.

Is that Diva? That can't be Diva.

I checked my immediate surroundings for the dog. There was nothing but grass and driveway and beautiful landscaping.

"Aren't you going to get that," Chip said, scrutiny in his eyes.

"What's that now?"

I looked down at my pants. The bark was coming from my pocket. It was my phone, because, of course it was. What sort of clever detective doesn't leave their ringer on full blast?

"Sorry about that." I pressed mute without looking at the screen and returned the phone to my pocket. "I just changed my ringtone; guess I'm not used to it yet."

"Right."

The skepticism in Chip's voice was palpable. He knew something was up. Since I had no idea how to deal with this actuality, I decided that the best course of action was to plow onward, to behave as though I were oblivious to any and all weirdness.

"So yeah. Wait, where were we? Diva, right? I was trying to get y'all to help with the search."

"No," Chip replied, an edge in his voice. "That's why you initially came over here and it seemed urgent, but then you started talking about immunizations."

"No, honey," Alexandra contended. "I was the one discussing immunizations. Owen was just—"

"Yes, Alexandra, you were the one talking about them, but Owen was the one that broached the subject."

"Is that right?" Alexandra pondered out loud. "I don't think that's ri—"

"Yes, it's right. It's also odd considering the dog search was such a pressing matter. So why did you bring up the topic of vaccinations, Owen?"

"I, uh..."

"Because it seems clear to me that you have some sort of ulterior motive."

"A what? Ulterior motive? I don't even know what that—"

"Come on now, don't play dumb with me."

Chip took a step toward me. His body posture was confrontational—shoulders back, jaw forward, muscles tightened. He wanted me to be intimidated, but I wasn't. I'm significantly more athletic than Chip. Also, he was wearing a salmon-colored dress shirt, and I was not going to get my ass kicked by a guy in a salmon-colored dress shirt.

"Oh, relax Chip-othy," I said, flipping to a casually confident voice.

"Don't call me that."

"What, Chip-othy? That's your name right, Chip-othy Starboard Stonecipher?"

"No. It's not. And you know it's not."

"Are you sure—"

"I'm done with you," he snapped. "Get off my property."

"No problem." I took two steps backward onto the sidewalk. "I'm off your property. You happy?"

It was a childish move—the move of an annoying sibling—but it was also funny.

"That is not—"

"What? Off your property? Because it is."

"You know what I meant."

"Of course, that's why I did it."

"Why you—" Chip cut himself off, biting back the insult.

"What?" I grinned. "What am I?"

"No, you know what? I'm done with your antics. I'm calling the police!"

"Sweet. Go for it."

He was bluffing. He had to be. I'd been an asshole, but not a call-the-cops level asshole. Plus, Chip and Alexandra are criminals and criminals don't voluntarily bring the cops to their house...

Unless I'm wrong, I thought. *Maybe they're not up to anything shady. Maybe they're just old money dickwads. Maybe...*

Chip pulled his phone out of his pocket and slid his thumb across the screen. I watched intently, eager for an answer. If he called the cops, then he and Alexandra were innocent. If he didn't call the cops, then they were up to something. I didn't know what exactly, but something. Probably cannibalism.

Chip held the phone down near his waist. I couldn't tell if it was for my benefit or the benefit of his eyes. Either way it gave me a clear view of his screen. He flicked away a cryptocurrency chart, slammed his thumb into the green phone icon, then with slightly less conviction into the keypad icon, then in a routine way into the nine, then rather hesitantly into the one, and then he looked up at me, his thumb hovering over the final digit, his face intent with deliberation. He wanted me to flinch, but I didn't. Instead, I shrugged my shoulders and tilted my head a bit to the side. It was the most irritatingly cavalier response I could think of and man did it work well. Chip's anger went up to eleven. He was legit old-timey cartoon level mad — red face, smoke from the ears, steam whistle sound — real Yosemite Sam stuff.

I stared at his phone in eager anticipation. A decision was coming. Chip was too pissed off to stay idle.

One last push, that's what he needs. Do it. Push.

So I did. I pushed. Not too much, just a little. Rather than running my mouth I offered a smile of the taunting, impish variety. It was the right move. I knew it instinctively. There was no way Chip could leave it alone. If he didn't press that button now, then he never would. And if he never would, then that told me all I needed to know.

Here it comes, the moment of truth.

Chip broke eye contact, looked down at his phone and —

"Look guys, I found Diva!"

Chapter 11

I like Tanner, but at that moment I wanted to tear off his shaved legs and beat him to death with them. His timing could not have been worse. Chip was about to reveal everything, but nope, Tanner ruined it. The frustration must have been evident on my face because Tanner's pep evaporated the second he laid eyes on it.

"Uh oh. Did I screw up? I thought we were supposed to find Diva."

"Yes," Chip echoed knowingly. "I thought we were supposed to find Diva."

"Of course we were," I said, shifting into the appropriately cheerful tone. "That's awesome that you found her. Riddhi and Ryan will be so glad."

"Happy to help," Tanner replied, the concern evaporating from his voice.

"Did you already let the rest of the search party know?"

"Not yet, I can call them right now."

"No worries, I got it."

I pulled out my phone and dialed Riddhi. She picked up immediately.

"What took you so long? We're out here traipsing through suburbia, getting devoured by mosquitoes, looking for a dog that's not lost, and you've just been doing what? Seriously, what have you been doing?"

Riddhi clearly had space between herself and the other members of the search party. She was free to say what she was thinking. I was not. Chip, Tanner, and Alexandra were all within a five-yard radius. It was going to be an interesting conversation.

"Hey, I got some good news," I said, completely ignoring her opening remarks.

"Don't you 'I-got-some-good-news' me..."

"That's right, we found Diva!"

"..You had one simple task..."

"Yeah, she was up here by the house."

"...and you couldn't even..."

"Uh huh, yeah, Tanner found her."

"...manage—Wait, what'd you just say?"

"Tanner found her."

"Owen, what are you talking about? How the fuck did Tanner find her?"

Oh crap. How did Tanner find her?

"Did you set that up or did he find her inside the house? How could he even get inside the house? Did you—"

"Excellent! See you in a sec."

I ended the call abruptly. Riddhi was not going to be pleased, but it had to be done. I needed to figure shit out posthaste and that was not going to happen with her in my ear.

"Are they all headed back?" Tanner asked, as jaunty as ever

"Yup. Everybody is pumped."

"Cool."

"Uh huh, yeah, cool." My response was lackadaisical. I was too flummoxed to come up with anything better. How the hell did Tanner get the dog? I ran through possible explanations in my head, but each seemed more implausible than the last. Then it dawned on me, a genius insight: I could ask him.

"So, how did you end up with Diva?"

Tanner looked confused. "Well, we went out looking for her and then I found her."

"Right, yeah, I meant where did you find her?"

"Oh, she was in the side yard between your house and Riddhi's. She must have found her way back home after she finished chasing that mouse."

"Vole," I corrected, because I'm an idiot.

"Huh?"

"Vole, Riddhi said it was a vole not a mouse."

"A vole? Is that a real thing?"

"Great question."

"I'm googling it." Tanner pulled out his phone and commenced typing.

"So, Owen," Alexandra cut in. "Now that Dilly has been located, perhaps we can go and talk some more about vaccinations."

"Yeah, sure, that sounds good."

"I'll join you," Chip declared with icy authority.

"Of course, the more the merrier," I replied.

Chip was thrown by my hospitable response, an understandable reaction given the hostilities we'd just been sharing. The idea that I'd welcome him into my house for coffee and a chat was unthinkable a few seconds prior. Whatever. It didn't matter that it didn't add up. It didn't need to. All it needed to do was keep him out of his house for a little bit longer. Elle had to be close to done in there.

"Vole," Tanner read aloud from his phone. "A small, typically burrowing, mouse-like rodent with a rounded muzzle. Huh, you learn something new every day."

Chip had no interest in Tanner's zoological aside. He ignored it, stepped closer to me, and spoke: "I don't know what you're playing at, Owen, but I'm having none of it." There was venom in his voice, almost enough to drown out the arrogance.

I opened my mouth to offer a snarky retort, but got distracted before getting it out. I'd spotted Elle in the distance. She was sprinting through backyards—the Stonecipher's, into Tanner's, into the Russians', into I don't know, I lost track of her. I assumed she was making her way around the-cul-de sac via backyards so that she could pop out with the rest of the search party. It was a good plan, but I honestly didn't care. All that mattered to me was that she was outside and away from the Stonecipher's place. That meant she was safe and my distraction duties were done. It was time to play the baby card and get the fuck out; I'd figure out how Tanner found Diva later.

"Oh!" I made a surprised face. "I think I just heard Lola on the monitor." I pressed the earbud in deeper. "Yup, that's her. Sorry, gotta run."

And without another word, I strode away, a smile of relief on my face.

Then Riddhi yelled my name.

Chapter 12

Before I knew it everybody was back. The entire search party, the entire cul-de-sac, all of them gathered around me. At first I was uncertain as to why I had become the coalescing point, then I looked to my right and saw that Tanner was standing next to me, Diva still tucked under his arm. The crowd wasn't gathered around me, they were gathered around the dog.

Good, I thought. *My presence won't be missed.*

I turned and started once more toward the house.

"Where are you off to?" Riddhi inquired, instantly halting my progress.

"I think I heard Lola on the monitor."

"No, you didn't."

"Yeah, I'm pretty sure."

"Oh really? Let me hear." Riddhi plucked the bud from my ear, held it up to her own, then tossed it back to me. "Nope, she's fast asleep."

"Are you su—"

"Fast." Riddhi stated again, a snap in her eyes. "Asleep."

And just like that my exit strategy was kiboshed. I covertly stuck my tongue out at Riddhi, but offered no further protest. She was right, I needed to stay and help. When the mess is a group effort, the cleanup should be as well.

Having assured my continued presence, Riddhi turned her attention toward the hero of the moment. "Tanner," she beamed. "Thank you so much! If Diva had disappeared on my watch Ryan would never have let me live it down."

"Oh, it was nothing."

"No, for real, you saved my butt. So tell me, how did you find her?"

A curious smile fleeted across Tanner's face. He glanced in my direction and then back to Riddhi. "Well, I was out looking for her and then I found her."

"Right, yeah, I just meant where did you find her?"

"Just there," he pointed to the side yard between Riddhi's house and ours. "She was laying in the grass sunning herself."

"Lounging in the sun, yeah, that sounds like Diva."

"So, we did our goal?" Boris interjected, matter of fact. "Dog is found."

"Yup, the dog is found!" Riddhi answered, the decibel of her voice indicating her words were for the group as a whole. "Thank you everybody for helping with the search."

"Happy to do it."

"That's what neighbors are for."

"I needed more steps today anyway."

Generic courtesy.

Safe mediocre joke.

Polite departing remark.

Etcetera.

Etcetera.

I didn't know exactly what the last few comments were, but I was happy they were being made. They portended a conclusion to the craziness, an end to the snooping mission turned shit show. But unfortunately, they were just a tease. Elle saw to that. She arrived just in time to stop everyone from dispersing.

"Excellent, you found Diva!" she said with convincing enthusiasm.

"Yes. The handsome one found her." Natasha replied.

"Don't call Owen handsome," Elle grinned. "It will go to his head."

"Who is this?"

"Owen," Elle replied louder and slower, as though Natasha's English skills were to blame for the confusion. "Don't call him handsome or it will go to his head."

"I was not talking about this one," Natasha gestured toward me. "I was talking about this one." She gestured toward Tanner. "The handsome one."

"Oh, I see." Elle adjusted quickly. "It was Tanner that found Diva. I thought you were talking about Owen."

"No, I said the handsome one." Natasha retorted, as though she could not have spoken with greater clarity.

"Sure, well, you know there's six men here and they're all handsome."

"This is not true."

I laughed. I couldn't help myself. Sure Natasha was knocking my looks but goddamn it, it was funny. I love interacting with blunt Eastern Europeans. Their words are like little hammers.

"Yeah, Tanner is the handsomest of the bunch." Riddhi agreed. "Look at that chin, it's like granite but stronger."

I laughed again. Ryan gave his wife a playful push on the shoulder. Boris nodded as though he were acknowledging an interesting and uncontestable new fact. Tanner gave an oh-you-guys wave of his hand. Chip turned and marched off in a huff. None of the reactions surprised me.

A moment of uncomfortable silence passed before Alexandra interjected a non sequitur, her tone divulging zero acknowledgement of her husband's surly departure.

"Owen, your shoes are dirty," she announced.

Everyone looked down at my sneakers, capitalizing on the offer to blow past Chip's tantrum without comment.

"Yeah, what is that? It's a weird color."

"Rust is what this looks like."

"Maybe mud?"

"No, it's too reddish to be mud."

"You know you scrub that with some baking soda and white vinegar and…"

The next five minutes were spent discussing stain-removal techniques. When I was younger I would have found it to be insufferable small talk, but not anymore. Lola's stained over half my wardrobe. If Riddhi and Ryan's boys hadn't gotten home and interrupted, I'd still be on the topic.

"Mom, Dad, why is the front door open?" Ajay inquired. He yelled the question from their front porch, a lacrosse stick with gear dangling off of it slung over his shoulder.

"I don't know," Ryan responded, mildly puzzled.

"Yeah, I don't know," Riddhi concurred while flashing me a you-idiot look.

"Don't worry about it, probably just an accident," Ryan said with a shrug.

"Yeah," I echoed. "Probably just an accident."

It was an accurate assessment. I certainly hadn't meant to leave the door open. I must have forgotten in my rush to get over to the Stoneciphers.

Ryan moved on without another thought. "Hey, babe, now that the boys are home, you want to go grab a bite to eat?"

Riddhi swiftly agreed. She didn't need to stick around. Elle was back and the mystery of Diva's escape had just been resolved, it was time to put a bow on this dumpster fire of an initial investigation.

Within a minute of Riddhi and Ryan's departure nearly everyone was headed back to their respective homes. Alexandra and I were the two exceptions. She wouldn't let me get out of there without firming up a time to continue our discussion. I was tempted to agree to something just to escape, but I didn't. I stayed strong, evaded like a champ, and by some small miracle got out of there a free man, my appointments calendar still unmarred by a bullshit anti-vaxx convo.

When I finally got back home, I immediately headed upstairs to check on Lola. She was still conked out so I tiptoed out of her room, walked directly to mine, and collapsed into bed like a felled tree. I slept like that—fully clothed, face down, arms at my side—until Izzy got home thirty minutes later. She woke me with a kiss on the cheek and followed it up with two questions.

"Rough day, huh?" Then, without waiting for a response. "Why is there blood on your shoes?"

Chapter 13

Lemon juice and salt? Maybe hydrogen peroxide? No, that will bleach the fabric.

I'm ashamed to say that these were the first thoughts that popped into my head after Izzy mentioned the blood. I'm okay with being a stay-at-home dad, and I'm proud to be married to a badass physician, but sometimes it feels like domesticity has consumed me; like the real Owen is gone, devoured by diapers and bottles and laundry and chores. It's a terrible feeling for anyone, but especially for a dude. I know that's not politically correct, but fuck it, it's true, or at least it feels true, especially in the wake of a particularly emasculating thought. I mean Izzy had just pointed out blood on my shoes, it was evidence in support of my suspicions, confirmation that something grisly had gone down at the Stoneciphers, yet what was the first thing that came to mind? Stain removal. Ugh.

"Are you sure it's blood?" I sat up and looked down at my shoes.

"Yup. I've seen a lot of dried blood and that's dried blood."

"You're positive."

"Actually, I'm negative—O negative." Izzy winked as she stripped down for a shower. "You see what I did there?"

"Uh huh, very clever."

"It was a blood-type joke. You get it? A play on words. You asked me —"

"Oh my God I get it, you turd," I wrapped Izzy up in a playful bear hug.

She squealed, gave me a kiss, then turned on the shower while asking me about the origin of the blood on my shoes.

I spent the next ten minutes filling her in on the afternoon's events. By the time I concluded, she'd finished her shower and was drying off.

"I don't know, babe," she said while scrunching her hair in a towel. "I mean I can imagine the Stonecipers trafficking in white collar drugs. I can even imagine them eating human meat—God knows they're obnoxious enough foodies. But serial killers? I just don't see it."

"What about the weird hum from the garage? Or the hesitation in calling the cops? Or the blood?"

"Well, the weird hum could be almost anything. There's an array of equipment that emits that sort of noise. Refrigerators, freezers, computer servers, amplifiers, HVAC units, ice machines..."

"Yeah, alright."

"What's next? The police thing."

I nodded.

"Well, you said it yourself. You were being an asshole but not a call-the-cops level asshole. Maybe Chip felt the same way. Maybe it was just an empty threat from the beginning. Plus, you can't be certain about whether or not he would have made the call because you got interrupted by Tanner, right?"

"Right."

"So there you go."

"And the blood?"

"Yeah, the blood is weird. Still, I feel like there are more plausible explanations than serial killers. And even if they are serial killers, why would the blood be in the yard?"

"Fair point," I nodded reluctantly. "But then again, I don't know. I mean you know how the houses in this neighborhood work. Everything drains into the side yards."

"That's true. I don't know what the developers were thinking."

"Right? They're like little swamps. It hasn't stormed in weeks, but that side yard was still marshy."

"And bloody."

"Yeah, and bloody."

"Alright, I'll admit that's a little odd."

I jumped off the counter and gave Izzy my finger guns celebration complete with "pew pew" noises and multiple holster draws.

She rolled her eyes, an amused expression on her face. "What are you pew pewing about? I didn't say that you were right. I don't think they're serial killers."

"True." I blew the smoke from each barrel and reholstered. "But you did concede that the blood was, and I quote, 'a little odd.' That's a pretty big win."

Izzy smiled, went onto her tiptoes, and gave me a kiss. It started as a cute kiss, but I successfully transitioned it into a sexy one. From there her hands went to my waist and mine to her butt. She undid my belt and then my jeans. I squeezed her ass with one hand while drawing her hips closer with the other. My clothes dropped to the floor. Her towel did the same.

Then Lola woke up.

Izzy went and got her.

I stayed in the bathroom with an erection and a frown.

Chapter 14

"Owen, babe, wake up."

"Huh?"

"Wake up. RPS me for it."

"What's that?

"She's awake. Rock, paper, scissors."

"Right. Yeah…Wait, no. Don't worry about it, I got her."

"Are you sure?" Izzy was slightly thrown by the departure from our routine.

"One hundred percent. You have that big case tomorrow. You rest up."

"Oh, okay," she replied, puzzled but pleased. "Thanks, babe."

"No problem, my love."

I gave Izzy a kiss on the cheek, grabbed my phone (Izzy's was the sound machine tonight, I made sure of that), exited the bedroom, and headed toward the nursery.

"What's up, girl?" I asked Lola with genuine pep. "You ready for another father-daughter stake out?"

She wasn't, but after I changed her diaper and got her a bottle she was.

As we settled into the wingback, I pulled out my phone. I intended to open the camera, but before I got to it, I noticed a bunch of new texts on the group chat I have with the girls. Based on a quick assessment it looked like I'd missed about twenty back and forths, although most of Riddhi's contributions were Bitmojis and GIFs, so really just half that.

The first text from Elle explained that she hadn't intended to break into the Stoneciphers, that she just saw a window cracked and impulsively climbed inside. The last text from Elle said: *No, I want to tell you both in person. Coffee at our regular time.* The last text from Riddhi was a cartoon of her dressed like an avocado, riding a ladybug.

I was tempted to search for a funny GIF to send back, but didn't want to get distracted, so instead just typed out, "I'll be there!" and pressed send. I didn't wait for a reply because there wouldn't be one because it was three in the goddamn morning.

"Alright, girl," I said, looking down at Lola, finally ready to commence with our surveillance. "Let's do this stakeout."

I sat up straight, opened the camera app on my phone, flipped it to video, and poised my thumb over the red button. Lola continued to drink her formula. We sat like that for the next five minutes. Other than the amount of liquid in Lola's bottle, nothing changed.

I was undeterred by the lack of action. I'm realistic, I know it's not how it is on TV. I know that actual stakeouts are arduous affairs, that they take days not minutes, that the bad guys don't show themselves at convenient moments—

"Lola, oh my God look at that!"

A white delivery van was making its way down the cul-de-sac. It moved at a slow and smooth pace. The driver was trying to avoid suspicion, but he was doing the opposite. No one drives that slow unless they're lost or up to something.

I pressed the record button on my phone.

Lola spit out the nipple of her bottle and made a velociraptor hatchling noise.

"Yeah," I replied. "I think you're right. It looks like the same vehicle that was there last night."

Lola fussed. It sounded like it had less to do with the van and more to do with air in her stomach, so I raised her to my shoulder and rubbed little circles on her back. That didn't work because that never works, so I set down my phone and changed the circles into a pat. She belched immediately.

"There it is!"

The gas expelled, we resettled ourselves in the wingback and watched as Alexandra, Chip, and the short delivery driver with the low-slung cap, emptied the van. Alexandra struggled to lift some of the boxes, and the driver had a hitch in his giddy-up, but the three of them still managed to unload the whole thing in less than five minutes. It was a marked improvement from the night before.

As soon as they were done, I held Lola out in front of me so that we could converse face to face.

"They were moving fast, huh, girl? There's only one explanation for that increased pace. The Stoneciphers know we're onto them. They're feeling the heat!"

Lola looked at me, shook her head no, and then spat up. The puke flew over my shoulder and landed on my phone, which was laying on the table, recording nothing but the ceiling.

Chapter 15

"Have you ever been to The House on the Rock?"

These were the first words to leave Elle's mouth the next morning. She didn't even greet us, she just handed Riddhi and me our coffees, sat down at her outdoor table, and asked the question.

"Elle, what the hell are you talking about?"

"The House on the Rock, have you ever been there?"

Riddhi and I shared a look of confusion then shook our heads no.

Elle carried on, undeterred.

"Alright, well The House on the Rock is this weird tourist attraction in Wisconsin. Originally it was just a vacation home built by some wealthy eccentric, but then it turned into something else. I don't know if the guy lost his mind or what, but as the years wore on, he started adding rooms onto the house—big rooms, more warehouses really, and he filled these warehouses with random curios: dolls, guns, miniature houses, suits of armor, carousel animals, automated instruments—"

"Creepy old stuff, we get it."

"Yeah, that's an understatement actually. I saw that place when I was twelve and I still have nightmares about it. I'd never seen anything like it, and I haven't seen anything like it since. Until yesterday."

"The Stoneciphers' place?" The skepticism was clear in my voice. "What are you talking about, they have parties there all the time, that place is straight out of an interior design magazine."

"Correct," Elle replied, her tone enlivening. "But only for the parts of the house where they host the parties."

"Okay, so what? The rest of the house is nothing but scary rooms filled with weird antiques?"

"Exactly."

"What? Seriously?"

"Yes. It's awful. It's like a sadistic antiquarian's fever dream. The study was nothing but taxidermied animals and vintage guns next to porcelain dolls and rusty toys."

"No way."

"Yes way, and that was the best one. Another room was filled with old fashioned children's clothes and used prosthetics."

"Jesus Christ."

"Yeah, he was there, too. Eerie Jesus paintings, graphic Jesus statues, weird crucifixes, basically an entire collection of the most disconcerting religious iconography I've ever seen."

Riddhi shivered dramatically; whole body, heels to head.

"Yeah, it was unnerving. Look at these." Elle pulled out her phone to show us pictures. They did not disappoint. If anything, she had undersold the freakiness. The place was a veritable cornucopia of ghoulish shit: prams next to antique surgical equipment, tarnished rattles beside rusted animal traps, theater masks, gas masks, plague masks, crude homemade masks cut from burlap. They even had an iron lung. Who the fuck owns an iron lung? I didn't even believe it at first. I had to ask the group for confirmation.

"Yeah, that's an iron lung," Elle replied.

"Yeah, that's an iron lung," Riddhi concurred. Then she whispered, "What's an iron lung?"

"It's like a polio remedy."

"Why do they need a remedy? Can't they just get off the horse and drop the mallet?"

"Polio not polo. One's a disease, the other—" Elle closed her eyes and took a deep calming breath through her nose. "You know what, not important."

I laughed. Riddhi may or may not have been joking. I'd put the odds at fifty-fifty.

"So what *is* important here?" Riddhi asked, plowing ahead with new questions. "What's the big takeaway? Is it that the Stonecipher just have a whole bunch of scary-ass rooms? I mean I'm not pooh-poohing it. That's good info to have, but it's not enough to get them thrown in jail or anything."

"No, there's more," Elle said, equal parts excitement and trepidation. "Actually, there's a lot more."

"Alright, out with it, girl."

"Okay, so the first thing—and it isn't all that odd, but it did seem worth noting—is that intermixed amongst all of the terrifying rooms was one somewhat normal room."

"Probably one of the kid's rooms."

"No, the children's rooms are downstairs, away from all the awful macabre stuff, and they're actually pretty ordinary. This room was different, it was in amongst the horrors, but it wasn't packed with terrifying old stuff, it just had a hospital bed in it."

"Like a modern-day hospital bed?"

"Yeah, a normal, contemporary, beige hospital bed with the rails and the electric recline and everything."

"Alright, what else was in there?"

"Nothing, just white walls."

"Cozy."

"I know. It was pretty awful, all cold and sterile. It's like the room was an obligation, like they had to do it but didn't want to. It doesn't make any sense. Why is it even there?"

"It's probably for old High Pockets Harry," Riddhi shrugged as though the answer was plain to see.

"Who?" Elle and I replied in unison.

"High Pockets Harry. That ancient white guy with the huge ears and the pants pulled up to his pits. The one that totters around the neighborhood every weekend."

Elle nodded her head in dawning comprehension.

I did the same and added an, "Oh yeah."

I knew exactly whom Riddhi was talking about. Izzy and I call him Shufflin' Sherman, but High Pockets Harry is better, so we'll have to make the switch. I never connected the old man with the Stoneciphers. I never connected him with anyone in particular. He's always just been part of the neighborhood, a crotchety but harmless accessory of suburbia.

"I didn't know he was connected to the Stoneciphers," Elle remarked.

"Yeah, me neither. Is he a relative?"

"Oh, I have no idea," Riddhi replied. "I just know that I've seen him coming and going from the Stoneciphers' place, usually during the weekend. If I had to guess, I'd say he's a relative. I mean he must be, right? Nobody that's unrelated is going to voluntarily spend time with them."

Elle nodded in confirmation while pursing her lips in contemplation.

Riddhi gave her an entire three and a half seconds to think before she interjected. "Alright, so what are the other things?"

"Sorry, what's that now?" Elle responded, returning to the moment.

"What are the other things?" Riddhi repeated. "You said there was a lot more. So what's the a-lot-more?"

"Blood," Elle stated simply.

"Blood, like human blood? From a murder victim?"

"I don't know the blood's origin, but it was there."

"Where?"

"A fair amount in the kitchen, a few drops near the study, and a few more near the door to the garage."

"Damn. That's a lot of blood."

"Yeah, certainly more than your average home."

"And what was in the garage?" I asked, excited for an answer to the mystery of the humming noise.

"I don't know, it was locked."

"Yeah, but you were inside the house. Why didn't you just open it up?"

"I couldn't, it had a padlock on it. Two actually."

"The inside door to the garage was padlocked?"

"Twice."

"Wow."

Images of freezers filled with dead bodies flashed through my head. It struck me as a reasonable reaction to the new information. A lot of dead bodies require a lot of freezers, and a lot of freezers make a lot of humming noise. In light of this reality, the padlocks made perfect sense. The Stoneciphers wouldn't want their kids stumbling across dismembered body parts while searching the deep freeze for salmon puffs or gelato or whatever the children of pretentious foodies eat while they're home from boarding school.

Elle and Riddhi must have been entertaining similarly disturbing thoughts. Their faces were grim and their mouths shut. Lola was the only one acting normal, but she doesn't understand anything so that tracks.

Naturally, Riddhi was the first to break the silence.

"Any other disconcerting discoveries?" she asked.

"Yes, one more," Elle replied.

"What's that?"

"Lye."

"Lye, like the acid-y stuff?"

"It's a base actually, but yes."

"Whatever, it's the stuff that dissolves things right?"

"Correct."

"Like... bodies?

"Yeah, it will dissolve bodies."

"Oh fuck."

"Oh fuck, indeed." Elle took a sip of coffee before finishing bleakly, "They had a lot of it."

Chapter 16

We talked about lye for quite a while. How could we not? It's a pretty odd and potentially grisly thing for a family to purchase in bulk. Did you know if you boil a body in that shit, it liquefies in four hours? That's a fact that the Internet seems a little too eager to share.

Despite lye's morbid appeal, we eventually managed to exhaust the subject. It was at that point I decided to communicate my new information. I told the girls how Izzy had identified the stain on my shoe as blood, and how Lola and I saw the Stoneciphers unloading more boxes in the middle of the night. This news paled in comparison to the revelations that Elle had brought to light, but it still deserved mention.

The group immediately tossed around theories as to what the boxes contained. Everything from money to torture equipment was put forward as a possibility. Riddhi and I made an enthusiastic case for the latter but Elle remained skeptical.

"I'll admit there's some evidence indicating that the Stoneciphers might be murderers," she said. "But I see nothing that suggests they're murderers of the perverted sadistic variety."

"Yeah," I retorted. "They're a classier, more refined type of homicide enthusiast."

"Your sarcasm is duly noted, Owen, but I still think I have a point. Not every killer is a torturer. Also—and more importantly—we have no evidence that they're torturers. In fact, we have limited evidence that they're killers."

"Limited evidence!" I countered. "There's a butt-load of evidence: A) blood all around their house, B) possession of body disposal chemicals, C) padlocked doors inside their home, D) rooms chock full of creepy shit, E)—"

"Yes, yes," Elle cut me off. "All I'm saying is that you need solid proof before you can go to the police."

"Yeah," Riddhi retorted. "We have that."

"Not enough. Not to report the Stoneciphers."

"Why, because they're rich? Who cares, we're all rich."

"True, all of us are well off, but we're not Stonecipher rich. Not even close. They're old money and that's a completely different thing. Plus, they're the Stoneciphers."

"So?"

"So, they're *the* Stoneciphers. That family is different. Everyone that's from here knows that."

Riddhi and I looked at each other, taken aback by the snip and rattle in Elle's voice.

"Sorry," she said, noting our reaction. "I don't mean to sound alarmist or anything. I've always hated the people that talk about them that way. It's always struck me as foolish, and that's why I've never brought it up before, but now... I don't know, maybe those people are right."

Riddhi and I stayed quiet and moved forward in our seats, compelled by the foreboding in Elle's voice.

"You see there's an aura that surrounds that family," Elle continued. "It's eerie and elusive, you feel it more than you know it, or at least that's how it is if you grow up here. And you have to grow up here to understand. It's the only way to cobble together the pieces: the muttered comments from your grandparents, the uncomfortable stirring at local social events, the whispered stories at children's sleepovers. Some of it's true, some of it isn't, it's nearly impossible to tell the difference, and people here don't want to. They'd rather stay in the dark with the pieces scattered. That's why the Stoneciphers continue to run this town like some sort of fiefdom. Fear and superstition have inoculated them against all threats to their station. The community has allowed them to become de facto nobility—

powerful and unassailable nobility. And as a result, a bad family has become an evil one."

Silence.

Riddhi and I just sat there slack jawed. Lola too. I don't know how, but she knew it was the appropriate reaction to what Elle had just laid out.

When we did finally muster a response, it was far from profound:

"What the hell?"

That's it. That's all we could come up with.

Chapter 17

"It was bananas, babe. Like scary bananas."

"Like boo-nanas?" Izzy replied with a wink.

"Oh, dear lord, you're the worst."

"If by worst you mean best, then yes." Izzy kissed me on the cheek, did the same to Lola, then walked over and opened the fridge. "Alright, so you're saying Elle's story about the Stoneciphers was bananas, so you think she made it up?"

"No, Elle wouldn't make something like that up. Actually, Elle wouldn't make anything up, not even for fun."

Izzy nodded, while slathering jelly onto bread. "So, what then? You think all the stuff she said about the Stoneciphers is true?"

"I don't know, maybe? I mean she didn't really say anything concrete. Like there were no specific stories. It sounded more like the prologue to an urban legend or something."

"Well then, that's probably what it is."

"If that's the case then Elle has really bought into it, and she's not the type to buy into that sort of thing."

"Weird," Izzy said, biting into her freshly constructed peanut butter and jelly. "If I were you, I'd just ask her. She's cool, she'll talk it out with you."

"Yeah, you're right," I replied.

And Izzy was right. Elle's awesome. I feel comfortable talking to her about almost anything. Unfortunately, this seemed to be the almost. I'm not sure why.

"So, then what's next?" Izzy asked before taking another bite of her sandwich. "You make your case to the cops?"

"No. Not yet anyway. Riddhi and I want to, but Elle's not there yet, and we want everybody on board before we do it. What do you think?"

"Huh?" Izzy turned her ear toward me indicating she hadn't heard my last sentence. I wasn't surprised. Lola was banging the bejeezus out of the rattles attached to her floor seat.

"Hold on," I said loudly, a finger raised in the air.

I walked over to the pantry, got out some liquefied sweet potatoes, warmed them, sat back down, and stripped Lola out of her shirt. I don't bother with bibs. It's easier to wipe the baby food right off her tiny little body.

"So, what do you think?" I asked again while testing the temperature of the sweet potatoes on my top lip.

Lola quieted, watching the little spoon of orange muck with anticipation.

Izzy bit the inside of her cheek and bobbed her head from side to side—her standard I'm-debating-with-myself face.

I decided to venture a guess.

"You think there's something weird about it all, but you don't think they're murderers. Am I right?"

"Mmm."

"I mean you'd be way more concerned if you actually thought they were slicing up bodies across the street."

"Yeah, when you put it that way I think you're right. I *would* be way more concerned if I really believed that. I suppose that means deep down I just don't buy it."

"Oh." I was disappointed—surprisingly so. It's not that I wanted serial killers in the cul-de-sac, it's… I don't know.

"I'm not saying I'd have the Stoneciphers babysit," Izzy elaborated. "And the idea that they're up to something illegal like black market pharmaceuticals or money laundering or some white-collar crime seems totally plausible, but serial killers? I just don't buy it."

"I get it, I do. But I think you're wrong, and I'm going to prove it." I was making a conscious effort to rally past my disappointment because nobody likes a sad sack.

"Yeah," Izzy smiled, happy with my turn toward upbeat and proactive. "How are you going to do that, O'Shea?"

"Uh, get more evidence, duh."

"What sort of evidence?"

"The irrefutable concrete kind, obviously."

"And how, pray tell, are you going to get this irrefutable concrete evidence?"

"Oh, I have no idea."

Izzy laughed, "Well, at least you have a goal."

"Indeed I do, Izzy Bang. Indeed I do." I looked upward and tapped my index finger against my lips. I saw a detective on TV do this once. You could really tell he was thinking hard. "I suppose we'll have to get back into the Stoneciphers' place. That's where the evidence is, so that's where we'll have to go."

"That makes sense, but if you could figure out a way to do it without committing a felony that would be great. I prefer the father of my child out of prison."

"Totally agree. Orange is not my color. The question is, how do I do that?"

I recommenced tapping my index finger against my lips. Izzy joined me. Lola smiled at us, sweet potato dribbling down her chin. Ten seconds passed before Izzy pulled her finger from her lips and pointed it to the sky, eureka-moment style.

"I've got it," she said. "So we can't go into the Stoneciphers' house uninvited because that's against the law, right?"

"Right. So...?"

"So then we just have to get invited."

"Of course!" I exclaimed like I totally got it.

I did not totally get it. I didn't even a little bit get it.

Chapter 18

"Your lawn is looking great. Is that a new mower?"

"Your lawn is looking great. Is that a new mower?" Dear God, man, listen to yourself. Are you just one hundred percent suburban dad now?

"Thanks," Tanner replied, talking loudly over the sound of the engine. He released the handle and the machine fell silent.

Nice, must be battery powered. The gas ones just keep rumblin—Nope. Shut up about the mower, Owen.

The blades no longer whirring, Tanner continued on at regular volume.

"I do think the grass is looking better," he said, surveying his front yard with pride. "The landscaping, too. And yeah, it is a new mower. The old one crapped out on me. I think the mud did it in. It doesn't seem to matter how long you wait after a rain, the side yards are always wet around here."

"I know, it's the worst. Whoever graded the lots in this neighborhood got more than a little carried away."

"Yeah, and you'd think the Homeowners Association would care, but nope. They're more concerned with the color of people's mailboxes and whether or not someone has an online business based out of their garage."

"Don't even get me started on the HOA."

I looked over at Riddhi anticipating another smiling face enjoying the talk. She was smiling, but it was more at us than with us.

"What?" I said, responding to her expression.

"Nothing, I'm just loving all this middle-aged dad talk."

"Oh good, me too," Tanner agreed, without a hint of embarrassment.

The reply made me like him even more.

We bumped fists while Riddhi rolled her eyes.

"Yes, yes, you two are adorable. I have to cut you off though because we've got cookies to deliver."

"Cookies!" Tanner exclaimed, genuinely pleased. "I love cookies. What flavor?"

"Chocolate chip," Riddhi answered, handing over a plate of the baked goods.

"Classic. And what did I do to earn this deliciousness?"

"Helped find Diva. I made some for everybody that joined in the search."

"Sweet, thank you." Tanner peaked under the saran wrap covering the plate. "And these are nut-free, gluten-free, and vegan, right?"

"What? No." Riddhi snipped, borderline offended.

Tanner smiled mischievously. "I'm just fucking around. I love nuts and gluten and vegans."

"Not sure that last one works."

"No, I suppose not," Tanner winked. He replaced the plastic wrap, took a step toward us, and then spoke in a more serious and confidential tone. "Say, did you already give some of these to Boris and Natasha over there?" He tilted his head in the direction of the Russians' house.

"Yeah, why?"

"Just curious."

"Just curious, get out of here with your 'just curious.'" Riddhi scolded. "What's going on? Is Natasha cheating on him? I knew it. It's because she's the taller one."

"What?" I laughed, amused as ever by Riddhi's logic.

"She's taller. Whenever the woman is the taller one in the relationship, she cheats. Everyone in India knows that."

"Riddhi, you're from Tampa Bay. You've never even been to India."

"Owen, quit distracting Tanner. He was on the verge of telling us about Natasha's boyfriend. Or is it a girlfriend! I don't know why, but a girlfriend would be better."

Tanner was enjoying the show. He's been in the neighborhood for a little while now, but this was his first full dose of Riddhi Chakrabarti-Czechowski. I was glad to see he was a fan.

"No, it's nothing like that," he replied. "Although that would be juicy. Honestly, I just wanted to get your guys' take on them. Everyone in the neighborhood has been extremely welcoming except for those two. They're standoffish and weird. It's like they're watching me from a distance. I don't know, I just have a bad feeling, and I thought you might know more about them based on the fact that they actually showed up to help look for the dog. That was the first time I've seen them do anything with the rest of the neighborhood."

"You're right," I said. "That was out of character. They're usually pretty cold."

"Cold!" Riddhi blurted. "Cold is a massive understatement. They're a couple of witch's boobies."

"Witch's titties," I amended.

"Good to know," Tanner said, through a laugh. "That's helpful information."

"Of course it is," Riddhi replied. "We always have helpful information. And now that that's been established, we really do have to go. The whole point of this cookie business is to trick the Stoneciphers into hosting a party, so I want to make sure to get over there before they leave."

"Well then, get out of here," Tanner said, taking the news about our premeditated subterfuge in casual stride.

After Riddhi and I bid Tanner adieu, I gave her some shit for blabbing about the plan then shifted the conversation toward our swiftly approaching interaction.

"Alright, so how are we going to do this?" I asked.

"That's a good question," Riddhi replied. "I don't think there's a hard and fast answer, we just have to play it by ear."

"Right." I concurred, sounding more confident than I felt. It was an easy accomplishment since I didn't feel confident at all. Truth be told, I still didn't fully understand the plan.

"What you have to do is use the Thank You Cookies as a conversation starter, and then you use the conversation to lure the Stoneciphers into hosting a party. If you do it right, they'll think the whole thing is their idea." That's how Izzy explained it to me last night, and then again this morning over coffee with Elle and Riddhi. It sounded like a straightforward strategy; so much so that I almost didn't ask follow-up questions for fear of looking like an idiot. Of course I *did* end up asking follow-up questions, because, fuck it.

"Wait, how is this going to work?" I inquired, as Izzy finished telling her idea to the girls.

"Well, the cookies serve as a—"

"No, the cookies part I get, it's the make-them-think-it's-their-idea part. How am I supposed to do that?"

Izzy gave me a look filled with both affection and pity then transitioned to a new topic. I gained no further knowledge on the matter, maintaining my status as a novice in getting-somebody-to-think-my-idea-is-their-idea. But that didn't stop the group from nominating me to be one of the two cookie deliverers. When I protested my selection, the girls countered by claiming that the Stoneciphers liked me best. I countered them by pointing out that Chip had reamed me out less than forty-eight hours prior. They responded by saying: "Exactly. That happened for a reason."

To which I responded: "Huh?"

To which they said, *Come on, you know,* via their facial expressions.

To which I said nothing because Lola had pooped herself and needed a change.

And that's it. We didn't get a chance to talk further. By the time I got Lola into a new diaper and down for her nap it was go-time, so I go-ed, or got, or whatever. I don't know. The point is that Riddhi and I had just rung the doorbell to a house of probable serial killers, and we were armed with nothing but her above average cookies, our below average wits, and a vague plan to do some sort of Jedi mind trick.

Chapter 19

Alexandra Stonecipher answered the door dressed like she was on her way to spin class, so when the first words out of her mouth were, "I was just about to head off to spin class," I wasn't surprised. What did surprise me was the abrupt shift in her demeanor as she moved her gaze from Riddhi's face to mine—harried and annoyed to sunny and welcoming in a flash. "But I do have a few minutes to talk," she added warmly, amending her declarative salutation from two seconds prior.

That was weird, I thought, as Alexandra guided us through her foyer and toward the posh barstools surrounding the stainless steel island in the middle of her kitchen.

"Would either of you like a refreshment?" she asked as we hopped up on the stools. "Kombucha? Coconut water? They're both homemade."

"Sure," I replied. "The first one sounds good."

I hadn't heard what the first one was, but I didn't care. I just wanted Alexandra to turn around so that we could give the place a quick visual inspection, perhaps confirm some of Elle's prior findings. Unfortunately, the opportunity didn't amount to much. During the time that our hostess was preoccupied, I spied a whole lot of nothing. Riddhi thought she might have seen some dried blood but couldn't say for certain.

"Here you go!" Alexandra set three glasses down on the island. "I really think you're going to love this. I know it's a lot of work to make kombucha at home, but it's worth it. You just can't trust the store-bought stuff, it's all pasteurized."

"Oh, for sure," I replied, claiming the nearest glass. "You're preaching to the choir here."

I had no idea what she was talking about. I thought kombucha was a type of monkey.

"We don't mean to hold you up," Riddhi said, sliding the plate of baked goods toward Alexandra. "We just came to drop off these cookies. I made them as a little thank you for all the people that helped look for Diva."

"Well, wasn't that nice of you," Alexandra fawned in an over the top aren't-you-sweet voice. "And you put them on such a cute paper plate. I haven't bought paper plates in years—you know, because of the environment and the aesthetics—I wasn't aware of how far they've come. These are almost as nice as plastic."

"They are cute, aren't they," Riddhi agreed. It was a generically courteous response, and it left me dumbstruck. In a normal situation Riddhi would have replied to Alexandra's backhanded compliment with the venom of a thousand cobras. The fact that she kept her fangs to herself verged on miraculous. It was a noteworthy testament to how seriously she was taking the plan.

"Yes, super cute," Alexandra concurred, putting the topic to rest. "So, Owen, have you figured out a time for us to sit down and discuss vaccines?"

"Oh… Uh…" I was not expecting the question. Looking to buy time I picked up my kombucha and took a drink. It was a bad choice. Imagine vinegar got a yeast infection and you're somewhere close.

"It's delicious, isn't it?" Alexandra beamed. "And so good for your digestive health."

"Mmmm." I forced a grin. "Mmm Hmm."

"I'm so glad you like it. And don't worry, there's plenty more."

"Yay," I replied, my teeth clenched against the bile tickling my uvula.

Riddhi tried to contain her laughter but two snorts escaped.

"Sorry, allergies," she explained.

"There are tissues in the bathroom." Alexandra pointed to the nearest door, then turned her gaze back to me. "So, what do you think, Owen? Is tomorrow a good day to meet up? Maybe lunch at The Bistro? Or we could do it at either one of our places, my schedule is open."

"Tomorrow, huh?"

"I can make any time work."

"Wellllll..." I drew the word out hoping I'd come up with something inspired by the end of it. I didn't so Alexandra plowed on.

"You're right, The Bistro's not great for lunch. We should definitely do one of our houses."

"Umm, yeah. That sounds..."

"Are you guys talking about vaccines?" Riddhi interjected, hopping back up onto her barstool.

"Yes." Alexandra and I answered in unison. Our words matched, but our tone did not.

"Well, you know that's interesting because a lot of parents at my boys' school have been encouraging the board to take some action on that front."

"Action." Alexandra sounded alarmed. "What sort of action?"

"That's a good question. I'm not sure exactly. Probably something like they did over in Riverside. You know, a stricter application of the state law or whatever. The kids over there really can't go to school until they've had their vaccines, there's almost no exceptions."

"God, what a travesty."

"Mmm."

"You know it's sick is what it is, forcing poison into children's veins."

"Right. Totally. Except..."

Alexandra's eyes snapped toward Riddhi. "Except what?" she demanded.

"Except aren't vaccines supposed to be good?"

"Good!" Alexandra thundered.

"Yeah. Good. I mean I know my boys are older and everything, but when they were little our pediatrician said it was good for them to get their shots. I don't know. There have probably been a bunch of new studies since then. I guess I just don't know too much about what's going on."

I was impressed with Riddhi's approach. She'd struck the perfect chord, provoking Alexandra's passion but not igniting her rage. It was the openness of the last few sentences that did it, the admission of possible ignorance. It encouraged Alexandra to teach rather than tirade, so that's exactly what she did... For forty painful minutes.

Riddhi and I feigned interest the whole time. It was excruciating. And then, after Alexandra concluded, Riddhi somehow managed to kick it up a notch.

"Wow, just, wow." Riddhi said, her jaw slack, her eyes wide, the very embodiment of aghast. "I'm shocked, seriously shocked. How is this still going on?"

"I know." Alexandra tut-tutted. "I'm just glad I could convince you two. The more allies the better."

"You really did convince us. We're here for you. Whatever you need, however we can help, just let us know."

"That is so sweet, but I don't think there's a lot we can do. I mean it's basically impossible to convince people of the truth on this issue. Especially with all the disinformation from the state health department and the American Medical Association. I think that terrible school board resolution is just destined to pass."

"It does seem likely," Riddhi nodded. "Although..."

"Although what?"

"Although you *did* just convince Owen and me."

Alexandra's face lit up. "That's right, I did."

"Yeah, so I'd imagine you could do the same with other people. I mean you explain it so well."

"You're right. I've been too quick to give up. I just need to teach people the way I taught you two, maybe at a big event or something."

"Like a party?"

"Yes, a big party where I can get in front of a lot of people all at once and win them over en masse."

"Brilliant. I love it. But where are you going to have it on such short notice? The school board is going to act fast."

"Good point," Alexandra frowned. "All the nice venues are booked at least a few months out."

"So that's it?"

"I guess. Unless…"

"Unless what?"

"Unless we have it here."

"Here?" Riddhi acted as though the idea had never crossed her mind. "Like *here*, here."

"Yes. Why? Do you think it's a bad idea?"

"No, I mean I wouldn't have thought of it, but now that you say it, I think it's a great idea."

"Yeah?"

"Absolutely."

"Wonderful!" Alexandra clapped her hands. "Then it's settled, we'll have the event here."

Riddhi and Alexandra kept on talking and making plans but I stopped listening. I was too blown away to pay attention.

Holy shit, I thought. *That's how you do it. That's how you convince someone that your idea is their idea.*

Then I thought: *Damn, that was scary easy.*

I spent the rest of the conversation doing a mental review of all the big ideas I'd had over the past few years—new furniture, crossfit membership, car upgrade, hairstyle change, wedding venue, honeymoon destination, house. After a considerable amount of time mulling over each of them, I realized that I had no clue which ideas were actually my own.

Well played Izzy, I chuckled to myself, *well played.*

Chapter 20

The contents of the mirror were disappointing, which was a real bummer because I was the one standing in front of it. I'd like to say that I didn't recognize myself but that would be a lie. I know what I look like. I know that I used to look better. I know that my attractiveness has been on a swift downward slide since the day Lola was born. I didn't always resemble a basset hound after a night of heavy drinking; parenthood did that to me.

I was pushing my cheeks up in a futile effort to remove the bags from under my eyes when Izzy walked into the bathroom.

"What are you up to there, babe?"

"Trying to fix this disaster," I replied, motioning toward my entire face.

"Ah, it's not a disaster. You look good. Distinguished. Anyway, nobody looks their best when they have a newborn."

"I didn't have the newborn, you did."

"I meant in the house, you ass." Izzy gave my arm a light slap.

"Yeah, but you're the one that actually had the baby and you look awesome."

"Eh, I still got this doughy center." She poked her belly.

"You're nitpicking. You look sexy as hell."

I gave Izzy's butt a squeeze, then moved my hand toward her lower back and pulled her in for a kiss. She kissed me back then gave my chest a playful push.

"Get out of here, I've got stuff to do before bed," she said, her tone coy. She wasn't sold on fooling around, but she wasn't uninterested.

"I know you've got stuff to do, and that stuff has a name, and that name is Owen Mickey O'Shea." I posed dramatically, showing off my body the way a game show hostess shows off a prize.

"Is that supposed to be alluring?"

"Oh, it's alluring alright."

Izzy was all smiles. She's a sucker for goofy playful flirting. She pulled me in by the waistband, moved her lips to my neck, and slid her hand down my boxers. My penis went from six to midnight in under a second.

"Mmm, Sloopy's glad to see me," she grinned.

"You have no idea."

She leaned in, her breath hot in my ear. "Tigresa misses you too."

"Yeah!"

"Yeah."

She took two of my fingers and guided them to where they were needed.

"Damn, babe. Tigresa's excited."

"Super excited."

I lifted Izzy up onto the bathroom counter, dropped to my knees, and buried my face in the welcoming warm and wet. The smell and taste immediately brought me back. Pregnancy had changed both, but evidently that change had been temporary. Original recipe Tigresa had returned.

I was tempted to stand up and slide inside, but I mastered the impulse. Instead, I stayed down and worked with my tongue. It has a higher success rate, and it didn't disappoint, getting Izzy to her destination in under four minutes. I think she was loud, but I can't say for certain because I couldn't hear a thing. Her thighs were clinched around my ears like a pair of sexy noise canceling headphones. It was crazy hot. I told her as much.

"Damn, babe," I said. "That was crazy hot."

Izzy gave me a massive grin, shook her head in the affirmative, then leaned back against the bathroom mirror. She was too winded to provide a proper vocalized response, but she didn't need to. Her body language made it clear that I'd done a good job and that made me happy.

"Alright, handsome," she said two minutes later, sitting up on the counter, her breath regained. "I'm ready for you now. Get that sexy ass over here."

I immediately did as instructed and made zero effort to hide my delight.

"Mmm, has Sloopy been this excited the whole time?" She asked, taking him firmly in hand.

It was my turn to be at a loss for words. It felt so good all I could do was let out a low moan.

"Oh, he likes that."

I closed my eyes and nodded my head.

"Good. What about this?"

She guided him slowly toward the warmth radiating from between her thighs. He trembled with anticipation of the wetness to come, every centimeter of the journey delightful agony until finally... nothing. And I'm not talking sweet oblivion nothing, I'm talking *nothing* nothing. Sloopy and Tigresa didn't even touch. Lola's crying interrupted them. And it wasn't the whimpering sort of cry you can ignore for a couple of minutes; it was the death-is-imminent sort of cry that demands immediate attention.

The moment we heard the noise, both Izzy and I took off running toward the nursery. I stopped after a few yards because Izzy had it handled, and because running naked with an erection is awful. By the time I arrived, Izzy had Lola wrapped up in her arms, both of them notably calmer.

"What was it?" I asked. "Did she fall out of the crib or something?"

It was a stupid question. Lola can barely roll over let alone climb out of the crib.

"No, I don't know what it was. A nightmare, I guess. Do babies have nightmares?"

"Of course," I said, not knowing the real answer but wanting to be comforting.

"Alright, yeah," Izzy replied, her face both relieved and affectionate. "Then that's probably what it was. Now why don't you go take a shower and get some sleep. I'll get her back down."

I smiled, nodded, blew both my girls a kiss, closed the nursery window, and headed off to the master bathroom.

"Don't hesitate to have a fun time in the shower," Izzy called out as I made my way down the hall. "I'm not judging."

I looked down at my recently healed hand, then at my erection.

"Yeah, I'll do that," I replied.

A minute later I was asleep on the seat that's built into our shower. I hadn't even touched Sloopy.

Chapter 21

I woke up in the shower two hours later. We have a tankless water heater so there was no blast of cold to wake me up. If my neck hadn't been at such an odd angle who knows how long I would have gone. Izzy certainly wasn't going to wake me up. Her ass was snoozing in the nursery. I found her there after my shower nap when I went to check on things. She was taking up most of the crib, her cute butt pressed against the rails.

"You turd, you even hog your daughter's mattress."

I spoke softly, but Izzy still stirred at the sound of my voice. I leaned over and woke her the rest of the way with a kiss to the cheek. She reluctantly opened her eyes, a confused expression on her face, drool on her chin. As soon as she spotted Lola and me, her look of confusion gave way to one of contentment. I reached out a hand and she took it. We stayed like that for a bit, the whole family gathered together: Izzy and me holding hands, her naked and crusted with saliva, me pruney fingered and sore in the neck, our daughter between us, asleep and oblivious. It wasn't a picture-perfect moment, but it was perfect, and we soaked it up. I'm glad too because the next moment was not great. It's when I looked up at the window and exclaimed, "Oh fuck!"

Chapter 22

I shouldn't have shouted profanity in our daughter's nursery while she was asleep, but I don't blame myself. That's how any parent would react to the sudden realization that their child's window had been closed when they put them to bed but then open when they came back to check on them.

"What do you mean it was open?" Izzy whispered sternly as she pulled me out into the hall.

"I mean it was closed when I put her in the crib for the night, but then when we came back to calm her down it was open. I just remembered that I pushed it down before leaving for my shower."

"Are you sure?"

"A hundred percent."

"Well, why didn't you say anything earlier?"

"I don't know Iz, I mean I wasn't firing on all cylinders. I'm massively sleep deprived, and we'd just been having sexy-time, so my mind wasn't exactly primed to be on the lookout for breaches in our home security."

Izzy took a breath. "Fair enough. I'm sorry I snapped, it's just scary."

"That's okay," I replied, accepting the olive branch. "I'm sorry too."

Our heads more level, Izzy and I attempted to figure out how the window had opened. We had quite a few theories, most of them terrifying: crazy people, burglars, baby snatchers. Fortunately, the most plausible of the theories was also the most comforting. Namely, that the window opened on its own.

When Izzy first presented this hypothesis, I scoffed. Then she reminded me that humidity and air pressure and wind can do crazy things, especially if a window frame is warped or spring-loaded. She also reminded me that we'd had a window open on its own once before.

"It was right when we moved in here," she said. "Remember?"

Her words sparked a recollection. "Yeah, the one up high above the entryway."

"Exactly. And I'm sure that's why we didn't freak out about it at the time, because it was so obvious what had happened. An intruder would never break into that window. It's fourteen feet up and opens into thin air, it would be pointless. And neither of us would ever open it because it's a huge pain in the ass. You'd have to get a ladder or—Actually now that we're talking about it, that's exactly what we did. Remember, we got out that big ladder, almost took a chunk out of the wall maneuvering it down the hall."

"Yeah, that's right." The memory was coming back with greater clarity. "It *was* a huge pain in the ass. I even took down that smoke alarm while I was at it so we'd never have to deal with getting up there again."

"Yes, you did," Izzy replied, her recollection also sharpening. A beat passed, then she added a follow up. "Wait, what did we do with that smoke alarm?"

"It's in the junk drawer in the kitchen."

"Right. Okay. Do we still have one on every floor?"

"We're good. I bought a plug-in one to replace it."

Satisfied with our home's fire safety status and our conclusion about Lola's window, Izzy relaxed and reached out her hand. I took it. We walked back to our room and climbed into bed. She fell asleep almost immediately. I didn't sleep the rest of the night. The explanation for the open window was sound, but I still couldn't shake the feeling that something was off.

What I saw the next night only made things worse.

Chapter 23

Lola was halfway through her nighttime bottle when something moved outside. I didn't see what it was. Probably a person, but I couldn't say with certainty. I only caught a glimpse in my peripherals. It seemed like the movement came from across the street, but it could have been closer. The neighborhood's old-timey street lamps create tricky shadows.

I sat up in the wingback and scanned the cul-de-sac. Nothing.

"Alright, girl, stay vigilant."

Lola kept drinking.

"Carb up first. Good idea."

I stood up and moved us closer to the window. We had the lights off and the blinds drawn so the risk of being spotted was low, but my adrenaline remained high. I could feel it above my Owen's Apple and across my chest—a pressure, both exciting and disconcerting. I think Lola could sense it in me. Her eyes were wider than normal, her body more rigid.

"It's okay, Lo. We got this."

I had no idea what I meant by "this," but it seemed to make Lola feel better. It made me feel better too. My excitement stayed put, but my disconcertion went down.

I peered through a gap in the blinds.

Our front yard was clear, so I shifted my gaze toward the Stoneciphers'.

"It's earlier than normal," I reasoned aloud. "Maybe we'll see some different activity. Maybe the Stoneciphers do even weirder shit at this time of night."

It was a reasonable guess, and it turned out to be kind of right. At least the first part. Because there *did* turn out to be activity that night, much of it unusual, it just didn't come from the Stoneciphers. It came from everyone else.

Chapter 24

The first of the night's happenings was innocuous. Tanner came home with a brunette. She had nice legs and wore a skirt that showed that she had nice legs. They arrived at his house, in her car, roughly fifteen minutes after the bars had closed. Tanner is single and handsome so the scene made perfect sense. I think I would have been more surprised if he hadn't come home with somebody.

Next came Prudence and Preston Peabody, the couple that live stage right of the Stoneciphers. I don't talk about them much because there's not a lot to talk about. That shouldn't be surprising, they're named Prudence and Preston Peabody for fuck's sake. It doesn't get any stuffier than that, nor more boring. Dear God, they're boring. It's like they go out of their way to live up to their names. At least that's typically the case. Not last night though. Last night was the opposite, especially for Prudence. Rather than cautious and sober, she was reckless and shit-faced. I could see it from fifty yards away. Anyone could have. It's fairly easy to spot a drunk person, and it's really easy to spot a drunk person when they drive their own car into their own mailbox. She wasn't going fast, but in a weird way that made it more egregious. It's hard to jump a curb when your speedometer is in the single digits.

As soon as I saw the crash, I headed out to check on everybody in the car, but then I caught sight of Prudence and Preston safely exiting their vehicle so I stopped. Neither of them was seriously injured which meant my immediate assistance wasn't needed. In all likelihood it also meant it wasn't wanted. I remember thinking: *If Izzy and I were in a drunken slow-motion collision with our own mailbox what would we want?* And then I remember thinking: *Space.*

It was the correct choice. The presence of Lola and me would not have made things better. The second Prudence emerged from the vehicle it was clear that she was the hottest of messes, the worst I've seen since college. She was holding her shoes in her hand the way that super drunk girls do, except they weren't heels, they were flats. The ballet style ones. At most those things lifted her a centimeter off the ground.

"When a centimeter of sole is too much sole, you're too drunk." That's what I told Lola.

She looked at me like the fount of knowledge I am, then turned her attention back to the Peabodys. I did the same. Prudence was waving angry drunken arms at nothing, while Preston was flopping down into the driver's seat.

The moment Preston got behind the wheel Lola cast a look of disapproval.

I shrugged my shoulders. "He can't do any worse than she did."

Once again I was correct, but just barely. Preston's performance was only a fraction better than his wife's. It took him a solid four minutes to move the car thirty yards into the garage. His path was circuitous and erratic and bisected at least one flower bed, but he did eventually get there, so all in all it was a win. And as a reward for that win, he got a urinating spouse.

The sight of Prudence peeing took Preston by surprise. She is not the pop-a-squat type of girl, yet there she was, pants down, goods out, pee pee flowing. It was refreshingly improper. Especially the way she was trying to shoot it onto the Stoneciphers' house. True, she didn't really succeed—most of her urine fell impotently onto the grass—but the fact that she even gave it a go indicated a level of balls-iness that was totally unexpected.

"The Stoneciphers must have done something seriously shitty," I informed Lola as I raised her up to my shoulder.

Lola concurred with a burp.

Across the street, Preston arrived beside his wife. I expected him to get mad at her or shake his head disapprovingly and then help her move inside, but instead, he followed her lead. Without a moment's hesitation, he pulled down his pants and started unloading his bladder alongside his better half. His intended target was the same as his wife's, but he was far more accurate. Every drop of his number-one connected with the Stoneciphers' wall, and when he finished, he added some spit to go along with the urine.

"What the hell did we just witness?" I asked Lola as the Peabodys ambled inside. "We have to talk to them. They must have something on the Stoneciphers. There's no way tha—"

Elle cut me off mid-sentence. Not with her words, with her appearance. All of the sudden she was just there, standing in her driveway, staring up at the night sky. I watched on as she moved her hands into her jacket pockets, then pulled them out, then patted herself down, then tilted her head back and breathed a sigh of frustration toward the stars. Something was wrong, or missing, or I don't know.

I considered going out to talk with my friend, but held off. She looked like she needed some alone time, so Lola and I gave it to her... mostly. We still watched of course, looking on as she gave up on the search of her pockets and headed off toward the side yard.

"Where's she going? There's nothing over there."

Captivated, I continued to watch as Elle proceeded toward the space between our houses. As soon as she got out of sight, I turned, exited the study, and made my way to the picture window at the back of our house. While en route I started mulling over whether or not it was cool of me to be spying on my friend. Before I could reach a conclusion, she re-entered my field of vision. She'd made her way between our houses and was proceeding toward the gardening shed at the back of her yard.

What the hell is she up to?

I ran through possibilities in my head, but came up with nothing.

After opening the shed door, Elle took a quick look over her shoulder then stepped inside. The small structure is windowless, so I couldn't tell what she was doing in there, and it annoyed me something fierce. I stared and squinted real hard, but that didn't help. The walls refused to let me see through them. It was a mystery.

Fortunately, that mystery resolved itself the moment Elle opened the door. The billow of smoke that emerged along with her looked like a legit weather front, a dense and defined cloud.

It made me laugh. How could it not? The whole visual was ridiculous: Elle, exiting a gardening shed in a fog of cannabis that would have irritated Snoop Dog's lungs. Had someone else told me about it I wouldn't have believed it, not from Elle. From literally any of my other friends, yes, but not her.

Oh, it's going to be so much fun giving her shit, I thought with a big grin on my face. Then I thought: *Wait, maybe I shouldn't give her shit because then she'll know I was watching her and that's weird.* Then I thought: *Wait, no, I totally do have to give her shit because watching her and not telling her really is weird. Creepy even. Basically, I'm morally obligated to give her a hard time.*

Having acquired an explanation for Elle's mysterious behavior, and having decided upon the most ethical course of action regarding how to handle my observation, I decided to call it a night. It had already been eventful enough. A car crash, two DUIs, two instances of public indecency, and one enthusiastic use of a controlled substance is a lot by suburban standards.

No, that's a lot by any standards, I thought, as I gently laid my daughter down in her crib.

Before exiting Lola's room, I checked her window. I didn't want it accidentally opening again. It was closed tight, but I still pressed both the locks as hard as I could and jammed the newly bought wooden dowel as deep into the track as possible. Then I pressed the locks again. Then, as I pressed the locks a third time, my gaze inadvertently shifted from near to far and I caught sight of the Russians. They were looking out the window through a gap in their blinds. It was a disconcerting visual that struck me as sinister. (Yes, I know that's hypocritical of me to say considering I watch the neighborhood every night, but they don't have a baby so they can't blame their snooping on anything but themselves.)

The subject of the Russians' spying was unclear. I couldn't tell where their eyes were aimed and the window from which they peered offered a view of the entire cul-de-sac. They could have been looking everywhere or nowhere. The latter actually seemed more likely. Nice residential areas can't have too many people sitting by their windows surveilling the neighborhood, right?

Or maybe not? I shrugged. *The suburban busybody is a cliche for a reason.*

Deciding that it was impossible to deduce the motives of Boris and Natasha from a distance of sixty yards, I moved my attention back to the rest of the cul-de-sac. I looked toward the Stoneciphers' place again, but there was still a whole lot of bupkis going on over there. No lights, no movement, no nothing. The Peabodys' was similarly placid. Other than the demolished mailbox and mangled flower bed their house was back to its beige, boring self. Tanner's was also unchanged save the addition of a second floor light, which was now on, presumably for some sexy time. I thought briefly of the brunette's naked legs because I'm human and I'm a straight dude, then I moved on to Elle and Sota's place. It too was back to the status quo.

"All right then," I yawned.

With Lola asleep and the action abated, the extent of my exhaustion suddenly hit. Gritty eyes, heavy body, lumbering faculties, all of it, the whole sleep deprived experience slammed into me in less than one-Mississippi. I rubbed my eyes, gave the locks on the window a final push, the dowel a final jam, then turned and—Headlights.

"Balls."

Screw it, man, just go to bed.

"No. I've come this far."

Having won the argument with myself, I shambled over to the window on the other side of the nursery. Squinting out from under leaden eyelids, I watched as a uniformed policeman emerged from an unmarked Crown Vic, straightened his uniform with three tugs and a smooth, then walked to Riddhi and Ryan's front door.

Riddhi opened it before he even knocked.

Chapter 25

What.

The.

Fuck.

Is this real life?

That's what I thought as I watched the policeman step into Riddhi and Ryan's house. It seemed ridiculous—all of it, the whole night, the whole week. It felt like my suburbia had become a made-for-television-movie suburbia.

What's next? A teen pregnancy pact? A call-girl coven?

Sweet Jesus, it was almost too much to wrap my head around. I mean suspecting the Stoneciphers was one thing, but all of this was something else. The Peabodys, the Russians, Elle, Riddhi, Ryan. It felt like I didn't know my neighborhood. Even worse, it felt like I didn't know my friends.

God, what a terrible thought: *Maybe I don't know my friends.* It kept me up, kept me pacing the living room floorboards, searching for a way to put my mind at ease. And finally, around dawn, I came up with a plan. It wasn't great, but it was something.

Chapter 26

"Friends, what the hell?"

That was my plan of attack. That's what I decided on after hours of pacing the living room floorboards. I'd just ask Elle and Riddhi straight up: "Friends, what the hell?"

The idea struck me as low-key ingenious. Seriously, how often do you see people ask their friends and family direct questions on uncomfortable matters? Not often enough.

Izzy woke up at the same time that my enthusiasm for my plan of attack reached its zenith. I explained it to her the moment she got downstairs. Her response was not what I had anticipated. She looked confused. It actually took me a second to recognize the expression on her face because it's not there very often.

I must have messed up, I thought. *Izzy doesn't get confused.*

And sure enough, I had. I'd skipped right to the friends-what-the-hell bit. I'd given no lead-in at all, nothing about the drunken Peabodys, or Elle and the gardening shed, or Riddhi and the policeman. It was a laughably huge oversight. Izzy must have thought I was drunk, and in a way I was. Not from booze, from tiredness. At some point sleep deprivation equals a .08 BAC.

Round two went better. I included all of the requisite background info and Izzy followed along with ease, preparing coffee while she listened.

"So, that's what I'm going to do," I said, the pace of my words quickening as I approached the end of my spiel. "I'm just going to ask them. I'm going to walk up to Elle and Riddhi like it's no big deal and say: 'Friends, what the hell?'"

I paused and looked expectantly at Izzy, my breathing slightly labored from the rapid way in which I had wrapped up the speech.

"Yeah," she replied, looking down at her coffee, her nose crinkled like she smelled a toot. "Clearly, that's what you should do. Hey, is something wrong with this coffee?"

"Um, yeah, it's French Roast. We're out of the Breakfast Blend. I'll buy some today at the store."

"You're the best!" Izzy's voice was upbeat, ready for the day.

"Alright I have to run. Love you!"

A kiss and she was out the door.

"Love you too," I replied, my words a bit tardy.

I mulled over Izzy's response while I poured myself a cup of coffee. Her casual no-duh reaction to my friends-what-the-hell plan surprised me. It shouldn't have though. She's not like most people, she doesn't hesitate to talk directly. To her there could have been no other plan. Realizing this made me feel stupid, but it also made me feel energized. The next step was evident. There was nothing left to ponder. It was time to go, time to talk to my friends, time to get some answers.

I ran upstairs to grab a hoodie and Lola before heading out to Riddhi's. In my closet I found a fresh and clean sweatshirt. In the nursery I found a disaster. It was bad, like an IED went off in a field of port-a-potties. And Lola was laughing. It seemed sadistic. It wasn't a time for giggles, it was a time for dry heaving. In fact, that's precisely what I did for the entire hour it took to clean everything up. It was brutal. I went through two rolls of paper towels, a bottle of disinfectant wipes, a scrub brush, and a handheld metal shovel. The shovel wasn't a deliberate choice, I just found it behind Lola's changing table while I was cleaning, but I was glad I had it. The main pile of poo was that big.

By the time I was done I barely had enough energy to throw everything away and get Lola downstairs and into her floor chair. I did not have enough energy to actually feed her. Instead, I just spread some pureed banana out on her tray, told her to go nuts, and fell asleep face down on the kitchen table. I didn't even bother to move the macramé runner that lies on top. So what if I woke up with a weird imprint on my face and a daughter covered in fruit. There are worse things. Like parenting.

Chapter 27

I woke up twenty minutes later when Lola started kicking her tray. The noise startled me. I went from face down on the table to upright in my chair in a flash. The macramé runner accompanied me on my ascent. Drool and sweat had fused it to my skin during the half-hour nap. The sight of it all made Lola's day. Her laughter was loud and unfiltered and heartwarming in the way that only a baby's can be.

I took a beat to enjoy my daughter's laughter, then I looked up at the clock. We were late for coffee with the girls, so I plucked Lola from her chair, ran upstairs, stripped off both our clothes, got in the shower with her in my arms, washed our bodies, washed my hair, attempted to wash her hair, gave up and left some banana in there, hopped out of the shower, got us both dressed, and jogged out the door toward Riddhi's.

On the way over I started to feel anxious about my chosen course of action, so I focused my attention in the distance and quietly voiced the decided upon phrase over and over like a mantra: "Friends, what the hell? Friends, what the hell? Friends, what the hell?" The plan was to simply increase the volume of my voice once I arrived at the table, that way it would be done and there would be no backing out. It was a wussy approach, but reasonable, and I suspect it would have worked. Unfortunately, we'll never know for sure. Stupid Alexandra Stonecipher saw to that. I almost saw her too late. "Friends, what the hell—" had already left my mouth.

Chapter 28

"Friends, what the hell—o, Alexandra! How are you doing today?"

"I'm doing quite well, thank you for asking."

"Alexandra came over to give us an update about the party," Riddhi said, bringing me up to speed.

"I prefer to think of it as an *event*," Alexandra corrected. "If we call it a party it downplays the serious and somber nature of the subject."

"Totally," Riddhi concurred, while making a finger-down-the-throat-puke-face behind Alexandra's back.

"I've narrowed it all down," Alexandra continued. "Decorator, bartenders, florist, musicians. Naturally, I have my favorites, but I try not to give all of my business to the same vendors over and over again. It encourages complacency."

I nodded in agreement while rolling my eyes in my mind.

"I also put together an initial guest list." Alexandra handed each of us a piece of paper that contained a large number of names. "I was hoping you all might look through it and give me some feedback, let me know if there's any personae non grata amongst the proposed invitees."

"Of course," Elle replied, her tone casual, as if she'd been asked to do precisely that a hundred times before.

"Excellent," Alexandra clapped. "Now I know most of the cul-de-sac is on the list, but I saw no way around that. The event is supposed to be educational in nature so I can't use my normal excuse for not inviting them—you know something about the event being tied to a philanthropic organization, or a members-only club."

Riddhi, Elle, and I all nodded. In my head I tried to calculate how many times she'd left us off a party list using that excuse.

"I think it will be fine though," Alexandra continued. "No one in the neighborhood is terribly uncouth. Heaven knows we wouldn't live here if they were. Nevertheless, I do question how at ease some of them might be. Boris and Natasha for instance. I know they haven't been in the country that long. An elegant event like this might make them uncomfortable."

"They'll be fine," I said, a bit snappy, my patience for the pompousness waning.

Riddhi and Elle glared at me. *Keep your shit together,* their eyes said.

"Yes, I suppose they will be," Alexandra agreed. "And I suppose it's immaterial anyway. I really don't have a choice now that Boris and Chip are in business together."

Interesting.

"Boris and your husband are in business together, huh?" I did my best to disguise the eagerness in my voice. "What's the venture?"

"Who knows," Alexandra replied. "Chip dabbles in so many enterprises, I can't keep track. Although I must say this one has occupied a great deal of his time as of late."

"Oh yeah?"

"Yes, it's actually been interfering with our home life a fair amount."

"I'm sorry to hear that," Elle commiserated.

"Oh, it's alright." Alexandra gave a wan smile.

"Is it alright?" Riddhi interposed. "Tell the truth."

"Well, no, I suppose it's not. It's actually quite frustrating. I'd really prefer he keep his work at work. I tell him that all the time."

"And does he listen?"

"No, not really."

Riddhi shook her head, "That's shitty. I hate when Ryan does stuff like that."

Alexandra gave a genuine smile, enjoying the unfiltered support. Based on her sheepish enthusiasm I surmised that she didn't have a lot of experience griping with friends.

"Still, I let him do it," she continued. "Even when it throws our home into disarray, even when he becomes a moody grump, I let him do it, and I make it work. The other day he brooded around the house all night because of some disagreement with Boris, and I didn't say a thing, I just shut my mouth."

"Sometimes that's the best way to handle it," Elle consoled.

"Yeah, and sometimes you've got to yell at him," Riddhi added, a consoling comment in its own way.

Combined, Elle and Riddhi were covering all the bases of friendship feedback, so I just nodded my head in general support. At times it's a little weird being the only guy in the group, like I'm intruding on sacred feminine rituals.

I didn't add anything more to the conversation until the venting fiesta reached its natural conclusion. It was hard for me to keep my mouth shut for that long, but it was worth it. The airing of frustrations seemed to put Alexandra at ease, and the more relaxed she is with us, the more likely she is to spill useful info. Plus, when the conversation finally did shift, it shifted in an interesting direction.

"Speaking of disasters," Alexandra said in response to I-don't-know-what. "Did everyone see the Peabodys' mailbox? It's completely obliterated."

"No," Riddhi replied. "When did that happen?"

"It must have been last night. It wasn't like that yesterday."

"Oh, I swear if it was my boys, I'm going to grind their bones to make my naan."

"No, it wasn't your boys, Riddhi" I interjected, kindly saving Ajay and RJ from a lecture.

"Are you sure? Because they're crazy little shits. Especially Ajay, he's totally the type of kid that's going to knock down mailboxes for fun."

"Yes, I'm sure."

"Like *sure*, sure? Like you saw it happen and there were definitely no middle-school-aged Cauc-Indian boys involved?"

I laughed. Riddhi's mash-up of Caucasian and Indian gets me every time. "Yeah, I'm *sure*, sure."

"So how did it happen then?"

Shit. I walked myself into that one.

"Uhh..." I took a sip of coffee to buy some time. I wanted to be straight up. I wanted to tell Riddhi and Elle everything about the Peabodys' accident. I also wanted to ask them why they didn't notice said accident last night. I mean they were awake. Were they too distracted by their clandestine cop meetings and late-night bong hits? Who knows? Not me because I couldn't go down that road with Alexandra present. Grrr.

Unable to improvise anything brilliant, I decided to stick with a reasonable approximation of the truth. Basically, I just described what happened but left out all of the stuff that made the Peabodys seem like they wanted to punch the Stonecliphers.

"That's a shame," Alexandra said as I finished my account, the tsk-tsk subtext conspicuous in her voice. "There's really no excuse for that sort of behavior, especially from them. You know they come from a good family. The Peabodys have been a staple of this town for almost as long as the Stonecliphers. It's quite sad to see them—what's the phrase—go off the rails."

What sort of catty oblique shit is that? I thought. "Uh-huh," I said.

"Anyway, what can you do? If alcohol has got the best of them, then that's the way it is, at least until they decide to clean themselves up."

"Well, I'm not sure it's like that. I don't think they're raging alcoholics or anything. I think they just got a little too drunk and made some bad choices."

"That's such a nice way to look at it, Owen," Alexandra reached out and gave my elbow an affectionate squeeze. I couldn't tell if it was mocking or sincere. "But I have a feeling you're being overly generous in your analysis. Chip and I have been seeing signs of the Peabodys' dipsomania for quite some time now."

"Mmm," I replied through tight lips.

My annoyance with Alexandra was reaching a breaking point, so I excused myself to go make another pot of coffee, regain my patience, and look up the word dipsomania.

By the time I returned, my friends had thrown me under the bus.

"Owen, you don't mind accompanying Alexandra on a quick trip over to Boris and Natasha's do you?" Elle asked. "She just has to drop something off. She wanted some company and we thought you'd like to go and leave Lola with us. You know, get a little breather from baby duty."

"Oh… uh…"

Alexandra looked up at me expectantly. Behind her back Riddhi gave me puppy-dog eyes. Elle flashed a saccharine smile and reached her arms out for Lola.

Ah, friendship. I thought.

"That sounds good," I said. "Let me just run to the restroom before we go."

I didn't really need to pee, I just needed to mutter some profanities and insults under my breath before departure. Of course, if I had known what awaited me at the Russians' place I wouldn't have muttered. I would have shouted my profanities loud and clear and with horror in my voice.

Chapter 29

It took me roughly zero seconds to contaminate the crime scene. The coffee in my mouth came out in a spray the moment I noticed the first body. It was followed soon after by the contents of my stomach when I turned and saw the second. Both Boris and Natasha were dead. No, murdered. No, butchered. There was enough blood to fill a kiddie pool. I remember thinking that at the time. Then I remember feeling gross for thinking that.

Dude, what the fuck? A kiddie pool? Why not an oil drum? Or a bathtub?

Then I realized that was a stupid concern. I had no control over which liquid container my mind deployed as a unit of measurement during a moment of trauma. Plus, it didn't matter.

What matters is that Boris and Natasha are dead. Killed. Brutally. Get it together, man. Shit, maybe they're not even dead. Maybe you're jumping to conclusions. Focus, Owen. Now!

And all at once I did. I took control. Disorientation and queasiness gave way to acuity and competence. Moving quickly, I pulled out my phone, dialed 911, set it to speaker, and placed it on the ground. While waiting for the dispatcher to pick up, I got down on one knee and checked Natasha for a pulse. There was nothing. Her body was above room temperature but not by a lot.

She must have been killed a while ago, I concluded based on no knowledge of forensic pathology.

As I moved over to Boris, the 911 operator picked up. She asked about my emergency, but I didn't answer right away. I was distracted, intent on getting my middle and index fingers onto the right part of Boris's neck.

"What's your emergency?" the dispatcher repeated, speaking louder the second go around. "Please respond if you can. What is your emergency?"

The increased volume of her voice grabbed my attention. I forgot about Boris's pulse for a second, focused on the call, and replied with as much poise and clarity as I could muster.

"My name is Owen O'Shea. I'm at my neighbours', Boris's and Natasha's, house. It's on Benedict Court. I don't know the exact address, but it's the white colonial with the red door at the end of the cul-de-sac. Both of them have been..." I looked around the scene trying my best to process the information analytically. It seemed like a stabbing, so I went with that, "...stabbed? Yeah, I think they've been stabbed, like a whole lot of stabs. There's a kiddie pool's worth of blood here."

Again, with the kiddie pool!

"Alright, Owen, help is on the way."

"Good. Right. Okay."

"Don't hang up, sir. Stay on the line with me."

"Yes. Got it. So, I'm checking for a pulse, is there anything el—Oh, God! Oh, that's gross."

"Are you okay, sir?"

"Yeah. Yes, I'm fine. It's just I was checking for a pulse and then I got distracted talking to you and when I looked back, I realized that my fingers had kind of slid into his neck."

"Into his open mouth, sir? Like, down his throat?"

"No like into his throat?"

"Like pushing on his skin? That's okay, that's how a pulse should be take—

"No like *into* his throat, like *actually* into it, like past the skin."

"I don't understand, sir—"

"Oh my God. It's like I'm fingering his throat, okay. Like I just accidentally fingered the open stab wound on his throat."

"Alright, Owen, if you could stop fingering the man's—"

"Yes! Of course, I stopped. I didn't just leave my fingers in his open neck wound."

"Good. That's good. Just remain calm."

Chapter 29

"Calm! I am calm."

"That's great. Really good work. That means you can give me a status update on the injured parties, right? Were you able to find a pulse on either one?"

"No, neither of them has a pulse."

"Alright, can you locate the primary stab wound on either of them?"

"I don't think so. I mean there are a lot of wounds. Like too many wounds."

"I understand, sir. Are there any signs of life at all?"

"..."

"Sir?"

"..."

"Owen?"

"No. There are no signs of life."

A pause followed my response. I didn't breathe. The 911 operator didn't breathe. Boris and Natasha obviously didn't breathe. No one breathed. Not even Alexandra—

Wait. Where the fuck is Alexandra?

"Alexandra!" I got up off my knees as I called her name. Blood covered my body from cuticles to clavicles. "Alexandra, where are you at?"

Probaby covering up evidence? I thought.

"Alexandra!" I called again, shouting now, the 911 call all but forgotten. "Alexandra, where are you?"

"Outside," she replied. Her voice sounded weaker than normal. Not a lot, but a little.

Enough for show, I mused grimly.

Alexandra kept speaking but not to me. I followed the sound of her voice out onto the front porch. She was on the phone, her words drowned out by the approaching sirens.

99

Chapter 30

Where did my abs go? What's this horizontal crease between my belly button and pubes? Is that new? Is it from my stomach fat folding up when I sit down?

I bent over a little at the waist while watching my belly.

Sweet God it is.

I knew I'd been on a downward slide ever since Lola was born, but I didn't realize the full magnitude of the decline until that moment. It's funny how standing in nothing but your underwear in front of the rapt eyes of the entire cul-de-sac forces you to take an honest look at yourself.

It's time to get back to the gym, O'Shea. Until then suck in your gut, people are watching.

I followed my own advice then asked the uniformed officer what was next.

"Leave your clothes where they are, step off the tarp, and turn around," she directed.

The police officer was attractive in a could-beat-me-up sort of way. Had I been less covered in my neighbors' blood, I would have found her instructions kind of sexy. As it was, I just found them irritating. I didn't want to deal with this shit. I didn't want to strip off my clothes and talk to the cops. I wanted to be left alone. I wanted to take a hot shower with a cold beer and a bar of that harsh gritty soap mechanics use. Lord knows my normal body wash wasn't going to do the trick. Energizing eucalyptus and aromatic juniper berry? Nope, not when you're covered in human gore.

After I stepped off the tarp, the police woman carefully folded it up around my clothes, slid the lot of it into a large evidence bag, sealed it, and then handed me a pair of gray sweatpants with a matching crewneck sweatshirt.

"Put these on while you wait."

The sweats were gigantic, XXL at least.

"Thanks," I grumbled sarcastically.

Once I got the clothes on, I really was thankful. They were clean and their roominess made me feel thinner.

"Better?" the officer asked.

"Better," I nodded.

"Good. Now stay here for a moment, Detective Nikolasdottir will be right over."

"Got it. Wait. What's the name?"

"Nikolasdottir."

"Like Nicholas and daughter?"

"Yeah."

I practiced the detective's name a couple of times and then eased down onto the bumper of the nearest vehicle. I figured I might as well take a seat. There was a gruesome crime scene to deal with so Nick-o-lus-dot-er (nailed it!) was obviously going to be quite a while.

She arrived ninety seconds later. I'd barely had time to locate Elle, Riddhi, and Lola in the gathered crowd. I hadn't had time to finish miming out to them what had happened. I was mid Psycho-style overhand stabbing motion when the detective tapped me on the shoulder.

"Owen O'Shea?"

"Huh? Yeah." I tried to turn the stabbing motion into a head scratch before turning around for the introduction. It didn't work.

"Don't worry, Mr. O'Shea, ya can tell your friends all about it as soon as we're done here. There's no need for charades."

"Charades? What... Pshh... Nooo..."

The detective gave me a friendly but knowing look that resulted in my immediate confession.

"Yeah, okay, I was doing charades."

"I appreciate your honesty, Mr. O'Shea, even if it was a bit tardy."

"No problem."

"I'm Detective Corey Nikolasdottir with the RPD." She showed me her badge with her left while delivering a shake with her right. Her hand was small but her grip was firm.

"Nice to meet you, Detective. I wish it was under better circumstances."

"Oh yah, I agree with ya there." She nodded her head while pulling out a pen and notepad. "So listen, Mr. O'Shea, I don't want to hold ya too long because I know you've been through a lot with the finding your neighbors murdered and all, but I have to get your statement while it's fresh. Procedure ya know?"

"Yah—I mean, yeah, I understand."

The *yah* had slipped out. I hadn't meant to mimic the detective's Upper-Midwestern accent. It was just too damn contagious. Fortunately, she didn't seem to notice.

"Alright then," she continued. "Why don't ya go ahead and tell me about this stabbing business."

"So they *were* stabbed. I was right?"

"Eff… Well, yah, they were stabbed, but I shouldn't have said that. Not before I took your statement. I just saw ya reenacting that Hitchcock shower scene earlier when ya were trying to let your friends know what happened, so I figured ya knew."

"Don't beat yourself up about it. I was pretty sure that's what had happened."

"Right. Well, that does make me feel a bit better. Now why don't you just go ahead and tell me what happened. As much as you can remember from this morning."

I did as instructed. I started at coffee with the girls and finished with the arrival of the police. Detective Nikolasdottir didn't interrupt, she just listened and scribbled down the occasional note. When I finished relaying the day's events, she asked me three questions:

One: "Did Alexandra Stonecipher say why her husband was upset with Boris?"

Two: "What did ya say Alexandra was doing when ya came out on the porch?"

Three: "Have ya noticed anything else odd around the neighborhood lately?"

The answers to the first two questions were easy. The answer to the third was not.

Chapter 31

Detective Nikolasdottir is easy to talk to. I think it's the accent. All those forward As and flat Os are just so friendly you can't help from feeling at ease. If you're not hyper-alert, you're bound to over-share. I know I nearly did.

"Have you noticed anything else odd around the neighborhood lately?" she asked. It was her third question. I'd answered the first two directly and started to do the same for the third.

"Yeah, quite a bit actually, like my frien…"

I faded out when I realized that a complete and candid account of recent neighborhood activity was a bad idea. Friends and harmless acquaintances would not come out of it looking great. Riddhi's late-night liaisons, Elle's covert drug use, the Peabodys' booze-fueled property destruction, I didn't want to tell the detective any of that business.

"Owen?"

"Huh? Yeah?"

"Like what exactly? What odd stuf—"

"The Stoneciphers!" The words squirted out of my mouth like a premature ejaculation.

"Okay?" Nikolasdottir seemed confused. "What about the Stoneciphers?"

"Well, they've been up to a lot of weird shit," I replied, recovering some of my composure. "I can go into detail if you'd like."

"Yah, alright."

I immediately told the detective as much as I could. I even brought up the stuff that Elle discovered when she snuck into their home. It was easy enough to pretend like that information had been gathered during one of our legal entries into the Stoneciphers' place.

Nikolasdottir listened attentively. She scribbled down notes and nodded her head at all the appropriate moments. It seemed promising. I even flashed Riddhi and Elle a thumbs up toward the end of my account when the detective wasn't looking.

Riddhi returned the gesture.

Elle mouthed the word *focus*.

Lola gnawed on her knuckles.

Why is Lola chewing on her fist? I thought, all other concerns evaporating. *What happened to Jafar? Please don't let that stupid giraffe be lost. If that sucker is lost, we are effed right in the A. I told Izzy we should have bought a backup—maybe a couple of backups.*

"Where's her giraffe?" I mouthed the question to Elle. She didn't understand so I pointed at Lola and mimed some exaggerated chewing. She didn't get that either, so then I tried to impersonate a giraffe. That also failed. *Fuck it.* I gave a never-mind wave and turned my attention back to Nikolasdottir. She was looking right at me.

"Sorry, Detective. I just noticed my daughter's toy giraffe is missing."

"I see. I'd actually already figured out the giraffe bit. Ya did a good job charade-ing out the long neck."

"Thank you."

"You're welcome."

"I don't know why my dummy friends didn't get it."

"Oh, I expect they're a little distracted by the whole homicide thing. Ya know, murders tend to dominate people's attention when they happen."

"Maybe people without teething babies."

"No, I think they dominate pretty much everybody's attention, regardless of whether or not they have a baby. The only exception I can think of is a person that's not interested because they already know exactly what happened."

"Yeah, I suppose... Wait. What?"

"Have a good day, Mr. O'Shea. Make sure you don't go anywhere."

"Go anywhere? Why would I? What the fuck?"

Chapter 32

My face cheeks started sweating. So did my butt cheeks. So did everywhere in between. It was not the nice, I-had-a-good-workout type of sweat either. It was the bad, you-are-the-primary-suspect-in-a-homicide-investigation-type of sweat. I was not a fan.

"You look like shit."

"Of course he looks like shit, Riddhi, he just walked in on a murder scene."

"Yeah, Elle, I know he just walked in on a murder scene, but he didn't look this bad a few minutes ago."

"Maybe it just hit him. Sometimes trauma takes a little while to process."

Both Riddhi and Elle turned their big eyes on me. So did Lola. So did the Peabodys and Tanner and Ajay and RJ and Ryan and Sota and nearly everyone else in the neighborhood. Clearly, the word had spread. I probably should have stayed quiet in front of the crowd, but I didn't.

"I look like shit," I explained, "because I just discovered Boris's and Natasha's dead bodies, and because that stupid detective thinks I did it."

There was an audible gasp when I delivered the second piece of information. A few people in the crowd actually stepped back. My friends stepped forward. Elle put a consoling hand on my shoulder. Riddhi started swearing and looking around for the detective.

"What the fuck! Where is that Viking bitch? I'm going to drag her over here by that beautiful blonde hair and slap her around until she explains herself."

"I don't know where she went, but I don't think—"

"I mean who the hell does she think she is strolling in here tossing around accusations after twenty minutes. What sort of detective work is that? I'll tell you what type it is: it's the shitty type. You know what? I bet her pasty ass did it. She's probably trying to frame you to get the attention off of her. Well, I'm not fooled. Uh-uh. Nope. Just because…"

Riddhi's diatribe continued for another two minutes. It was nice. That sort of unadulterated support makes you feel good. My mom was the best at it, but Riddhi is a close second. She even sounds like my mom when she gets going. And she's convincing too. Even when her insults and assertions are completely baseless, you can't help from being swayed. By the time she wrapped up, the sentiment of the crowd had shifted back in my favor. People were standing close to me once again, their suspicions and ire now focused on Nikolasdottir. A few of them actually booed the detective when she came out to make a statement. I didn't join in because it seemed tacky, and because I didn't want to get myself in even deeper shit, and because I was distracted. There was a lot to process.

Chapter 33

"Babe, you okay?"

"Yeah, I'm good."

"That's a lie, you are not good. You just walked in on a murder scene. No one that just walked in on a murder scene is good."

"True. I meant I'm good given the circum—Hold on, how do you know that I just walked in on a murder scene?"

It had suddenly dawned on me that I had forgotten to call Izzy.

"Well, I definitely didn't hear it from my husband, you ass."

"Sorry, Iz, there was a lot going on."

"It's fine. Actually, it's not fine, you should have called, but I get it. You were in a pretty crazy situation."

A brief silence passed in which Izzy looked up at me, inhaled heavily, then exhaled the same way. I could see an array of emotions enter and exit her body along with the oxygen. After another deep breath she wrapped her arms around my waist and hugged tight.

"I'm just glad you're okay," she said. "I don't know what I'd do without you."

"You're smart and hot, you'd be fine," I winked.

"That's correct, but I'd still be a wreck."

I brushed her hair away from her face and kissed her forehead. "That's sweet."

"It is." She wiped away a tear. "Now, enough of that. Tell me what the fuck happened."

"Okay, but first you tell me how you heard about everything that went down."

The answer dawned on me before it left Izzy's lips. We said it at the same time.

"Riddhi."

We both laughed.

"Of course Riddhi told me," Izzy went on. "She immediately tells all her friends everything. She told me when she thought her food processor was haunted, and when her radiologist said she had dense breasts, and when Ryan wanted to do the sexy librarian role play."

"I still don't see how a guy can be a sexy librarian."

"Because it's impossible." Izzy shook her head and waved a hand. "But we're getting distracted. Get back to the story, tell me what happened. And start with the stuff from last night. Detail all that craziness in the cul-de-sac that you were talking about this morning, it might be relevant."

I proceeded to give a meticulous account of everything that had happened since Izzy went to bed the previous night. It took quite a while to get through it all, partly because we stopped to talk some stuff through, but mainly because Lola woke up and demanded a diaper change, and then formula, and then burping, then more formula, and then more burping.

"So that's all of it," I said, concluding my account as I wet a washcloth under the warm tap. "What do you think?"

It was a broad question, but it seemed like the right one. There were a lot of threads to choose from and I wanted to see which of them Izzy pulled on first.

I handed her the washcloth and waited for an answer.

"I think a number of things," she replied, while wiping Lola clean.

"Like?"

"Like first off, I think this Detective Nikolasdottir woman is lazy and terrible at her job. She should be focusing on people who might have actually killed Boris and Natasha not on the person that just happened to find their bodies."

I smiled at Izzy's indignation. Her defense of me wasn't as bombastic as Riddhi's, but it was just as reassuring.

110

"Thanks for the support, babe." I squeezed Izzy's hand affectionately, then lifted Lola out of her high chair, laid her down on the kitchen table, and got to work dressing her in fresh clothes. "So, what else do you think? Anything about any of our neighbors?"

"Absolutely. I have thoughts on pretty much everybody, so I should be systematic about it, go clockwise around the cul-de-sac beginning with the Peabodys—athough, that's a tough place to start, considering I'm not sure what to make of their behavior. They're always so proper and boring, it's hard to even imagine them driving drunk and then urinating on their neighbors' house."

"I know."

"It's just so unlike them. But the fact that it *did* happen says one of two things to me: Either the Stoneciphers did something unconscionably shady that made the Peabodys act totally out of character, or the Peabodys' actual character isn't what we think it is."

"Interesting."

"It is. And if the latter is the case—if we really don't know the Peabodys' character—then that's probably because they really don't want people to know their character."

"Why?"

"I don't know, but I can't imagine it would be anything good. And if it's something bad, something they really want to keep secret, then maybe they'd be willing to kill a couple that witnessed their lapse."

We sat quiet for a minute running through the possibility in our head. It seemed far-fetched, but not ridiculously so.

"Alright, we're moving clockwise," I said, getting things going again, envisioning the cul-de-sac in my head. "So, the Stoneciphers are next. What are your thoughts? I mean I know they're up to no good, but Alexandra acted pretty much how I would have expected someone to act when we found the

Russians' bodies this morning, save maybe the phone call. Plus, last night I didn't see her or Chip do anything."

"That doesn't mean they didn't do anything."

"True."

"I don't know. To be honest, prior to today I thought you, Riddhi, and Elle were going a little crazy with the whole the-Stoneciphers-are-murderers business."

"But now?"

"Now everything is different. Now that there actually *has* been a murder in the neighborhood, I feel like the Stoneciphers have to be the number one suspect."

"Agreed. I'm totally on board. Those damn Stoneciphers... But why do we think that?"

"Well, if you suspect people are murderers before there's a murder, and then there *is* a murder, then it seems pretty reasonable to be suspicious of the people you already suspected."

"That's a very confusing sentence," I laughed. "But I'm like ninety-nine percent sure I agree with you."

"Good. So that brings us to Tanner whom we can eliminate."

"Right, because he's so cool."

"No, because he was with that girl all last night. You saw her come over and I saw her leave in the morning."

"So, you were checking her out too?" I smirked. "That's hot. Maybe we can talk to Tanner, get her number, see if she's interested in meeting with an adventurous married couple."

"You're the worst."

"What?"

"Even when we're trying to solve a murder you're thinking about sexy time."

"Well, yeah."

Izzy smiled indulgently and rolled her eyes. "She wasn't even that hot."

"Did you see her legs?"

"Yes, they were too muscular."

"Get out of here."

"Plus, her dress was too tight."

"Yeah, like sexy—"

"No, not like sexy too tight, more like put-on-weight too tight."

"What? You're crazy."

Izzy gave a dismissive wave of her hand, picked Lola up, and carried her to the tummy-time blanket.

"So where are we at?" she asked, as she walked back toward me.

"Well, the next house is Boris and Natasha, and they can't really be considered suspects," I replied. "So, I guess we're at Elle and Sota's."

"Yeah, the Elle thing doesn't seem like a big deal to me."

"What?" I was a bit surprised. "You don't think it's weird that Elle sneaks out to her gardening shed to smoke weed in the middle of the night?"

"No. I think it makes sense."

"Really?"

"Of course. Like one out of seven adults smokes weed, so it's not surprising that Elle is one of them. And now that Sammy is older it makes sense that she would go out to the shed to do it. It might be uncomfortable out there, but I guarantee you that it's more comfortable than having your first grader walk in on you smoking a bowl."

"Alright, when you say it like that it does make a lot of sense. I guess I'm just surprised that she hasn't told us. She knows we wouldn't care. In fact, it would be nice to have a hook-up so we could get high every once and a while."

"Agreed."

"I should probably just ask her."

"Yes." Izzy spoke, plainly. "You should."

I nodded in agreement, then moved things along. "Okay, so that covers Elle, and the next house is ours, and we know what we were up to, so that brings us to the Chakrabarti-Czechowskis."

"Jesus, that's a mouthful. Riddhi shouldn't have hyphenated."

"I kind of like it. It's a challenge, like reading *Fox in Socks* out loud."

"Well, your opinion is wrong," Izzy smiled. "But we're not going to debate that now, because I actually am a little concerned about Riddhi's late-night cop meeting. I mean what could that have been about?"

"An affair?" I said, tossing out the first idea that came to mind.

"Yeah, it could be. But I hope not, Ryan's a good guy."

"Agreed."

"Then again if it's not an affair, it could be something worse."

"Like what?"

"I don't know, but if she's meeting with the cops, and not telling us about it, then I suspect it's nothing great for us."

"Shit," I frowned. "I guess that's true."

At that moment I felt worse than I had all day. I was tempted to grab some ice cream, plop down on the couch, and mope. But I didn't. I refused to spiral downward. Instead, I finished the conversation with Izzy, and resolved myself to talk to Riddhi and Elle first thing in the morning. It was time to follow through on my friends-what-the-hell plan, time to ask them about everything straight up, face-to-face.

Despite the awfulness of the day, I went to bed that night feeling good, my spirits buoyed by the simple, tangible, and proactive course of action I had decided upon. I woke up the next morning feeling the same way, good, ready to go.

Then I went and got Lola.

She had little red dots all over her body.

My first reaction was: *poor girl.*

My second reaction was: *fuck my life.*

Chapter 34

Chicken pox. That's what Lola had. I figured that's what it was as soon as I saw it, but when Izzy confirmed the diagnosis, it still felt like a little jab to the belly.

"Shit." That's all I could muster in response.

"Yeah," Izzy nodded. "It is shitty. Fortunately, it seems like a pretty mild case. Some acetaminophen and an oatmeal bath and she should be fine."

"Okay," I nodded, convincing myself. "Not a problem."

"Are you sure? I can take off work, babe."

"Nope, there's no need. Lola and I got this. We're gonna acetaminophen and oatmeal bath all over the place."

"And by 'all over the place' you mean use the acetaminophen as directed, right?"

"Yup, as directed all over the place."

"Perfect. Also, calamine lotion will help. Also, if you can get her to keep mittens on that would be good, and if you can't, then just make sure her nails are cut so that she doesn't scratch herself."

"Done and done."

"Great. I guess I'll get ready for work then."

Izzy headed back toward our room. Halfway there she stopped, turned around, walked back, gave me a kiss, and said, "You're an amazing dad."

I smiled. I knew Izzy felt that way, but it was nice to hear.

"Thanks, my love," I replied.

"No need for thanks, it's just true. You *are* an amazing dad."

"And husband," I added with a wink.

"Yes, and husband."

"And lover."

"Oh my God you're the worst."

Izzy gave me a playful push then headed to our room. As she walked away a final thought occurred to me so I yelled it.

"Hey, babe, one last question."

"Uh-huh."

"It's okay if Lola is around other adults, right?"

"Yeah, as long as they've had chickenpox, it shouldn't be a problem."

"Sweet," I said.

It was not sweet. Over the next thirty minutes I learned that neither Riddhi nor Elle has ever had chicken pox. Stupid Alexandra Stonecipher has though.

Chapter 35

The next nine days were not good for my mental health... or my physical health... or my emotional health. Basically, my entire well-being took a hit. I saw very little of Izzy, Riddhi, and Elle, whom I love, and a whole lot of Alexandra and Detective Nikolasdottir who suck. Also seven of the nine days were rainy. Also I couldn't sleep.

Izzy's absence wasn't her fault. She came home as much as she could, but calamities conspired against her. There was a horrible accident on the highway and an even more horrible one at the county fair. The latter of these was truly bananas and not in the good way. The video of the incident went viral. One of the whirly rides spun out of its bolts and into a crowd. Nobody died but there were a whole lot of broken bones so all the orthopedists were slammed. The department hasn't been that busy since the osteogenesis imperfecta convention was in town. Izzy actually had to work through the night a couple of times.

Riddhi and Elle were similarly blameless for their absence. If you haven't had chickenpox, you haven't had chickenpox. There was nothing they could do about that. Plus, they made up for their lack of physical presence by calling a lot. I kept the talks short though. They were too tempting. Sure, I wanted to speak to them about their late-night escapades, but I wanted to do it face-to-face. Difficult conversations are better that way— more uncomfortable, but better. The visual component reduces misunderstandings, and I wanted no misunderstandings. Riddhi and Elle are my best friends, and, assuming that they're not up to anything massively shady, I want to keep it that way.

So, with no Izzy, no Riddhi, and no Elle, it was just Lola and me against the world. Although technically it wasn't the whole world, it was just a horrible neighbor and a folksy cop, but that was enough. I saw Alexandra every damn day and Detective Nikolasdottir every other. The former for party planning, the latter for conversations that verged on interrogations.

I suppose the silver lining of the whole thing was that I got to know Tanner better, albeit under less than ideal circumstances. I would have preferred our friendship evolve over the course of time via repeated social interaction, not under the umbrella of attorney-client privilege, but what can you do. I'm certainly not going to complain.

I didn't even have to ask him to be my lawyer, he just volunteered as a kindness. Detective Nikolasdottir stopped by, and he noticed, so he did the same, knocking on the door shortly after her arrival. His soil stained jeans and gardening gloves indicated that he had been out working on his yard. It was pure luck that he saw the detective pull up, a fortune of timing to the benefit of yours truly. And man was it fortunate. I would have been screwed if he hadn't been there. I was so sleep deprived I might have admitted to anything, especially with Nikolasdottir's homespun Minnesotan shtick turned up to eleven. Thankfully, Tanner kyboshed all her maneuvers. He let me respond to questions that would help the police find the actual killer, but nothing more. Anything that resembled an effort to trap me got shot down immediately. It was both great and seriously troubling. Great in that I got a good lawyer and established a real friendship, troubling in that I was continuing to be questioned for a double murder.

And then there was Alexandra Stonecipher, the snobby, murderous cherry on top of my lonesome, pox-laden sundae. Tanner couldn't do shit about my meetings with her. Lawyers simply don't have a well-defined role in the party planning process. I wish they did though. Those meetings were excruciating. Never in my life have I had to weigh in on so many decisions that I didn't care about. Color schemes and dress codes and waiters' uniforms. Ugh. Alexandra even had us establish a shared aesthetic language. I told her I didn't have an aesthetic language to begin with, so there was nothing for us to reconcile, but she just laughed and said, "Oh, Owen, you are too funny," which is a sentiment I generally agree with, so I didn't fight her on it. I should have though. That vocab nonsense alone took an entire morning. It was so bad I almost quit, almost exploded, almost told her off and blew up our chances of figuring out what the hell her and Chip are up to. I didn't care if it meant they'd continue to get away with horrible stuff. I didn't even care if it increased the likelihood that I'd go down for the murders of Boris and Natasha. At that moment prison didn't seem all that bad. At least I'd get some sleep. Also nobody would ask me to make a motherfucking mood board.

Seriously? A mood board?

"I'll tell you my mood, Alexandra: pissed."

That's what I wanted to say when she asked me to make one of those ridiculous collages. It's a good thing I didn't though. Partly because that's not really what mood boards are about so I would have looked foolish, but mainly because our final meeting made the entire painful, party-planning ordeal worth the effort.

Chapter 36

"Owen! Hello." Alexandra looked surprised when she answered the door. "I thought we were meeting at your place."

"Were we? I'm sorry, I guess I had a brain fart."

I hadn't had a brain fart. I never had any intention of having Alexandra over. I only offered at the end of our previous meeting because it seemed rude not to, and because an unexpected visit to her place was more likely to yield incriminating evidence, something that our previous meetings had not.

"Well," Alexandra said, doing her best to compose herself, "that's not a problem. Mental lapses happen to the best of us. Why don't you just come on in. We'll sit and chat where we always do."

I walked in and sat down in a big squishy chair in the living room. It is not where we normally talk. I figured if I was going to try and throw Alexandra off, I might as well commit.

"Oh, I suppose the parlor is alright," she said, plainly displeased by the change. "You just settle in and I'll go to the kitchen and throw something together."

"Sounds great," I smiled.

Alexandra exited in a hurry. She returned a couple of minutes later with a bizarre combination of food: bagels and lox, a black olive assortment, and some Filipino dessert I'd never had before called pichi-pichi. As far as I could tell there was no rhyme or reason to the day's menu, a stark contrast from the carefully curated offerings she normally brought to the table.

"I apologize for the farrago of food," Alexandra said, tucking a stray hair behind her ear. "This is all I have on hand. Just some recipes I've been working on."

"No worries. Looks great."

Alexandra was back out the door before I'd finished my sentence. It was weird. She was acting wildly off-brand:

distracted, disheveled, serving food without a theme. None of it was Alexandra Stonecipher behavior. Sure, she wasn't expecting us, but that couldn't account for this level of discombobulation. *Fishy.*

I looked down at Lola, eager to share my suspicions, but she was conked out, the back of her hands covering her eyeballs like that scary monster from *Pan's Labyrinth.* She only sleeps that way when she's down for the count. I was on my own.

"I'll be there in a moment, Owen," Alexandra said loudly from the kitchen, her voice strained. "I just have to..."

The sentence remained unfinished, hanging awkwardly in the air. It was further evidence that something was up, and it was time to figure out what. So, I stood up out of the comfy chair, laid Lola down near the back of it, kissed her forehead, put some pillows on the floor just in case she started rolling like never before, and then crept toward the kitchen.

I held my breath with each step that I took. A lifetime of soccer has given me creaky knees and ankles, so cracks and pops are inevitable, yet by some small miracle I made it to the destination in silence. Once there, I settled into a manageable crouch behind the bar where I immediately heard Alexandra's voice. A few seconds later it was joined by another, and then a third—or maybe not. I couldn't be certain. There was not a third person talking, but it sounded like there was a third person breathing.

"As I said," Alexandra whispered sternly. "I didn't know he was coming over. If I had known I would have told you."

"A likely story," retorted the second voice. It was Chip Stonecipher. I was about ninety percent sure... maybe eighty... okay, seventy.

"Yes, it *is* a likely story, because it's a true story."

"Pshh."

"You can 'pshh' at me all you want, it doesn't change the fact that I'm telling you the truth. That should be obvious. I don't want to get caught either. That wouldn't benefit me at all."

"No, but it's not as harmful to you."

"And why not? I'm also a Stonecipher."

"By marriage, it's not the same, dear."

So it is Chip.

"You're right, it's not the same. It's more serious. You were born a Stonecipher, I became one by choice."

"Yes, but you're still relatively new at it. You don't fully appreciate the microscope we live under, the attention that the local public pays to our—"

"Don't condescend me. I know precisely—"

"No, you *don't* know, Alexandra. You—"

"Oh, shut up, Chip. Just run off to the garage and disassemble the rack."

A rack! That's like a medieval torture instrument. Holy shit they're even more messed up than I thought. Sadistic killers with vintage tastes. How do you even get a—

Chip took a couple of steps. It brought me out of my mental tangent, refocusing my attention on the conversation.

"Yes, yes, whatever will bring this argument to an end," he said, heading toward the kitchen's rear exit.

"Good," Alexandra snapped. "And take Great Uncle with you."

So, there is a third person. Boom, two for two.

"Fine. Come along, Harold, you treasonous old coot. We'll leave Alexandra to plan her party with the idle neighbor."

Idle! What the fuck does that—

Alexandra started to move, which made me realize that I needed to move. Hustling, I made my way back to the living room, picked Lola up, and settled into the chair.

"Sorry for the delay, Owen," Alexandra said, arriving a few seconds after me.

"No worries," I replied, doing my best to control my heavy breathing. "Anyway, it's Lola and me that should be apologizing to you. We came over unannounced, we're the reason you're having to scramble around."

"That still doesn't excuse my frenzied state." Alexandra shook her head. "My hostessing skills should be more adaptable."

"Well, I think you're doing great," I shrugged.

Alexandra reached out a hand, squeezed my forearm, and flashed me a smile that was both sincere and something else— Understanding? Affectionate? I don't know. "That's very kind of you to say," she beamed.

From there our conversation proceeded in a friendly and productive direction. Inevitably, Alexandra annoyed me a few times, but I didn't get sassy or puckish in response. I kept my cool, kept Alexandra at ease, and after a while successfully segued us to some individual tasks on our computers.

By the time I asked if Lola and I could use the bathroom, Alexandra was so immersed in her work she didn't even look up from her screen. She just let us breeze off into the depths of her house as if she had nothing to hide.

So breeze we did, first to the bathroom to turn on the lights and fan and make it look like we were inside, and then down the hall, and then down another hall because the Stoneciphers' house is fucking gigantic, and then to the door that opens into their garage. I tried it immediately, but it didn't budge. Of course it didn't. The door was double padlocked, just as it had been for Elle. It was stupid of me to even try.

"It's actually good that didn't open," I whispered to Lola.

My mind flashed to images of what we might have walked in on: Chip and his ancient uncle dismembering a body, or tanning somebody's skin, or playing jacks with human teeth.

In lieu of barging in, I put my ear to the door. I hoped to hear voices, preferably Chip narrating his horrors loudly and intelligibly so that I could get a recording of it, but nope. I got nothing, not even the loud ominous hum that saturated my last eavesdropping-on-the-Stoneciphers'-garage experience.

"Nada," I whispered to Lola.

"..." she agreed.

"Maybe we can see something through the crack at the bottom."

I shifted my daughter into a different hold and squatted down. My knees and ankles cracked loudly. It echoed down the hall.

"Chip, what noise is that? It doesn't sound like you're doing what I told you to." Alexandra spoke at a reasonable volume, but it seemed loud, partially because of the amplifying effect of their fancy marble floors but mainly because of her proximity. She was close. The turn of a corner from one hall to the next, that's all that separated Lola and me from getting caught.

Shit.

I tried the door to our left. The handle stood fast.

Shit, shit, shit.

I moved to the door to our right.

Yes!

Lola and I slid into the room, my hand over her head to prevent a noggin-bump. The second we cleared the threshold I closed the door behind us, swift but controlled. It came to a rest on the frame seconds before Alexandra's arrival. The knob was still twisted in my hand when I heard her first knock on the door to the garage.

"Chip."

Another knock.

"Chip."

An angrier knock.

"Chip!"

I gently released the knob in sync with Alexandra's third round of knocking. The latch made a distinct noise, but the thumping of her fist provided sufficient camouflage. She didn't hear a thing.

I took a step back and exhaled heavily, cheeks puffed out, eyes closed. Anxious sweat was pouring out of my armpits and down my sides. I used my T-shirt to blot it up, then I used another part of my T-shirt to wipe down my face, then I returned to the door and pressed my ear up against it. I was just in time to catch the beginning of the Stoneciphers' argument.

"What do you want, Alexandra?"

"I want to know that you're doing what I asked."

"Yes, I'm disassembling the rack."

"Are you? Because I don't hear anything."

"That's because I'm currently talking to you, dear."

"Ah, yes, very clever, Chip."

"I thought so."

"Of course you did, because you're arrogant."

"Arrogant, no. Astute, yes."

"Astute, that's quite the joke. An astute man wouldn't have gotten us into this mess. That business with Boris and Natasha was haphazard and greedy, nothing more."

"We've already discussed this. Things did not go as planned, but that doesn't mean it was a mistake. Poorly executed perhaps, but not a mistake."

"Semantics, dear."

"It's not semant—You know what? It's not worth it. I'm not having this conversation right now. I'm not hashing this out through a door. Why don't you just go back and plan your party with that shiftless mick."

"It's not a party and Owen is not shiftless."

But I am a mick? Well technically, sure, 54% according to ancestry. com, but still.

"Okay, Alexandra, whatever you say."

"No, you can't play that card."

"What card?"

"You know the card you're playing. Surrendering. Acting as though you're the victim of my tyranny."

"That's not a card, it's just reality."

"Oh my God, the histrionics. I can't talk to you when you're like this."

"Perfect, because I don't want to talk to you."

"Fine. But that contraption better be disassembled and destroyed by tonight. We can't be found with it."

"Oh my God, yes, I know."

"And dispose of the ether as well."

Ether! That's how they knock out their victims!

"That's not quite how it works, dear."

"Chip, just close your mouth and—"

Alexandra stopped mid-sentence, interrupted by the sound of my waking daughter.

Chapter 37

Lola makes a big show out of waking up: long stretches, loud yawns, miscellaneous baby noises. Normally it's cute. Too bad this wasn't normally. This was hiding-in-the-neighbors'-weird-security-room-hoping-that-they-don't-find-out-that-we're-spying-on-them-because-if-they-do-they'll-probably-kill-us.

"Chip, did you hear that?" Alexandra's query was quiet but pressing. I heard it clearly despite the door between us. She must have turned toward Lola and me.

"Hear wha—"

"Be quiet."

"I was just respon—"

"Quiet!"

"Yes, dear." Chip's voice was more muffled than his wife's, but I could still make out the contemptuous sarcasm.

A moment passed. Lola made another noise. I'd moved us away from the door, but she was still loud enough to be heard.

"That!" Alexandra demanded. "Did you hear that?"

"…"

"Chip, did you hear that?"

"…"

"Chip!"

"Oh, I'm allowed to answer now? Because a second ago—"

"Yes, yes, your point is made. Now answer my question."

"I might have heard something. It's possible that the rat is back."

"I don't think so, it didn't sound like a rat, and it didn't sound like it was coming from the wall."

"Alright, then what did it sound like?"

"I'm not sure what it sounded like, I think it's coming from the security room though."

127

"What!" Chip's voice took on a bit of urgency. "You need to get in there and check it out."

"But what if it *is* a rat. I'm not dealing with that. You come out here and investigate."

"I would, Alexandra, but the door is quadruple locked as you know."

"Unlock it then."

"That will take forever."

"Well then, you better get to it."

"Fine. Hurry up and unlock your side while I do mine."

"How did my side get locked?"

"I had Great Uncle Harold do it. I figured I should take extra precautions since we have an unemployed slug in our house."

"Owen's not unemploy—"

"And speaking of our derelict neighbor, where is he at right now?"

"He's not the one making the noise if that's what you're insinuating. He's in the front bathroom changing his daughter."

"Sure he is, dear."

"Oh, shut up, Chip."

"I will if you go get your keys and unlock your side."

"Fine, give me a second."

The sound of Alexandra's departing footsteps gave me hope. I'd been looking around the room for a way out but found nothing. An entire wall of tiny televisions airing security footage of more rooms than I could count, a large stainless steel desk, and two luxurious office chairs, that's all the space contained. There wasn't even a closet in which to hide.

Shit, girl. We're going to have to exit the way we came in.

Lola stretched her arms out in the direction of the screens.

Good idea.

I took a few steps toward the wall of monitors, moving my eyes from one small display to the next, searching for Alexandra.

Christ on a bike, how many security cameras do they have? How many rooms do they have? There's like six foyers. Why do they have six foyers? And why is this one screen just the inside of a drawer? What a waste of a security cam—Wait, there she is!

I spotted Alexandra. She was in her kitchen, digging around in a drawer.

"Alright, daughter of mine." My whisper was serious. I knew Lola wouldn't understand my words, but I hoped that she'd get something from my tone. "Alexandra's in the front of the house, we have to go now, and we have to be super duper quiet. Shhh."

Holding Lola tight to my chest, I opened the door, made my way into the hallway then closed the door carefully behind us. I could hear Chip unlocking things out in the garage. He was being sloppy about it, rattling the keys and locks, grumbling indecipherably in frustration. The noise was welcome. It gave cover to my footsteps as I proceeded down the hall. It also gave me the confidence to bounce a little as we went. Lola likes bouncing. More importantly, it keeps her tiny mouth shut.

This-is-work-ing. This-is-work-ing. This-is-work-ing.

I repeated the phrase in my head as we went, bobbing with each syllable.

Lola smiled up at me.

We turned from one hallway to the next and then ducked into the first room on the right. Alexandra was still a ways off, but I wanted to play it safe. There was no need to make the entire journey in one shot, no need to push luck that had already been shoved.

"We'll just stay in this room and wait for her to pass by," I explained to Lola, my voice as soothing as I could make it. "Once she's turned the corner into the other hall we'll sneak out and go back to the living room, easy peasy lemon squeasy."

But it wasn't easy peasy lemon squeasy. It was more like shit show shit show lemon shit show.

Lola's caboose is what gave us away. The bouncing had succeeded in keeping her mouth quiet, but it only served to agitate her second noisiest body part. The toot that she released was a master class in flatulence on par with the work of any adult. I honestly couldn't believe it came out of her tiny body. At least at first, then the shock gave way to pride, which quickly gave way to concern. Alexandra hadn't heard, she was still out of earshot, but she would soon be within noseshot, and that smell wasn't going anywhere. We were hosed. We couldn't stay put and wait for her to walk by because she was not going to walk by. She was going to come in and investigate. She had to. You can't smell something like that in your own house and not look into its origin. That would be irresponsible. There might be a plumbing issue or a geological anomaly or worse.

We gotta get out of here.

I turned to see what hiding places or escape routes the room had to offer.

That's when I saw Great Uncle Harold.

Chapter 38

I shrieked. I had never shrieked before. Not once in thirty-one years. That said, I had never been surprised by an elderly man standing silently in the corner of a room filled with model trains and old pictures of homeless people before either. Perhaps it's my standard reaction to that particular scenario.

"Chip! Hurry, I do think it's an animal. Not a rat though. Whatever it is, it just made a strange noise in Great Uncle's hobby room. It smells awful too, like refuse or sewage or something."

I could hear Alexandra move down the hall as she spoke, hurrying toward the garage. Chip offered a loud response, but I couldn't make it out. He was too far away and I was too busy staring at Great Uncle Harold, terrified, holding my breath, waiting for the old man to open his wrinkly mouth and give us away.

A second passed in silence.

Then another.

And another.

Harold stood rooted to the spot, his glassy eyes aimed in our direction, the seal of his lips unbroken. Tentatively, I took a step. The quiet remained, so I took one more. Then one more, then again, and again, steadily moving toward the window in the corner. The old man's gaze followed our progress, the movement of his head oddly mechanical, as if he saw but didn't comprehend. With each step I gained more confidence in his continued silence.

Maybe he can't speak. Or maybe he's lost his mind. Or maybe—

The door to the garage opened. I could hear it hit the wall as Chip barged through. We had seconds.

Fuck it.

I covered the last few yards to the window with abandon, no longer worried about spooking the old man. Great Uncle Harold was either going to rat us out or he wasn't, we couldn't do anything about it now. All we could do was get out of the room, cross our fingers, and pray that the ancient train enthusiast had lost his marbles, or at least his ability to communicate.

I popped the latches on the window and slid it open. It was as smooth and silent as a ninja. Lola and I were not. I banged my knee into the sill on the way out, then muttered swear words under my breath to mitigate the pain. Lola laughed at me.

Again with the laughing, you little monster.

I returned the window to its closed position as the door to the room opened, disappearing out of sight before the Stoneciphers entered. I was tempted to stay hidden from view and eavesdrop, but I knew I couldn't. I had to get back. Alexandra is an obnoxiously conscientious host, even in her frenzied state she was bound to come and check on us soon. So I took off, hauling ass toward the Stoneciphers' front door, hoping that it was open, hoping that Lola and I could get through it and into the comfy chair before Alexandra's return.

And we did. We even had a bit of time to spare. I don't know exactly how long, but it was enough to catch my breath with enough left over to realize that I'd just made two big mistakes.

Chapter 39

Mistake one: I had left the bathroom door closed with the fan and light on.

Mistake two: I had voluntarily re-entered the house of probable killers who may or may not have just been told that I was snooping around their place, and, consequently, may or may not be feeling a tad homicide-y toward me.

Not great.

I started to stand up as soon as mistake number two dawned on me, but it was too late. Alexandra was already entering the room. I held my breath as I waited to see if Chip was going to enter behind her. If they were going to kill me, then surely they were going to do it as a team.

Alexandra said something as she settled into the love seat on my right. I didn't process a word of it. The entirety of my attention was still fixed on the hall, my body tight with anticipation, ready for the emergence of Chip with a weapon in hand.

Gun? No. Knife? No. He'll probably have some sort of bizarre medieval weapon that only rich maniacs use—a flail or some shit like that. How am I supposed to deal with an effin' flail? You rush a gun, you run away from a knife, what do you do against a spiky ball on a long-ass chain?

"Throw stuff I guess?" I looked around the room for heavy objects.

"What's that now?" Alexandra queried.

"Huh?"

"You just said something."

"Did I? No, I don't think—"

"Yes, you said something about throwing stuff."

"Oh, *throwing stuff.* Uh-huh, I did say that. I said that out loud and on purpose..."

Alexandra stared at me, earnest and eager for the continuation of my reply.

"Sorry, I um…" My mind groped desperately for a plausible explanation. "Honestly, I don't even know. I'm just so tired."

"Well, of course you are." Alexandra leaned toward me and gave my shoulder a squeeze. "You're taking care of a sick daughter all by yourself. That's more than any man should bear."

"Oh, well I wouldn't—"

"It's really quite remarkable. God knows Chip would never take that much parental responsibility upon himself."

"That's very nice of you to say, but it's not just me. I mean Izzy's great, she works her ass off and is super helpful when she's home. Plus, Elle and Riddhi are—"

"There's no need to be humble, Owen. I see how hard you work for Lola."

"Uh, thank you."

"And I see how underappreciated you are."

"Uh huh." *What the fuck is happening?*

"And that makes me sad."

"Okay."

"To watch a good man get taken advantage of like that, it's just—"

"I don't think anyone is taking advant—"

"Shush, shush, shush." Alexandra moved her finger to my lips, her arm extending awkwardly over Lola's head. "There's no need for modesty…"

This is weird.

"There's no need to downplay yourself…"

But good, I guess.

"Because I see you…"

Great Uncle Harold must have kept quiet.

"I really see you…"

Or maybe not?

"I know who you are..."

Oh, shit, she does know.

"Not just on the outside but deep down..."

The old man blabbed.

"I see the entirety of Owen..."

Is this a threat?

"And the entirety of Owen is..."

About to get murdered?

"Alexandra!" Chip's voice was a whip, its sharp crack halting Alexandra's exposition.

"Yes, dear," Alexandra answered, her tone sweetened cyanide.

"I think I discovered the problem. You should come back here for a minute."

"Of course, dear." Alexandra turned toward me. "Sorry, Owen, I'll just be a minute."

"Yerb."

Yerb isn't a word but it's what I said. The nonsense reply was an appropriate reflection of my confused mental state. I had no idea what to make of the situation. Had Alexandra been threatening me? Commending me? Venting? Flirting? Who the hell knew? I can tell you who didn't: Me, Owen Mickey O'Shea. And I didn't wait around to figure it out.

As soon as Alexandra left the room, Lola and I got our asses out of there. I yelled an excuse toward the back of the house as we left, something about Lola having an accident and needing to get her home. I also said that we'd left the door to the bathroom closed and the fan on because Lola had made it stinky.

Alexandra must have heard because she told us to wait a second. I pretended not to hear her and hustled out the door, across the cul-de-sac, and into our house. As we stepped inside, I stole a quick glance back at the Stoneciphers' place. It was quiet save the window occupied by Great Uncle Harold. The old man was staring at us, his gaunt face half-hidden by a curtain, his eyes unblinking.

Chapter 40

A cold and sticky gloom filled the space between my vertebrae. My body shivered in a bid to shake it free, but the sensation remained. The disconcertion was there to stay, driven in deep by the sight of Great Uncle Harold's withered husk of a face as it stared out the window at us.

"I'm definitely going to have nightmares."

That's what I told Lola as we stepped inside our house, and that's precisely what happened. A few hours passed, I put Lola down for the night, walked to Izzy and my bedroom, face-planted down on the mattress, and the bad dreams began. Three to be precise, one followed by another followed by another.

In the first nightmare I was playing chess in a dark room against an even darker figure. All was silent save the drip from a leaking roof and the whimpers of my daughter, both of which emanated from somewhere in the black. The game was going poorly and it filled me with dread. Something depended upon it, something unknown but grave. I looked at the board for hours, searching desperately for a move to change the tide of the match, but it was futile. There was nothing. And as my hope faded the dripping noise grew louder, and the whimpers of my child louder still.

In the second there was fire. Every house in the cul-de-sac was ablaze, consumed by flames that lit up the moonless night. And in the middle of the street stood the Stonecipher family, smiling at the inferno. Next to them knelt the Peabodys, leashed up like dogs. And on the other side sat a wolf, handsome, free, and salivating.

The final nightmare took me back to the moment I discovered Boris's and Natasha's bodies. It was different though. Different from how it had really been. In the dream I was naked and the entire neighborhood was watching. I tried to talk to the crowd but my mouth refused to open, so I tried to run, but slipped and fell in the blood. And there I stayed, floundering in the carnage, unable to escape until my wife woke me with a shake of the shoulder.

Izzy was a welcome sight, a beautiful and loving face pulling me from the nightmare parade. Unfortunately, the relief she offered was fleeting. The moment I processed what she was saying all of the fear and anxiety returned.

And this time it wasn't a product of my dreams. It was reality.

Chapter 41

"Owen! Owen, wake up!"

I stirred. My head was an anvil, my eyes silt. It took effort and concentration to sit up. I needed a minute to regain full consciousness and get my shit together, but Izzy didn't give it to me. She couldn't.

"Owen!"

She gave my face a firm slap.

"Owen! The police are here."

My brain's operating system kicked on, the rainbow wheel cursor giving way to a flurry of opening windows. It was too much to take in at once. I paused for a beat, waited for the cascade to conclude, and honed in on the foremost display: the moment at hand.

"Alright, the cops are here." My words were quick and clear.

"Yes," Izzy replied, matching my composure.

"Many cops, not just Nikolasdottir?"

"Correct, there are at least three cars outside. They're knocking at the door. What should we do?"

"Fuck. Okay." I took a second, looked up toward the ceiling, and clicked through the mass of open windows on my brain's desktop. Given time, Izzy and I could sort through it all together, try and figure out what was happening and how to handle it, but there was no time, so there was no handling it. There was only one option.

"You get Lola so she's not scared," I said. "I'll get the door."

"Okay," Izzy replied, composed as a well-drilled soldier. She kissed me and headed to the nursery. I went downstairs and opened the door for the police. They didn't say hello. Instead, they greeted me with handcuffs and warrants and my Miranda rights.

Chapter 42

Police handcuffs suck. They're way worse than the ones Izzy and I use for sexy time. There's no fuzziness, just unyielding steel. Of course I knew that before, but it still surprised me. The reality was so much worse than I expected. By the time I got to the interrogation room my wrists were ringed with bruises.

"Your arms got a little banged up there, eh? Sorry about that."

I looked up at Detective Nikolasdottir. She was holding two coffees, one of which she offered to me. I wanted to give her a big middle finger, but I figured that was a bad idea, so I made a muddled noise of displeasure and accepted the beverage instead.

"Cream or sugar?"

She set a couple of each down on the cold metal table. I took the cream, added it to my cup, and stirred. Nikolasdottir watched intently as if close observation of my coffee preparation would help her crack the case.

Oh brother, she thinks she's in the fuckin' BAU.

I rolled my eyes.

"Something wrong, Mr. O'Shea?"

"Well, I'm in an interrogation room at the police station getting questioned for a double homicide that I had nothing to do with, so, yeah, could be better." I couldn't help the smart-ass from coming out. I was too tired and too hangry to keep it in.

"So ya' know that you're here for the murder of the Russians then!" Nikolasdottir replied, jumping on my words like she'd caught me in something.

"Yeah, the police officer kind of gave it away when he said: 'You are under arrest on suspicion of the murders of Boris and Natasha Smirnov.'"

"Oh. Yah, I suppose."

"Also you've been out to our house to interview me about it like four times."

"That's true."

"Come on, Nikolasdottir, you know I had nothing to do with this."

"You're probably right. It's more than likely a screw up. I bet we can clear it up in no time. I just need ya to run through the day's events once more for me. But on the record this time, with a tape rolling. No big deal."

"Sure."

"Okay, great. Why don't we start—"

"I was being sarcastic, Nikolasdottir! Obviously, it's a big deal, you just sent three cop cars to arrest me."

"Well now, that was just a precaution, ya know. I—"

"No. No, I don't know. I don't know why you keep focusing on me, and interviewing me, and suspecting me. It doesn't make any sense. If you're going to investigate somebody in the cul-de-sac it should be the Stoneciphers. They're the shady ones."

"And why do ya say that?"

"Uh, because they're terrible."

"How so?"

"Well, I'm almost certain that they're doing something illegal in their garage."

"And what do ya think that is?"

"I don't know, probably murdering people."

"Now that's quite an accusation, Mr. O'Shea."

"Yes! It is! You want to know how I know it's quite an accusation?"

"How do ya kno—"

"Because you just accused me of it!"

"Oh yah. Yah, I see. I walked into that one, didn't I?"

"Mmm."

"Alright then, why don't ya take a couple of breaths, calm down, and explain everything to me."

"Okay, fine." I sat up in my chair, attempted to suppress my irritation, and mulled over where to begin. This was a good chance to tell a person with actual authority about the Stoneciphers' misdeeds. I couldn't let my anger, or my skeptical view of Nikolasdottir's competence get in the way of that opportunity. "I suppose it started a while ago, pretty much as soon as Izzy and I moved in. That was a few years back now, two thousand and—"

"How about something more recent," Nikolasdottir interrupted. "Why don't ya start with Alexandra Stonecipher? Maybe tell me what ya two were talking about when ya discovered the bodies of Boris and Natasha."

"Oh my God." I shook my head and rubbed my temples in frustration.

"Now don't get upset, I'm just tryin—"

"Lawyer."

"What's that now?"

"Lawyer. I want my lawyer. Get Tanner over here."

"Well, ya do have the right to an attorney of course. But if ya could just talk to me about that day—"

"Absolutely."

"Great, then—"

"As soon as my lawyer gets here."

"Listen, Mr. O'Shea, I'm trying to do ya a favor here. It looks bad if ya wait for your lawyer. It looks like you're trying to hide something, and innocent people don't try and hide things."

I had a retort, but I bit it back. "Lawyer," I said again, simply.

"Alright, then fine." The detective made a show of collecting her things. "I guess I'll leave ya alone until your attorney arrives."

Nikolasdottir left the room. I immediately put my head down and fell asleep. It turned out to be a pretty good nap. The chair was hard, the table was cold, and the lights were loud, but none of that mattered. I was too exhausted for it to matter. Plus, there was no baby monitor sound in the background and that was a welcome reprieve. I didn't realize how much I needed a break from that static hum until I got one. The part of my brain midway between my eyes and the back of my skull relaxed for the first time in months. I think that means parenting a newborn is more draining than getting interrogated for a double homicide.

Nah, that can't be right.

But maybe.

Chapter 43

"Owen."

"Huh? What? I got her, babe. You go back to bed." I lifted my head, wiped the drool from my chin, leaned over, and gave Izzy a kiss on the cheek. Her face was scratchy. I looked over to see why. That's when I realized it wasn't her face it was Tanner's. It was the rest of him too—arms, legs, torso, all the parts that comprise a human being.

"The kiss was nice, but you're still going to have to pay me in dollars," Tanner jested as he pulled stuff from his briefcase.

"Shit. Sorry, man, I'm a bit out of it." I rubbed my eyes then looked around the space to try and reorient myself. Bright, white, sterile, the aesthetic of the interrogation room had not improved during my nap. "Did this room get even uglier?"

"No, it's actually gotten a lot better," Tanner replied.

"Really?"

"Yeah," he winked. "I'm here now."

I smiled, encouraged by the levity.

Tanner shuffled some papers into a neat pile, set them down on the table, and turned toward me.

"Listen, Owen, here's the deal." His voice turned more serious—not in a dire way, in a business way. "I know you. I think you're a good guy, and I think you're innocent."

"Thanks, I think you're—"

"But none of that matters. Not really anyway. Sure, if you tell me you're guilty I have to make sure that you don't perjure yourself or whatever, but that's about it. All that really matters is that you listen to me and do what I say. Understand?"

"Understand."

"Good. Now what I say is this: shut up. Just completely shut up. Do not open your mouth at all, not even to breathe. Pretend

144

your life depends on your lips staying locked together, because your life depends on your lips staying locked together. Got it?"

I nodded my head.

"Perfect. Good start. Now let me tell you what to expect. Detective Nikolasdottir is going to come in here and try some bullshit interrogation tactics on you. They're not going to work because I'm here, but she's going to try them anyway. I don't know why she does it. Maybe because she's a dummy and thinks that the interrogation techniques will work even with an attorney present, or maybe because she's just really persistent and figures it's worth a shot. Regardless, it's going to happen, so be prepared."

I nodded again, my lips growing pale from my top notch keeping-them-shut.

"She'll probably begin by trying to build up a rapport," Tanner continued. "You know, shoot the shit about something completely unrelated to the murder, try and get you to feel comfortable talking to her. It doesn't matter that y'all have already talked a bunch at your house because she needs you to be comfortable here and now in this eyesore of an interrogation room. Actually, I'm guessing she already started doing the rapport thing. That or she jumped right into talking about the crime scene in the hopes of getting something out of you before I arrived."

I held up two fingers to indicate that she had done the latter.

"Okay," Tanner nodded, processing the information. "But you didn't tell her anything about it, right?"

I silently confirmed.

"Good. Well then as I was saying, she's going to start with the rapport building schtick. Then when she's done with that, she'll ask you some basic biography questions that she already knows the answers to. The goal of those questions is to just get you responding. The questions themselves are innocuous, but the motive behind them is not, because once somebody starts talking they tend to keep talking, and that's bad, so don't talk at all. Just shut…"

Tanner waited for me to finish his sentence.

I stayed quiet.

"Nice, you're a quick study."

I shrugged and nodded in faux modesty. I don't know if it was the arrival of Tanner or the nap, but I was feeling better about everything.

"After the biography questions, she'll come back to the day of the murder. She'll ask you a bunch of questions about a variety of details in order to try and find inconsistencies that she can use against you later. But she's not going to find any inconsistencies because you're going to stay shut up, right?"

I nodded again.

"Excellent," Tanner continued. "Then comes the hard part— Actually, it's not really hard because all you have to do is stay quiet, but it is hard because she's going to say some shit that you're really going to want to respond to. First, she's going to leave the room for a bit, then she's going to come back with a folder, or a box, or something else that looks intimidatingly like evidence, and then she's going to tell you that it *is* evidence and that it all points to you."

My eyes widened. My heartbeat quickened. I knew that cops could lie about stuff during an interrogation, but knowing it and being prepared to experience it are two very different things. As I processed Tanner's words my throat got a lump in it—a legit lump. I'd always thought that was just an expression, but nope. It's real and it sucks. It feels like you swallowed a hard-boiled egg dipped in sawdust and fret.

"Don't worry," Tanner continued, his voice confident with a hint of nurturing. "It's all bullshit. Even when a person is actually guilty it's usually bullshit. They're just trying to shake you, that way when they go to their finishing move, you're more likely to go along with it. And let me tell you, their finishing move is effective—brilliant really. They basically get you to confess directly without directly confessing."

Huh? My face said.

"Yeah, it's a little confusing. See what happens is the detective asks you if you committed the murders by asking you a different, seemingly more benign, question that asserts you committed the murders. Something like: 'Why did you decide to stab them? Was Boris being annoying? Because I know he can be annoying, all your neighbors have said so.' And see, if you admit Boris was being annoying, or simply that he can be annoying, then you've basically admitted to the murders."

Goddamn that seems shady.

"I know," Tanner said, reading my expression. "It's borderline at best, but that's how they do it. That, and sometimes they ask questions where they give you two alternatives to choose from, both of which admit to the crime, but one of which seems way more reasonable than the other. So, for instance they might ask: 'Did you stab them because of your hatred of immigrants, or because you thought they might hurt your child?'"

Fuck.

"Yeah, it's crazy unscrupulous. You just naturally want to say yes to the protecting-your-kids option because it's reasonable and human, and because the other choice makes you sound like a xenophobic nutjob, but the second you do that, you're screwed. And that's how they get you. That's how innocent people end up confessing. It's awful, but it's not going to change any time soon, and that's why you need to stay shut up. Got it?"

I took a deep breath and gave one more nod.

"Alright, I'll go let them know that we're ready." Tanner stood up and moved toward the door. "Hopefully, they realize that you're going to stay quiet and decide to end things early, but don't count on it. Detective Nikolasdottir is not the type to let things—"

"O'Shea, you can go."

Chapter 44

Tanner was a yard from the door when Nikolasdottir flung it open and pronounced my freedom. His expression was pure astonishment. Maybe because he was certain that the detective would put us through the whole interrogation no matter what, but probably because the door almost broke his perfectly proportioned nose as it swung passed.

I was equally surprised. Not by the door part, by the letting-me-go part. I mean *I* knew I was innocent, but Nikolasdottir didn't seem to, and I figured it was going to take a while for her to suss it out.

Guess not.

"Uh, okay then," I said, standing up. "So, I can just leave?" It felt awkward, like I was in elementary school asking for the potty pass during a spelling test.

"Yah, go ahead," Detective Nikolasdottir replied. She stepped to the side and gestured toward the door.

I looked over at Tanner for confirmation that I was free to go. I didn't want to fall victim to some stupid miscommunication based tragedy. It would be just like me to get shot for not hearing. Izzy would feel sad, but also vindicated. *I kept telling him that he needed to listen better.* That's what she would mutter through her tears as she identified my body. At least that's what I suspect she would mutter. Fortunately, we will never know for sure because after a couple of seconds Tanner got his shit together and responded to my appeal for guidance with a bemused shrug of the shoulders and a nod toward the door.

Cautiously, I exited the interrogation room and then the police station. Tanner walked behind me. On the way out he yelled something about filing a civil suit against the department for false arrest. He sounded confident and pissed off and a tad arrogant, which is exactly what you want your defense attorney

148

to sound like. It made me feel better but not all-the-way better. Confusion still tempered my enthusiasm.

"What just happened?" I asked, as the precinct doors closed behind us.

Tanner laughed then replied: "I have absolutely no idea."

Chapter 45

"…and then Nikolasdottir just let me go."

"Without an explanation?"

"Yup."

"And you have no idea why?"

"None."

"And Tanner doesn't know either?"

"No, he seemed just as confused as I was, maybe more."

"But he's a defense attorney, he should have some inkling."

"It didn't seem like it. He said that he had absolutely no idea, and that something must have fallen through."

"Well, that's not no idea," Izzy retorted, her voice equal parts exasperation and relief. "Something-fell-through is an idea."

"Yeah, I guess that's true."

"No, it's definitely true."

"Okay. So do you have any idea what that something-that-fell-through is?"

"Yes," Izzy said, matter of fact.

"What?" I asked, excited and nervous.

"I think it's a trowel."

"A trowel? Like the thing bricklayers use to spread mortar."

"I guess so, yeah. Listen, after they took you away, I lost it—like furious lost it, not crying lost it."

"I'd expect nothing less."

"Thanks, babe." Izzy smiled and gave my arm a squeeze. "Anyway, they didn't know how to handle me. If I was some burly dude, they would have just taken me outside and put me in the back of a squad car, but I'm a tiny woman and I was holding a tiny baby, so that wasn't an option. The optics would have been terrible, and they did not want that, not with all those people looking on, so instead they assigned some rookie to watch me."

"Oh God."

"Yeah, I ate that kid alive."

"I have no doubt." The thought of a baby-faced officer trying to control Izzy at her maximum-fierce was hilarious. It overpowered the gut punch feeling that accompanied the mental image of my wife and child getting gawked at by our neighbors while the police searched our place.

"Basically, the kid just followed me around the house saying, 'Mam, please calm down,' while I berated everybody," Izzy continued.

"That sounds right."

"But then after a while I realized that reaming people out probably wasn't the best use of my time, so I stopped yelling and started observing, and the young cop was so happy that I'd calmed down that he let me go wherever I wanted, which means I got to see exactly what the police were up to. That's how I figured out that they weren't doing a general search of our house, but rather were looking for something specific."

"A trowel?"

"Exactly. A trowel. It took me a while to work that out though. At first, I just heard people saying, 'Did you find it yet?' With nobody mentioning what the *it* was. But eventually some uniform officer replied, 'No, no trowel,' and as soon as he said it, he got awkwardly silent, and the cop to his left shot him an admonishing stare like he'd fucked up, and then nobody mentioned it again."

"Interesting."

"It is." Izzy paused briefly to let me take in the information, then floated a query: "So do you have any idea why they were looking for a trowel?"

"They must think it's the murder weapon, right?"

"Yeah, I think that has to be it," Izzy agreed. "Honestly, I thought that before I asked the question, I just didn't want to be the first to say it out loud."

"I get that. It's not the most comforting thought." I moved the ice pack that was wrapped around my left wrist over to my right while mulling over the idea of a trowel as the murder weapon. "It also doesn't really make sense," I added. "Isn't a trowel a flat metal rectangle with a handle centered on the back of it? You couldn't stab somebody to death with one of those. You could bludgeon them, sure, but not stab them. And Boris and Natasha were one-hundred percent stabbed."

Izzy shook her head as she typed something into her phone.

"You're right about the metal rectangle with a handle centered on the back, that is a trowel, but it's not the only type that bricklayers use. There are a bunch of different kinds, see." She turned the screen my way. It was populated by dozens of images of trowels. They all had metal parts for applying mortar and handle parts for holding, but other than that varied widely in size and shape.

"Well that's interesting, but it just makes me more confused."

"Why is that?"

"Because it doesn't make any sense. I mean how the hell could the police know to be looking for a trowel? That's way too specific. You couldn't narrow the murder weapon down to that just from looking at the wounds, could you?"

"No way. I mean you could narrow it down but not to something that specific. Even if you had the actual murder weapon, the most you could do would be to say that a certain trowel is compatible with the wounds."

"Right. And if they already had the murder weapon then they wouldn't be over here looking for it."

"True."

"So then, what the hell?"

"I don't know, babe... Unless."

"Unless what?"

"Unless somebody told them to look for a trowel."

"Like specifically? As in: 'Search the O'Shea place for a bloody trowel.'"

"Exactly."

"Well, if that's the case, that's not good."

"No, it's not."

"It means... What? That the Stoneciphers are trying to set us up?"

"It means somebody is."

I shook my head. "It's gotta be the Stoneciphers. They're the only ones that make sense."

"Well, I agree that they make the most sense, but they're not the only ones—"

"Oh shit." I interjected, cutting Izzy off as a light bulb clicked on in my head.

"What?"

"The Stoneciphers filled in the windows to their garage with fieldstone just a few months ago. That means they have a bunch of trowels lying around."

"Fuck." Izzy exhaled.

"Yeah," I echoed. "Fuck."

We both quieted, running through the implications of this newest realization in our heads. After a couple of minutes, she broke the silence.

"So, one other thing," she said.

"Yeah?" I tensed up, preparing for more bad news.

"I'm fairly certain that the police were told where in the house to look."

"Like somewhere specific, like a room?"

"Precisely. Take a sec and look around."

"I am, everything seems okay."

"Exactly, and that's weird. Everything should *not* seem okay. The cops were just here searching for a murder weapon, the whole place should be upside down."

"You're right. So why isn't it?"

"Because they were only focused on the nursery."

"Seriously?"

"Seriously."

Izzy walked me up to Lola's room. The sight of it filled me with fury and disappointment—fury at the cops for tearing apart the room of our daughter, disappointment in myself for having allowed it to happen. It didn't matter that there was nothing we could do to stop it, I still felt like a failure. A parent shouldn't let that happen to their child's room regardless of the circumstances.

Rather than speak I walked in and started picking up. Izzy did the same. We proceeded in silence for a while, cleaning up Lola's room and the space between our ears at the same time.

"I should have asked to see the search warrant." Izzy declared some twenty minutes later, breaking the quiet. "I bet the nursery was the only room listed."

"You think so? Is that even possible?"

"I'm pretty sure, yeah. I mean I'm basing this on one semester of Con Law, but I think a warrant is supposed to describe the specific area to be searched and the specific thing—or things—to be searched for."

"But you said there were cops all around the house, not just in Lola's room."

"There were, but they weren't really searching in the same way. They were looking around, but they weren't opening anything up or rifling through stuff. Think about it, it would take them forever to search our whole house for something as small as a trowel. If they had a search warrant for the entire place they'd still be here and you'd still be in jail."

I nodded my head gravely. "So why would the search warrant be so limited?"

"I don't know."

"But if you had to guess."

"Well, if I had to guess I would say it was because their evidence is thin. That would make a judge hesitant to issue a broadly written warrant."

"Thin like what?"

Izzy shrugged.

"Maybe an anonymous tip?" I posited.

"Maybe," Izzy nodded. "Probably not that alone, but that in conjunction with the fact that you discovered the bodies and other circumstantial stuff."

"That's not good. That seems like even more evidence that I'm being set up."

"Yes, it does."

"Fuck me."

"Maybe later," Izzy smiled, her expression haggard but warm. "After we figure this out."

***

I only slept for an hour that night, and the Stoneciphers haunted every minute. In the dream I was unable to move or speak. All I could do was watch as they took turns laying bricks, gradually sealing me into a wall in their garage. They didn't talk as they worked, but they did smile. And when a tear dropped from my eye, their smiles grew, and grew, and grew, and when it seemed they could grow no bigger, their mouths cracked at the corners, and then ripped, and then tore. Upward and upward they tore, until they reached their ears. Then there was a pause, and growing tension in their faces, then the sound of popping knuckles and slurped noodles, and all at once the base of their ears split and their grins continued northward, up to their audio canals and then down them, down into the depths of their skulls. And then, when I thought the horror show had concluded, the blood came. It poured in uniform sheets from every inch of their smiles, covering the bottom half of their faces in red, streaming off their chins and pooling on the floor. A gory treat for the wolf at their feet.

Chapter 46

I walked outside and the shit followed me. I mean that both literally and figuratively.

When you empty Lola's diaper pail the dirty nappies come out in a long string. It looks like a pearl necklace for a noseblind giant. It's unwieldy and smelly and an all around pain in the ass to dispose of. Usually, I do my best to carry it out to the garbage in a dignified fashion, but not today. Today I just dragged it behind me. I dragged it all the way out to the curb, flipped open the garbage lid, sloppily heaved it in, flipped the lid closed, and walked away. The last few diapers on the strand didn't even make it inside the bin, they just hung there like a dog's tongue on a hot day. It wasn't classy, but I didn't care. Let the HOA write me a warning. Let passersby furrow in disapproval. It didn't matter. Our family's shit was already on full display. A few more diapers weren't going to change anyone's perception.

"How did it go?" Izzy asked upon my reentrance.

"What, the trip out to the garbage? Good, I guess."

Izzy flashed me a come-on-man face.

"What?" I replied.

"You know what. That wasn't just another trip to the curb. That was your first time outside since the cops brought you in. How was it? Was everybody out there gaping at you, or were they being more discreet? You know, checking you out from the corner of their windows."

"A little of both."

"Interesting. I had my money on the windows. It seems classier."

A moment passed in silence. I could tell Izzy wanted to get serious so I stayed quiet and waited for her to change the tone of the conversation.

"O—" Her voice cracked. She paused, steadied herself with a sip of coffee, and then continued on, resolute. "Owen, how are we going to handle this? Are we going to keep to ourselves until this disaster gets sorted out, or are we going to move, or are we going to act like nothing's wrong, or what? What's the plan? I'm behind you no matter what, I just want to know."

I took a second before replying. I wanted to make sure my voice was sure and confident, and when it came out, it was.

"I think we should live our lives as normally as we can, and if people act weird or suspicious, we address it head-on, as candidly as possible."

"I like that," Izzy smiled.

"Good," I said, and brought her in for a kiss. "I like it, too."

We held each other for a while, secure and warm in one another's arms. It was nice. I could feel the tension trickle out of my body with each breath.

I could stay here all morning, I thought.

Then Lola started crying and my phone buzzed.

Chapter 47

A text from Riddhi, that's what the buzz was. She sent it to the group chat. The ensuing conversation went like this:

Riddhi (Neighbor — Loud):

Owen, just saw you taking out the garbage. You look like shit.
What happened!?! Are you okay? Did they arrest you?
Did they check your butt for contraband? OMG they did, didn't they.
That should be illegal. That's like unconstitutional.
You gotta tell us all about it. Do you want to meet now?
Should I bring some Preparation H over to help with your asshole?
It's leftover from when I had RJ but it should still work.
I don't think that stuff expires.

Me:
Let's talk tonight. We can meet
up before the party.

Me:
And yes, bring the Prep H.
They didn't search my butt but
I could still use it.

Elle (Neighbor — Fashionable):
Wait, so you're still going to
Alexandra Stonecipher's thing?

Me:
You bet your ass.

Elle (Neighbor — Fashionable):
Good for you. Excited to talk!

159

Riddhi (Neighbor—Loud):
*Are you betting Elle's ass
because the police destroyed
yours?*

Me:
*You're on to me. Shhh! Don't
tell Elle.*

Riddhi (Neighbor—Loud):
Eddie-Murphy-zipping-his-
lips GIF

Elle(Neighbor—Fashionable):
Unamused-Hermione-
Granger-slow-clap GIF

Me:
Ha. Y'all are the best/worst

Me:
Meet at Riddhi's at 7:00?

Riddhi (Neighbor—Loud):
Michelle-from-Full-House-
"You-got-it-dude" GIF

Elle(Neighbor—Fashionable):
Young-Keanu-Reeves-
thumbs-up GIF

Me:
Ron-Burgundy-riding-a-
unicorn-on a rainbow
"I-friggin-love-you" GIF

And in that mature and articulate fashion our plan to meet up
was set. I was excited to see my friends. I was also excited for
the party. Weird, I know, given the circumstances, but true. And
to my credit the party did turn out to be exciting. Bad—really,
really bad—but exciting.

Chapter 48

The night didn't start off horribly. Sure, our babysitter canceled because her parents had some concerns about the whole watching-the-child-of-a-murder-suspect-at-said-suspect's-house thing, but we found a replacement right away. We didn't even have to ask. Sota, Elle's husband, just volunteered. He had a business call with his firm's Tokyo office that night so he couldn't go to the party anyway, and since both his son and Lola would be asleep, he could do both the kid watching and the teleconference at the same time.

"I'll just text you if she starts crying, and I can't get her because I'm on the call," he reassured.

To which I replied: "Cool."

And it was cool. Normally. But given all the shit that had happened, I was feeling less cool about pretty much everything, and that definitely included my daughter. In order to alleviate my concern, but not seem untrusting or overly protective, I surreptitiously slid the tiny bluetooth that's connected to the baby monitor into my ear, thus giving me the ability to listen in for myself. No one saw me do it except for Izzy, and she just smiled and mouthed the words "good idea."

The night's positive trajectory continued at Riddhi and Ryan's. I hadn't seen my friends in weeks and the simple act of spending face-to-face time with them had a restorative effect that exceeded my expectations. I was still tired and haggard and muddled, but I wasn't exclusively tired and haggard and muddled. I was those things plus happy and present. It was nice. Fun. Rejuvenating. So, I let myself enjoy it. I didn't ask about Elle's drug use or Riddhi's late-night liaison with the cops. I didn't posit hypotheses about the Russians' demise, or the Peabodys' weird behavior. I didn't even discuss the Stoneciphers and their evil machinations. I just laughed with my friends and they did the same. I'm sure they wanted to ask me questions about the interrogation and the search of the house, but they didn't because they knew I needed a break. They knew it the second they saw my face, and they were kind and decent enough to give it to me. It was great. Unfortunately, it also turned out to be regrettable. If only I had talked that stuff out with them then.

Chapter 49

I blame the hors d'oeuvres. Not totally, but partially. Of course, I'm at fault as well, but I'm sure I would have done better if I'd had something in my stomach. Something to absorb a bit of the booze, something to keep me from getting hangry, something to lubricate the gears in my brain.

"Uuuggglechk."

We'd been at the party for five minutes and I was already dry heaving.

Elle, Izzy, Riddhi, and Ryan all looked at me in alarm.

"You okay?"

"What the hell was that?"

"Sorry I—guhhhaaahhhg," I actually heaved. Not a lot, just my most recent bite back up into my mouth. I immediately spat the regurgitated bit into a napkin, looked for a trashcan to toss it in, failed to find one, wrapped the first napkin inside of two more napkins, and slid the wad into my pocket.

"Gross," Riddhi looked at me the way a debutante looks at a porta-potty. "Owen, did you just put puke in your pocket?"

"Yes," I inhaled deeply and closed my eyes in embarrassment. "Yes, I did. Was it obvious?"

"Oh, for sure."

"Yup."

"Clear as day."

"Shit. Do you think anyone beside you guys noticed?"

"Yes."

"One hundred percent."

"Absolutely they did."

"Balls." A second passed then I shrugged in upbeat resignation. "Oh well, can't do anything about it now."

Izzy smiled, plucked a glass of wine from a passing tray, and handed it to me. "Here, get the taste out of your mouth."

"Thanks, babe." I took a sip. It was delicious, so I took another and swished it around my mouth. "What the hell did I just eat? I thought it was sushi but it was not sushi."

"It smelled like the pickled ejaculate of an aging fisherman."

"That's good, Riddhi," I replied, light sarcasm in my tone, a third wave of bile in my throat. "You really paint a portrait with your words."

"I don't know why you're getting testy with me, you're the one that's been working on this party with Alexandra. Don't you know what the caterer is serving?"

"Actually, no." I gulped some more wine. "When I brought up food, Alexandra said she had it under control, so I left it at that. I figured she had a go-to caterer or something."

"It's probably just that one dish," Elle said diplomatically. "Here, try this." She plucked something from the nearest tray and handed it to me. It looked like a hard-boiled egg that had been bullied its entire life, all bruised and down on itself.

"Uh uh, I'm not trying that." I shook my head for emphasis.

"No way, girl," Riddhi declined. She touched the tip of her nose while she spoke in case it turned into a not-it situation.

"Dear God you guys are babies," Izzy chided. "Give me that." She snatched the mystery food from Elle's outstretched hand, popped the whole thing into her mouth, and got to chewing.

The havoc wasn't immediate. The bad egg was craftier than that. It lured Izzy in, got her comfortable, gave her assurances that everything would be all right, and then... Ka-Blam! It attacked.

All at once Izzy's eyes widened, her mouth frowned, and her brow furrowed. Her skin tone shifted from average Korean to scared albino. Perspiration bloomed from the pores on her forehead and neck and shoulders and knees—knees that were visibly shaking, suddenly unsound, too weak to do their job.

"Babe, you look bad. You need help?"

Izzy nodded with intensity.

"Bathroom?" I asked while draping her arm over my shoulder.

Izzy nodded again, her mouth clenched tight.

Riddhi hit her husband in the arm and told him to help. He quickly slid under Izzy's other shoulder, and we made our way to the bathroom. Izzy is short, and Ryan and I are tall-ish, so it was awkward, but we got there.

As soon as we arrived, Izzy dropped to her knees in front of the toilet. Speaking into the porcelain bowl she said: "Ryan, you're a good friend and I appreciate you. Now get the fuck out of here." Then she puked hard and a lot. Ryan had already turned away, so he didn't see, but he definitely heard. It was loud.

Unsure of how to be of service, I stepped into the bathroom, closed the door behind me, turned on the fan, and held Izzy's hair. Her thick raven locks were already up in a high bun, so I wasn't really helping, but it was the only move that came to mind, so I did it anyway. She puked two more times.

"Ugh," Izzy exhaled heavily. She lowered the lid, flushed the toilet, turned around, and sat on the floor.

"You okay, babe? Never mind, that's stupid, you're not okay. I meant, like, do we need to take you to the hospital?"

She shook her head, ripped off a piece of toilet paper, and wiped her face.

"Was it food poisoning? No, it couldn't have been, it was too fast."

"You're right, it wasn't food poisoning." Izzy had post-throw-up voice—lower and more tentative than normal. "I don't know, I think it was just a visceral reaction to that texture and taste. I really thought you were overreacting when you ate that not-sushi, but after I tasted that egg, I think you might have been under-reacting."

"I was absolutely under-reacting. It was way worse than I let on. I'm super stoic, like a Spartan."

"A Spartan, huh? Sexy. If I hadn't just puked, I'd make a move."

"Go for it. I don't mind. You still look super hot."

Izzy laughed. "Thanks, babe." She held out a hand and I helped her to her feet. "We'll play later, I promise." She gave my cock a playful squeeze over my pants. "Now get out of here and let me get cleaned up."

I slapped her butt then did as instructed.

On the way out I contemplated whether or not pre-baby Owen would have hooked up with Izzy after she puked from a bad meal? Maybe parenting had lowered my standards? Maybe I'd become so hard up that I was willing to take anything I could get?

Nah, I concluded, *I've always taken anything I could get.*

Chapter 50

It was about forty yards from the bathroom back to where my friends were standing. I intended to spend the entire walk thinking about hooking up with my sexy wife later that night, but the eyes and the murmurs ruined it. There were a lot of them. It's remarkable that I didn't notice earlier. It must have been going on since the moment I stepped into the party. Evidently, the warm glow of fun times with friends had inoculated me against the glares and whispers of others, but not anymore.

Trying to mask my unease, I grabbed a glass of wine from the bar and casually made my way back toward the group. En route I caught snippets of various conversations. Nearly all of them dealing with yours truly:

"Do you really think he did it?"

"...covered in Boris's and Natasha's blood."

"Izzy can do better..."

"...remember the 'mud' on his shoe?"

"His poor daughter..."

The talking didn't make me feel pissed off, it just made me feel impotent. I fully accepted that people were going to gossip. If the situation were reversed, I'd do the same. The problem was that there was no way for me to efficiently and effectively combat the rumors, no way to win people over. It was too widespread. There were too many groups to talk to. I couldn't have fifty different conversations at once. I had told Izzy that we should live our lives as normally as possible, that we should address people's suspicions candidly and head-on, but those words now struck me as unworkable.

When I was three-quarters of the way back to the group I realized my glass was empty, so I did a one-eighty and returned to the bar. It meant hearing more people whisper about me, but it was worth it. It had been ages since I'd gotten a buzz, and it was feeling nice. It was also making the gossip more tolerable.

"Scotch, right?" the bartender said as I bellied up to the bar.

He was wrong, I don't even like hard liquor, but I didn't correct him. At that moment it sounded good.

After I got the drink I said thanks, left a tip, took a step away, tasted the drink, surprisingly enjoyed it, swallowed it down in one, returned to the bar, and ordered another. That's when I noticed both Tanner and the Peabodys. They were standing in a tight circle to my right, engrossed in conversation. Half of me wanted to be nosy and ease my way into earshot, but the other half thought that was trashy and I should mind my own business. The two sides quickly duked it out in my head and the nosy part won.

"That's terrible."

Those were the first words I made out as I inched over toward their discussion. They came from Tanner. He was shaking his head in compassionate frustration.

"Indeed, it is," Preston Peabody confirmed. "Is there anything you can do for us?"

"Unfortunately, that's not really the type of law I practice."

"No, we know, but Prudence and I still think you would be a good addition to our legal team." Preston held out his hand to his wife. She gave it a supportive squeeze. "Just the idea of having someone on our side that we know, someone that we are confident will speak openly and honestly and directly, that's very important to us. We already have attorneys with the requisite legal expertise, we want to add you because we trust you."

Tanner nodded contemplatively. He was warming to the idea. "Okay, that seems reasonable enough. Let me think it over." He took a sip from his highball glass. "But speaking of candor and transparency, I want you to know, before we do anything official, that there's a slight conflict of interest here. I mean they found me and hired me and brought me into town. They even helped me find my house. We parted ways soon after, but still, there's a history there."

Prudence and Preston nodded their heads.

Prudence spoke: "We already know. The fact that you told us up front like this is why we don't care."

"Indeed," Preston added, echoing his wife. "Also, you've proven that you're willing to stand up to them. Not too many people in this town can say the same."

"Well, don't think too highly of me yet," Tanner jested amiably. "But I am leaning toward yes. I'll let you know for sure by end-of-business on Monday, sound fair?"

Both of the Peabodys nodded their heads, shook hands with Tanner, and left. I watched as they walked out the front door. It was early, the evening's events hadn't even started, but I wasn't surprised to see them go. I'd been far more surprised to see them there in the first place. People don't normally attend parties hosted by enemies whose property they've vengefully peed on.

It's curious, I thought.

And since I was now a little drunk, I said it out loud as well: "It's curious." Just like that, right to Tanner's face.

"What's curious?" Tanner replied, taking my interjection in his stride.

"The Peabodys, I'm surprised they came. I didn't think they were very big fans of the Stoneciphers."

"Ha, yeah, you hit the bullseye with that assessment. But it's pretty hard to forego a Stonecipher event, even if it is for a stupid cause." Tanner held up his hand, apologetically. "Sorry, I know you helped plan this."

"No—I mean yes, I helped plan it, but there's no need to apologize. I also think it's a terrible cause."

"Oh, good. I thought it was weird that you were helping with this thing, you didn't strike me as a big fan of the measles."

"Nope. Mumps and rubella, maybe, but not the measles."

"That's funny." He took a drink from his glass then made an I-just-remembered face. "Oh my God, is this the party that Riddhi was talking about that day you guys gave me the cookies? The one you were going to trick Alexandra into hosting?"

"Yeah, actually. I can't believe you remember that."

"Well, it's not every day you hear someone talk about tricking someone else into having a party."

"Touche."

"So, why'd you two do it if you don't like the cause?"

"That's a good question."

I took a long sip of scotch and mulled over how much I should say. It was pretty Machiavellian what we were up to— getting Alexandra to host a party and then offering to assist in the planning of said party in order to snoop. Not exactly something to brag about.

I should probably stay quiet. I thought. Then I thought. *Fuck it. Tanner is cool, and he kind of knows already. Plus, he's my lawyer. It's good to tell your lawyer.*

My drunk-ass blabbed for the next ten minutes. I told Tanner everything. Everything we'd done, everything we suspected, all of it. None of it seemed to surprise him. He just nodded and quietly took in the information. Even when it was clear I was done, he still didn't speak, he just stood there in contemplation. After twenty seconds of dead air, I couldn't handle it any longer.

"Any thoughts?" I prompted.

"Many," he replied.

"Well, that's cryptic as hell."

"Sorry, it's just a lot to take in. I need to process." He took a step closer and leaned in confidentially. "I will tell you this though: I don't think you guys are crazy."

"That's good." Then an idea struck me. "Hey, why don't you come over and talk to Elle and Riddhi. Maybe they can do a better job of explaining than I did."

"Yeah, okay, just let me get another drink first."

Tanner polished off the dregs at the bottom of his glass then turned toward the bartender. I scanned the crowd while I waited for him. A large number of people were still gawking at me. They tried to hide it, but they did a terrible job. There's no way that half the attendees were interested in the shitty painting to my right, it was just a convenient spot for them to move their eyeballs once they realized I was looking their way.

"So, this is what zoo animals feel like," I muttered to myself.

"No," Tanner chimed in, handing me another scotch. "People don't pretend to look away from zoo animals, they just stare unapologetically. Kind of like that." He nodded toward my two o'clock.

I looked in the indicated direction and caught sight of Chip Stonecipher. His eyes were locked on me, his expression an unnerving mix of seething and disgust.

"That stare is more than unapologetic." I said, turning toward Tanner. "That's—I don't know—something not good."

Tanner agreed, and we both turned back toward Chip. He hadn't moved. His glare sent ice down my spinal cord then up and around my backbone, C1 to S5, every vertebra abruptly besieged by a penetrating cold.

Fuck, I thought. *That dude wants to kill me.*

And for the first time I realized precisely what that meant. I don't know why it hadn't hit me before. It should have. Riddhi, Elle, and I had been saying that the Stoneciphers were murderers for weeks, and we'd been investigating them for nearly as long, but up until that moment my body and mind had not fully processed what that meant. Now that my entire being was up to speed on the situation, I was feeling less enthusiastic about the whole endeavor.

Owen, what the hell are you doing? You have a good life. You have a smart and sexy wife, a newborn baby, good friends, financial stability, why are you dicking around with a serial killer investigation? Dislike of your neighbors? Curiosity? Boredom? Those aren't good reasons. Forget this shit. Don't let boredom get you killed. Get a hobby. Go back to work. Start coaching again. Something. Anything. But not this.

Having decided on a responsible course of action, I looked up at Chip, matched his stare, and slowly extended my middle finger.

Chapter 51

I didn't stop with the middle finger. Instead, I mouthed the words *You're done, asshole,* and then blew Chip a kiss. It was a terrible decision and it felt super good.

"Bold move," Tanner laughed.

"I couldn't help myself. He's just such a…"

"Prick?"

"I was going to say arrogant twat, but prick works. Still, I shouldn't have done it. I mean he's a serial killer, or probably a serial killer. I just talked smack to a probably-serial-killer. That's bad."

"Yeah, I'm not going to lie, it was a mistake."

"Entertaining though, right?"

"Very," Tanner smiled, then slapped me on the back. "Come on, let's go talk to Riddhi and Elle."

Feeling a strange blend of amused, proud, and scared I walked with Tanner toward the group, sipping from my new glass of scotch on the way.

"He's back! And he's brought a friend." Riddhi said, greeting Tanner and me enthusiastically.

"Hey!" Elle and Ryan cheered, raising their glasses.

Apparently, they'd all gotten drunk while I'd been away. That's okay. I wasn't jealous. I was getting there as well. I was, however, envious of the rolls in their hands. They actually looked like edible food and I was in desperate need of precisely that.

"What are those?" I said, pointing at the bread.

"I dunno," Ryan replied, his mouth full. "Pretty good though. Tastes kind of like a pretzel."

"Want one?" Riddhi asked, pulling three rolls from I-don't-know-where.

"Yes." I snatched a roll and shoved it greedily into my mouth. Ryan was wrong, it tasted exactly like a pretzel.

"Where's Izzy?" Elle asked. "Still in the bathroom?"

"She's not here?" I replied, stopping mid-chew.

My thoughts went dark fast. I'd been at the bar for a good ten minutes; Izzy should have returned already. Instinctively, I looked toward Chip. If anyone had done something to my wife it was that seersuckered asshole. But nope, he was still standing in the back of the room near the podium, staring at me with hatred in his eyes.

I met his gaze and scratched my cheek with my middle finger, doubling down on my previous insult.

Alright, if not Chip, then who? I thought.

The answer came immediately: *Alexandra.*

I scanned the rest of the room in search of her and came up empty. Chip's no-better-half was AWOL.

Shit.

Increasing concern evident on my face, Elle piped in with a supportive elbow squeeze and some comforting words: "I'm sure Izzy's still in the bathroom."

"Yeah," I said, projecting a confidence I did not feel. "Yeah, you're right."

"You want me to go and check on her with you?"

"No, that's fine. I'm sure you're right. I'm sure she's okay. And privacy is the nicest thing we can do for her. She hates throwing up around other people."

"I gathered that," Ryan said, injecting some levity. "I've never been dismissed in such a harsh yet polite manner. What'd she say, Owen: 'Ryan you're a good friend and I appreciate you. Now get the fuck out of here'?"

"Ha, yeah, I think you got it exactly. She's great at finding that fine line between sweet and brutal." I forced a smile, but inside I wasn't smiling, I was itching, anxious to go and check on Iz. Elle was right, she was probably still in the bathroom, but

I wanted to know for sure. The impulse to leave the group and find her was overwhelming, my legs hummed with the desire. Yet I stayed put. I needed Tanner to hear everything that Riddhi, Elle, and I were about to tell him, and I needed him to think that it wasn't crazy, and that outcome seemed far more likely if I stayed. So, that's what I did. I took another sip of scotch, stole another glance at Chip's scowl, and got the ball rolling.

Chapter 52

"Shut your face!"

Riddhi was equal parts excited and indignant. The information that I had gathered on the Stoneciphers over the last week made her want to shower me with praise, but the fact that I had not immediately shared said information made her want to give me a titty-twister.

"No way," she continued. "No way! You actually heard the Stoneciphers say that? You heard them talk about not wanting to get caught, and that they had ether, and that shit went bad with Boris and Natasha, and that they had a rack—whatever the fuck that is—you heard all those words leave their mouths?"

"A rack is like a medieval torture device. And yes, I heard them say all of that."

"Well, what the hell, Owen?" Riddhi actually attempted a titty-twister. I blocked it with my drink-free hand. "Why are you just telling us now?"

"I don't know, probably because I got arrested very soon after I gathered the information, so telling you guys what I'd discovered wasn't tops on my priority list."

My reply was heavy on attitude. I hoped it would be enough to chasten Riddhi and prevent further questions on the matter. I really, *really* did not want further questions on the matter. They would be too difficult to answer. I'm not good at lying to people that are close to me, and if Riddhi continued in that vein I would be forced to do exactly that. There'd be no other option. Because the truth is I wouldn't have told Elle and Riddhi even if I hadn't been arrested. At least not right away, not until they told *me* some stuff. Sure, the Stoneciphers' behavior was shady as a cave, but theirs wasn't great either. They had secrets too. Elle with her covert marijuana use, and Riddhi with her late-night cop meetings. Seriously, what was that shit about?

Elle's secret seemed so silly and unnecessary that it made me question what else she was hiding, and Riddhi's was so huge that her continued silence on the matter made me wonder if I was completely wrong about her.

My ears warmed and my face reddened just thinking about it all. I took another sip of scotch and clenched my jaw in a bid to suppress my negative thoughts, but it was to no avail. All I got was a little bit drunker, a little bit huffier, and a little bit sore in the molars.

Riddhi must have sensed something was off because she let it go and letting things go is not her forte. "Yeah, I suppose getting arrested gives you an out," she said. "Anyway, now that we know all that stuff, we have to figure out what it means, and I think it means exactly what we already thought."

"And what's that?" Tanner asked, his tone earnest.

"Uh, duh, that the Stoneciphers are nutjob psychopath killers. Keep up, man."

"I'm keeping up, you sass monster," Tanner replied.

We all smiled. His good-natured riposte was a positive sign.

"Bringing the heat," Riddhi grinned. "I like it, you're gonna fit right in."

"Of course I will, I'm wonderful," Tanner winked. He took a sip from his glass and then shifted into a more serious tone. "Anyway, I obviously know that you guys believe the Stoneciphers are engaged in something nefarious, but do you honestly, deep down in your bones, think that they're murderers? Because if we're going to pursue this further, I want to know with absolute certainty that everyone is there."

"Wait, by pursue you mean like legally, like actually get the cops involved and the legal system and whatever?"

"Yeah. Assuming that you all feel similarly and that the evidence you cite is legitimate, I think we should absolutely follow that course of action. And speaking as Owen's legal counsel, I love the idea. It would be extremely helpful to have a couple of serious alternative suspects to offer the police."

Elle. Riddhi. Ryan. Myself. All of us nodded our heads.

"Okay, not to be a stickler, but to be a stickler, I'd like to hear everybody actually say that they're on board."

Riddhi: "You bet your cute ass."

Ryan: "Yeah, I'm on board."

Me: "Yes."

Elle: "…"

"Elle, what the shit?" Riddhi admonished.

"Oh, calm yourself," Elle retorted. "Clearly, I'm on board, especially since that incompetent Detective Nikolasdottir is treating Owen like the prime suspect. It's just that before we dive into the deep end here, I'd like to remind everybody exactly what we're getting into with the Stoneciphers."

"Oh my God, again with the scary Stonecipher bit."

"Yes, again with the scary Stonecipher bit because the Stoneciphers *are* scary."

"No shit, we think they're killers."

"Yes, of course, but it's more than that. It's their history, it's their influence over this town, it's… I don't know. Listen, Riddhi, you're right, this would be frightening no matter what. Trying to prove that your neighbors are murderers is serious business, but when said neighbors are the Stoneciphers, and the town is this town, then it's extremely serious business, potentially life-cratering business."

"Yes, bu—"

"No, she's right." Tanner said, cutting Riddhi off, his words firm and solemn. "I haven't lived here long, but it didn't take long to figure out that the Stoneciphers are something different. They're smart and powerful and controlling, and they have a shocking amount of sway here. If we're all going to do this, then we should all be aware of exactly what we're getting into."

"Yes, thank you." Elle gave a grateful gesture toward Tanner. "That's all I'm saying. I just want everybody going into this with their eyes wide open."

"Alright," Riddhi relented. "I get it. I'll stop being all cavalier about the Stoneciphers. But it doesn't really change anything, I'm still on board."

"Good." Elle smiled, appeased. "So am I."

"Me too," echoed Ryan.

Everyone else having chimed in, all eyes shifted in my direction.

"Why are you all looking at me? I'm in. My life is already inches away from cratering, I've got nowhere to go but up. Same goes for Iz—Oh fuck, Izzy. Where's Izzy? She should for sure be here by now."

I looked toward the bathroom hoping desperately to spot my wife on her way over. But she wasn't on her way over. She wasn't anywhere in sight. And worse, neither were the Stoneciphers.

Chapter 53

I took off across the room. It was crowded but I went in a straight line anyway, plowing aside all those in my path. Delicious drinks and bad food were spilled, fancy dresses and dapper suits ruined. People grumbled and exclaimed and demanded apologies and I said nothing. Izzy's life was in the balance, I didn't care about some woman or the stain I'd left on her Loo-boo-tons. I didn't even know what the fuck Loo-boo-tons were. What I did know was that Izzy was out of sight, and so were the murderous Stoneciphers, and together those two facts added up to bad.

"I'm coming, Iz!" I yelled, midway to the bathroom in which I'd left her. If she was still there, she might be able to hear me, but I suspected that she couldn't, because I suspected that she wasn't. Something in the marrow of my bones told me that the bathroom was empty, that Izzy was gone and not of her own accord.

Shit, shit, shit.

I kept plowing through the crowd.

My heart pummeled the inside of my ribs.

Blood rushed through my veins.

I felt my pulse everywhere.

Eardrums.

Eyeballs.

Butthole.

Everywhere.

Thumping.

Thumping.

Thumping.

Shit, is this what a heart attack feels like? Doesn't matter. Gotta move.

I went up on my toes.

Looked for my destination.

Fifteen yards to go.

I charged onward.

The crowd thinned.

The bathroom neared.

Come on, Iz. Be there.

But I knew she wouldn't be. I could feel it. My brain was already contemplating my next move as I knocked on the door.

"Iz! Izzy! You in there?"

Of course she's not. So where? What would the Stone—

Moaning.

"Izzy?!"

More moaning, "Yeah."

My wife sounded miserable, and I was delighted. Not about her being miserable, about her being there. Sick in a bathroom is bad, but dying in a torture chamber is worse.

"Oh, thank God," I said, my tone borderline ecstatic.

"No—uuuggghhh—this is more of a—uuuggghhh—curse God situation."

"Right, yeah. Sorry." But I wasn't really sorry. I was too relieved to be sorry. "I'm just glad you're in there."

"Where else would I be?"

"Oh. Uh."

And that's when I realized I'm an idiot. The Stonecipher weren't going to attack Izzy in the middle of their own party. What the hell had I been thinking? No serial killers are that blatant. At least not ones that want to get away with it.

Attempting to cover up for my stupidity, I quickly shifted gears into caring husband mode. "Is there anything I can get you, babe?" I asked. "Any way I can help?"

"A ginger ale or Sprite would be awesome," Iz replied, her voice still weak.

"No problem. I got you."

I doubted the Stoneciphers had anything as ordinary as ginger ale or Sprite at the party, but I didn't care. I wasn't going to let that inconvenience spoil the moment. All that mattered was that Izzy was alive and well—or rather alive and sick, but all things considered, that was close enough.

After a couple of minutes of searching, I located a bottle of ginger ale. It was the most pretentious soda I'd ever seen: small-batch, locally sourced, organic. Whatever. I didn't give a shit about the provenance of the beverage so long as it made Izzy feel better.

I grabbed it and headed back, searching for the Stoneciphers on the way. Unfortunately, they were still nowhere to be found. I did spot the gang though. Elle, Riddhi, Ryan, Tanner, none of them had moved. Their expressions hadn't changed either. They still seemed to be engaged in a serious conversation, presumably about how to best take down the Stoneciphers.

Unless it's not about that, I thought.

The idea startled me. It was unconscious and unwelcome, a product of my hangry, sleep deprived, and increasingly inebriated mind. I tried to push the notion from my head, but the effort had the opposite effect.

What else could it be about? I thought. *Are Elle and Riddhi telling Tanner and Ryan all the secrets that they withheld from me? God, that's shitty. Why wouldn't they talk to me about that stuff? We're close, right?*

It was the paranoid thinking of someone void of confidence. I'd never experienced anything like it, at least not until the last few months, not until fatherhood started germinating previously dormant seeds of self-doubt. I hate those seeds. I do my best to stifle their growth, but it's hard.

I'm sure it's nothing, I told myself. *Elle and Riddhi are good friends. Stop psyching yourself out, Owen. Think about something else, like your wonderful wife that is currently vomiting in the bathroom.*

"Hey, babe," I spoke softly to the thin column of space between the door and the frame. I figured Izzy didn't want the whole party knowing about her tummy troubles. "I found that ginger ale for you if you're still interested."

"Thanks, my love," Izzy said, cracking the door and accepting the soda. "I appreciate you checking on me and helping me out. I think I'm going to take this ginger ale and sneak back home."

"Of course, let me just go and tell our friends that we're leaving."

"No, I want you to stay. Have some fun."

"What? No, I'll—"

"Yes, absolutely. You spend all day everyday with our baby, you deserve to have a good time with some adults."

Izzy's tone was painfully earnest, and since I didn't want to challenge her in her weakened state, I did as instructed without further dispute.

That was nice of her, I thought, as I turned back to the party. *I wonder if our roles were reversed, and she was the one staying with Lola all the time, if I would be as considerate and appreciative? I doubt it. Not because I'd be ungrateful of her efforts, but because it wouldn't occur to me.*

It was an accurate realization about myself, and it made me feel kind of shitty. Or perhaps that was the booze, or the empty stomach, or the booze and the empty stomach, or the sight of my friends continuing to share their secrets with people that weren't me. I don't know. Either way I was being a mewling sadsack in a doom spiral. Gross. I plucked a drink off a passing tray and made a resolution to get out of my own head and have fun.

That's when Alexandra Stonceipher grabbed me by the arm.

Chapter 54

"There you are!" Alexandra exclaimed.

"Correct," I replied. It was an accurate albeit curt response. I was too drained to do better.

"*Correct.* That's funny. Owen, you are too funny."

"True."

"*True.* There you go again. You are hilarious. Brevity really is the soul of wit." Alexandra wrapped her arm around mine and started walking us away from the crowd. "But listen, in all seriousness I was hoping to get a word with you before Chip and I go up to give our little address."

I didn't give a shit about their scientifically dubious speech, and I was tempted to say as much. Fortunately, I mastered the impulse. I may not have been in a great mental state, but I was collected enough to know that I wanted to stay in Alexandra's good graces.

"Sure," I said, as chipper as I could muster. "What do you want to talk about?"

"One second, let's just duck in here first, get some privacy."

She led me into a room I'd never been in before. I *had* seen it though. On Elle's phone. It was the first room she showed us a photo of, the one filled with taxidermied animals, antique toys, porcelain dolls, and vintage guns.

Alexandra saw me taking in the space.

"I know, it's awful," she said. "It's Chip's study though, so I have to live with it."

"No, it's—"

"Terrible, I know. Especially these hideous animal busts. Although I suppose I should consider myself lucky. At least he had these ones stuffed before he brought them home. I really despise it when he goes hunting and then brings it home to clean himself. He does it right in the garage—or in the kitchen now. It's disgusting. You'd think he was some sort of hillbilly, not a Stonecipher."

I wasn't sure how to respond, so I settled on a non-committal "Urmm" sound. Alexandra interpreted it as an expression of support.

"Exactly," she said, while preparing two drinks at the liquor cart. "But enough about Chip. Let's take a seat and talk about something more fun."

She handed me a scotch on the rocks and gestured toward a couch that looked part crocodile. I accepted the booze and sat down. As I eased into the seat a shiver took hold of me. I blamed it on the chilly room, yet it felt like something else. I thought about asking Alexandra if I could close the window, but before the words left my mouth she sat down next to me, kicked off her shoes, curled her feet up behind her, and started talking.

"You know, Owen, I really have enjoyed working on this event with you."

"Uh, yeah, me too." Her proximity confused and annoyed me. There were two other chairs, why didn't she curl her stinky ass feet up on one of them?

"I'm so glad to hear it," she beamed. "I was worried that the sentiment was only on my side."

"No, not at all," I lied.

"That's wonderful! I really hope we can continue to do things together. I don't want to stop spending time with you just because our event has concluded."

"No, of course not." Thoughts of additional intelligence gathering opportunities ran through my head.

"Excellent." She gave my arm a squeeze. "Because I must admit, spending time with you has really rejuvenated me. It's so different from spending time with Chip and all his friends and family. Don't get me wrong, it's wonderful being a Stonecipher, but it's also taxing. It just entails so much. So many things are expected of you, and some of those things take their toll."

"Mmm, Mm-hmm," I replied, a convincing effort at empathetic understanding. "It can be tough adapting to your spouse's family. Is there anything in particular that's taking its toll?"

"Well..." Alexandra seemed hesitant.

"Sorry, that was impolite. I didn't mean to pry. I was just thinking that some additional information might allow me to be a more helpful friend."

Dear God, Owen. Listen to yourself. She'll never buy that overly compassionate bull—

"That is so kind of you..."

Or maybe she will.

"Really, Owen, it's incredibly thoughtful..."

Wow, how gullible is this woman?

"You have such a good heart..."

Too gullible, that's the answer.

"Actually, it's not just your heart..."

Definitely too gullible to be the dementedly clever serial killer you think she is.

"You're a genuinely good person..."

Maybe I've been wrong about everything.

"Truly, all of you is good..."

Or have I?

"...your mind..."

Maybe this is all part of it.

"...your spirit..."

Maybe this is a trap.

"...your humor..."

Maybe Chip is lying in wait.

"...your broad shoulders..."

Maybe this is the moment they kill me.

"...your strong arms..."

What was that noise?

"...your full head of hair..."

Oh shit, what is she doing?

"...your green eyes..."

Fuck, she's going to attack me.

"...your lips..."

Ah!

Pouncing like a cougar, Alexandra was on me.

Chapter 55

I wasn't expecting the frontal assault. It struck me as a low percentage play. Sure, Alexandra is somewhat fit, and I'm in the worst shape of my life, but the odds were still in my favor.

"Wait. What?" Those are the genius words that left my mouth as Alexandra's teeth bit into my neck. I followed them up with, "Ow!" as she dug her nails into my back.

"Shut up, you like it," she snapped, her claws moving toward my nipples.

"I do?"

"Yes, you do!"

"Okay."

It was not okay. I was confused. This was not the sort of attack I'd imagined.

In fact, it might not be an attack at all, I thought. *It actually seems more like—*

My insight was cut short, driven from my head by the sudden presence of hands around my throat.

What the—

Fuck.

Chip!

Chapter 56

The pressure was immediately unbearable. You know when your ears hurt because they won't pop at the end of a flight? Getting choked is similar to that except multiplied by a bajillion and replicated throughout your skull. My eyes, my cheeks, my nose, my scalp, all of them felt as if they were going to explode, like blood and gray matter were going to erupt forth and spatter the room. It was bad. I was in trouble, and if I didn't fix it fast, I was going to be dead.

I moved my hands up to my assailant's wrists—*Chip's wrists, right? Yes, it had to be*—and yanked down. The grip around my neck loosened for a blink but nothing more. A second yank proved even less effective. The attacker was ready for it, and even if they hadn't been they would have been fine. Their positioning was far superior. I was seated on the sofa with a hundred and thirty pounds of snooty homicidal housewife on my lap, while they were in the textbook choking stance. I didn't stand a chance.

Shit.

I needed to do something else. Eyes protruding, legs kicking wildly, I moved my hands to the site of the chokehold, trying desperately to dig my fingers in between the attacker's palms and my neck.

"No! No! No!" Alexandra said, chastising my effort while slapping at my hands... or the attacker's hands... or both of our hands. I don't know. Either way it wasn't helpful.

"No! No! No!" More slapping.

Ow! Fuck!

Alexandra's gargantuan diamond ring cut the underside of my chin as she delivered the last of her smacks. The violence and urgency of the chokehold should have prevented the pain of the cut from registering in my brain, but it didn't. It just added to my growing tally of ouchies.

Ouchies?! I thought. *C'mon, Owen. You're getting murdered and you're calling it an ouchie. Who are you?* Then I thought: *I'm a dad. That's who I am. I'm a dad, and a husband, and I can't be either of those things if I'm dead, so I better figure this shit out.*

Fingers still clawing at my assailant's grip, I moved my eyes swiftly around the room in search of something to help me escape. My gaze landed on the antique rifles mounted on the far wall. They were old and ornate, but they'd work.

Yeah, sure, they'd work if they were loaded and if they weren't ten yards away. Stupid idea, Owen. Next.

I spotted the tumbler of scotch I'd been drinking on the nearby end table. It was made of thick, heavy glass. A blow to the head with that and my attacker was bound to go down. I reached out to grab it.

Nope.

My arm was too short, the grip around my neck too tight.

What else?

I scanned the room again. Nothing.

Shit.

Panicked, I instinctively returned my hands back to fight my assailant's. The instant my fingers reconnected with the chokehold it became clear that something was different. The grip around my neck was weaker than it had been before. Wetter. More slippery.

The blood!

For the first time in my life, I was pleased to be injured. Every drop of blood that descended from the cut on my chin was helping loosen the hold of my attacker, lubricating the space between his hands and my neck. Gradually but steadily my fingertips bored in, hollowing out a gap for my windpipe to do its job.

"Hhhuuuhhhggguuuzzz."

That was the sound of my first breath. It would have been funny if it weren't so terrifying. I attempted another.

"Hhhuuuhhhggguuuzzz."

The second sounded just as bad as the first, but it came more easily.

"Heeezzz."

The third was even better—quieter, less difficult, more effective. All at once my brain and body were back online. The oxygen flooded in, hitting me like a shot of strong liquor. I felt tingly, alert, amped. And that's when it struck me: I couldn't pull away from the strangler, but I could push into them.

Putting the idea into action, I slid down in my seat as far as the chokehold and Alexandra's weight would allow, planted my feet firmly on the ground, bent my knees, and pushed off, exploding backward toward my assailant. Taken by surprise they fell clumsily onto their back, Alexandra and me going down with them. We all landed in a pile on the hardwood floor, Alexandra on top, me in the middle, the attacker on the bottom. I could hear the wind leave the strangler's lungs in a gust as we hit the floor, his grip on my neck giving way at the same time.

Finally free, I shoved Alexandra off me with my left and rolled to the right. As I crawled away, I struggled to regain my breath. Each inhalation was a blessing for my lungs and a curse for my throat. It felt as if the air passing through my trachea was filled with splinters and vinegar. Luckily my attacker was in even worse shape. He honked like an emphysemic goose, every molecule of oxygen knocked from his chest. It was an awful noise and it made me smile.

Good, I hope it hurts.

I shuffled around one hundred and eighty degrees on my hands and knees, eager to look at my assailant. I knew it was going to be Chip Stonecipher there on the ground, but I still wanted to see him with my own eyes. Maybe I'd spit at him, or swear, or laugh sadistically at his ridiculous attempts to catch his breath.

Alas, my expectations didn't quite match reality.

Chapter 57

I identified Chip right away. He *was* the assailant, the asshole trying to throttle me to death. That wasn't the part that defied my expectations. My initial reaction to seeing him struggle for breath, *that's* the part that defied my expectations. For some unknown and unconscionable reason my first impulse was not to laugh or swear or spit at him, instead it was to check on him and make sure that he was okay. Weird.

Thankfully, that terrible idea passed quickly. It took precisely one inhale to get rid of it. I looked at Chip, felt an urge to help, took a breath, the breath burned like lava, the pain reminded me that I'd just about died and that Chip was the reason and that Izzy was almost widowed and that Lola was nearly fatherless, and all at once my impulse to help him became an impulse to kill him. But I didn't. I was good—or, at least, good-ish. Before I left, I *did* do a two-legged jump onto his belly like I was a kid on a trampoline. It was great. All the progress he'd made in recovering his breath went bye-bye in one bounce. I exited the room to the sound of the loudest goose honks yet. The noise actually prevented me from delivering a withering remark to Alexandra on the way out, which was too bad because I had some good ones.

Oh well, I thought as I charged out of the room, through the crowd, and onto the stage. *I'll just tell everybody the remarks... Or maybe, I'll tell everybody everything.*

Chapter 58

I was still laboring to catch my breath when I stumbled onto the platform and grabbed the microphone.

"Hhhhh."

My mouth opened, my lips and tongue moved, but all that came out was a rasp. Evidently, the strangulation had done a number on my vocal cords. Not good. It's tough to tell everybody everything when you can't tell anybody anything.

I snatched up the nearest beverage I could find and drank it down. I had no idea whose it was, and I didn't care. As long as it brought my voice back, I was on board.

"Hel— Hello."

The liquid had helped but only modestly. Even with the microphone's assistance the words drew few people's attention.

Shit, I gotta get going. Chip and Alexandra won't be long.

And right on cue they appeared, emerging from the hallway on the far side of the room. I picked up another random glass of wine, drank some, and tried my voice again.

"Hello everybody, could I please have your attention."

A few more people turned toward me. Not enough though. I needed to hurry up. Chip and Alexandra were almost halfway to the stage.

I drank again and tried again.

"Hel—"

I didn't even bother to finish the word. My voice was still too feeble. Alexandra and Chip were at the foot of the stage.

Shit. Shit. Shit.

It was go time. It had to be. I poured more wine down my gullet, braced myself for a brutal pain in my throat, and shouted.

"LOOK AT ME!" Then I patted the top of the mic to make that awful popping noise and shouted again. "LOOK AT ME! LOOK AT ME! LOOK AT ME!"

It worked. It sounded petulant and it hurt like hell, but it worked. All eyes were on me. Of course they were. I was on stage, I was loud, I was disheveled and bloody, and I was a suspected murderer. If that's not must-see viewing, I don't know what is. And since I hate to disappoint, and since I was seriously over it, I went ahead and kicked things off with a bang.

"CHIP AND ALEXANDRA STONECIPHER ARE SERIAL KILLERS!"

Boom. No preamble, no preface, no nothing. I just jumped right into the deep end. Cannonball, motherfuckers!

The crowd didn't know what to make of it, murmuring uncomfortably. I looked over to the gang for encouragement but found little. Tanner appeared to be devising my legal defense in his mind, Elle had her hands over her eyes, Ryan was shaking his head in disbelief, Riddhi was slapping her cheeks like the kid from *Home Alone*, and Izzy was nowhere in sight.

Well then screw it. I thought, feeling indignant. *I'll do it on my own.*

Visions of the great detectives from books and television popped into my head: Sherlock, Poirot, Jessica Fletcher. They always solved the case by giving a thorough account of the evidence while standing in front of a crowd.

I can do that. Can't I?

As I pondered the question, Chip climbed onto the stage to my right. I turned in his direction and flicked my shoe off my foot toward his face. It hit him in the ear, which somehow made him angrier than if it had hit him in the testicles.

"You stay right there, you crazy strangler man," I yelled.

It was a poor insult, but I was in poor shape. Whatever. It did what it needed to. It succeeded in getting Chip even more pissed off. He wanted his hands around my throat again ASAP, it was plain to see, but since there were a lot of people that *could* see, he was forced to hold back. Instead of tackling me and throttling me, he gritted his teeth, swallowed hard, and strained his face into something that vaguely resembled bemusement.

I took another drink of wine in order to buy myself a few seconds. I had everyone's attention, but I still needed to decide how to present my case. The accomplished detectives of fiction are always calm and methodical when they lay everything out. It makes sense. You come across as logical and level-headed. The audience trusts you and is able to follow your train of thought. Unfortunately, calm and methodical aren't really in my wheelhouse. I'm more of an excitable and tangent-prone kind of guy, so I went ahead and took it in that direction.

"Alright folks, listen up." My voice was gravelly but strong, like I played piano in a smoky bar back when bars could be smoky. "I know you all think I'm a murderer because the Icelandic detective lady took me in for questioning and then searched our house—which may have been done illegally by the way, but that's a whole other thing that we don't have time to get into right now, so I won't, but yeah. Anyway, the point is this: I DID NOT MURDER BORIS AND NATASHA. That's important so let me say it again. I, Owen Mickey O'Shea, did NOT murder Boris and Natasha. But I know who did: THE STONECIPHERS!"

I pointed at Alexandra with my left hand and Chip with my right then paused for dramatic effect. The crowd gave little in response. Riddhi tried to help out by providing a gasp, but people could tell it was forced.

"Nothing?" I said. "No one is impressed with that revelation?" Crickets.

"Well, that's probably just because you haven't heard all the evidence. We've got a shit ton of evidence."

The gang caught my eye. They were shaking their heads and making the cut-it-out gesture. I obliged with a revision.

"And by *we*, I mean *I*. *I've* got a shit ton of evidence that *I've* collected."

Reluctant shrugs from the crew. They didn't want me to continue, but as long as I kept them out of it, they weren't going to be adamant in their objections.

Wusses, I thought.

"Yeah," I went on. "A shit ton of evidence, so much evidence that I can't even remember it all without my notes, but I'm gonna give it a go anyway."

The crowd's interest seemed to rise a bit as I held up my hands in order to tick off the facts on my fingers.

"Let's see, I've got blood in the Stoneciphers' house, blood in their yard, shady late-night deliveries, freaky ass rooms filled with scary ass shit, chemicals for decomposing bodies, chemicals for knocking people out, a torture chamber in the garage, probably frozen dead bodies in the garage, whispered conversations about destroying evidence, a business relationship between Chip and Boris that turned sour—aka motive, but that's not to say that they need motive, because the Stoneciphers kill for sport, the evil bastards. Oh, and I didn't even mention the fact that they just tried to strangle me to death. Like just now, right before I came on stage. We were in the study and Alexandra held me down while Chip crushed my windpipe. That's why I sound like this—like I gargled wood chips—because they tried to kill me."

Now the audience was giving me something. They looked intrigued and excited. Momentum was shifting in my favor and Chip could tell. His face had transitioned from anger to anger mixed with fear.

"This is all nonsense," he protested, attempting a tone of confused and mildly annoyed. He sold it well. I might have bought it if I didn't know better. "Most of what you just said doesn't even make sense to me."

"Come on, Chip, don't play dumb."

"No, honest to God, I'm at a loss. I mean the blood in the house, I'd imagine that came from cleaning animals after one of my hunting trips. Where was the blood? The kitchen?"

"Some of it."

"Well, there you go. And what did you say about chemicals? Something about decomposing bodies?"

"Right."

"I don't even know what that could—"

"Oh yes you do, you maniac. You guys have more lye in your house than anyone could ever need. What else could you possibly be using it for other than getting rid of dead bod—"

"Cooking." Chip interrupted coolly. "Alexandra has been using it for cooking. I agree we ordered far too much, but she insisted."

"Chip, you know I like to practice before I serve my food to guests," Alexandra protested, her tone that of a spouse who has debated the topic many times before.

"Yes, I know, dear. But let's be honest, no amount of practice is going to make lutefisk or century eggs palatable. Food cured in lye is just bad."

"Bad? Bad! Are you saying—"

"I'm not saying you're a poor cook, I'm merely saying that lye is a terrible way to prepa—"

"Yeah, okay, Stoneciphers." I interrupted, my manner as dismissive as I could make it. I wasn't buying their explanation, but others were. I could see it on a number of the faces in the crowd. They weren't relating to the odd content of the dispute, but they *were* relating to the familiar tenor of a marital squabble. "I'm sure that you bought buckets and buckets of lye just to"— air quotes—"cook with."

"We did. We—"

"Uh huh, sure. I mean it smells like BS to me but whatever. Let's say for argument's sake you really did buy all that lye for cooking and not for dissolving bodies, that still doesn't explain the blood in your yard."

"Yes, you mentioned that, except I have no idea what you're talking about."

"Sure, you don't." I spoke as though Chip had proven my point. "And it also doesn't explain the rooms filled with creepy antiques."

"Those are my Great Uncle Harold's."

"Right, right. And I suppose it's his ether, too?"

"His what?" Chip's voice cracked. He sounded nervous, sheepish, like he'd finally been caught.

"Ether. You know, the stuff you use to knockout your victims before you drag them to your garage-slash-torture-chamber-slash-morgue." Chip shuffled uncomfortably. "Yeah, that's right. I heard Alexandra telling you to get rid of the ether and disassemble the rack. And you didn't want to, did you? I could hear the reluctance in your voice. You probably didn't think it was necessary, not with me around to take the fall. You thought you could just wait for me to get locked up and then start right back up torturing people on your rack, and throwing their corpses into your loud-ass freezers. Well, surprise! You can't! Because I found you out. What do you have to say about that?"

I looked over at Chip, ready to enjoy the panic on his face.

He was smiling.

"I don't have to *say* anything," he replied, "I can just show you." He stepped down off the stage and headed toward the garage. "Come on everyone."

Chapter 59

What was that smug grin all about? Can't be good. That snooty butthole's got something up his sleeve. It's probably a clean garage. Stupid, Owen, you didn't think that one through. Chip knew he was having this party so he knew he needed to get rid of all the incriminating stuff. He's going to show everybody a normal rich-person garage with a few luxury cars and some skis and golf clubs and you're going to lose all credibility. Fuck.

I intentionally dawdled in order to avoid talking to people. I needed time to think things through, to anticipate the Stoneciphers' next move and devise a counter.

My friends had other ideas.

"Owen, what the shit?" Riddhi chided. She said it in her whisper voice, so it was at a normal person's speaking volume. A couple at the back of the pack looked over their shoulders at us before continuing on toward the garage with everyone else.

"Yeah, not the best approach," Elle agreed.

"I know, I know, I'm sorry. It's just—"

"Owen, I love you like a brother, but there's no 'just' here. Zero." Riddhi was fired up.

"Zero? Really?" I snapped back. I felt irritable and defensive.

"I think Riddhi's right on this one." Elle chimed in, speaking like an intervention specialist. "It was a very ill-advised move. Especially when you consider that we'd just had a conversation with Tanner about taking concrete steps toward bringing down the Stoneciphers."

"Ill advised?" Riddhi piled on. "Yeah, I'd say it was ill advised. I'd say it was super fucking stupid. Now we're not going to be able to collect more evidence, or organize our case, or catch the Stoneciphers off guard, or anything like that. And now they're going to be prepared, they're going to button up the hatchlings and all that crap."

"Batten down the hatches," Elle corrected. "And, I agree, it's going to be much harder to get them now. I think our only hope is that there really is a torture rack and a freezer full of dead bodies in that garage."

I shook my head, frustrated and fuming. The rational part of me knew that my friends had a point, but the pissed off part of me wasn't interested in what the rational part of me had to say.

"I don't understand," Elle continued. "Why didn't you consult us before you went up on stage and made all those pronouncements?"

"Um, I don't know, maybe because the Stoneciphers had just tried to kill me."

The gang's faces flipped from anger to contrition.

"Yeah, you all forgot about that little chestnut didn't you?" I went on. "So maybe I didn't do a great job consulting with you guys before my big speech, but given the circumstances, I think you can cut me some slack. I mean my brain was literally deprived of oxygen. Plus, I'm starving and exhausted. And don't even act like you two consult with me about everything." I looked accusingly at Riddhi and Elle. They seemed at a loss, so I elaborated. "Come on, you know what I'm talking about. Elle you're sneaking off to smoke weed in your shed in the middle of the night, and that's not bad, but it is weird, because you know we wouldn't care, so why be sneaky about it? And you, Riddhi, you're having clandestine meetings with the cops for I don't know what reas—"

"Wait, what?" Ryan was taken aback. He looked toward his wife for an explanation.

Riddhi shook her head. "That's crazy talk."

"No, it's not," I retorted. Her denial galled me. "I saw it with my own eyeballs. A uniformed officer got out of an unmarked Crown Vic and knocked on your door and you let him right in. It was three in the morning or something crazy like that. Clearly, you didn't want anyone in the neighborhood to notice what you were up to, so I have to assume it was something bad."

Ryan's expression shifted into an amused smile.

Riddhi's showed dawning comprehension. "Owen, you idiot. That wasn't—"

"You know what, save it," I interrupted. "I don't want to hear it right now. I've got other stuff to worry about. Who knows what Chip is saying in that garage? I need to be there so I can call him on his bullshit."

"Owen, wait. If you'd just listen—"

But I didn't feel like listening, I felt like stomping off childishly, so that's what I did.

Chapter 60

Everyone was backed up in the hallway waiting for Chip to unlock the door to the garage. "Alright, it's a big space," he announced as he prepared to open the door. "There's enough room in there for everybody, so there's no need to rush. I don't want anyone getting hurt because of all this silliness."

The crowd assented.

Chip opened the door and stepped inside. Everyone followed, calmly and orderly, just as he'd asked. It felt disconcerting, like they were shuffling compliantly toward the laced Kool-Aid. Despite my apprehensions I followed suit. By the time I stepped through the threshold and into the garage there were only a few spots left—enough room for one person to the left and five or six to the right. Still feeling huffy, I went left, ensuring myself a space away from my friends. Then, as I settled into my spot, it struck me: I was finally in the Stoneciphers' garage!

Quickly, I scanned the room—top to bottom, left to right. Then I did it again, and again. The third time wasn't the charm. I still couldn't figure out what I was looking at. There were no fancy cars or skis or golf clubs, but there were also no torture tools or freezers full of dismembered corpses. There *were* racks, although they weren't the pain-inflicting kind I expected. Indeed, the entire garage was full of racks. Racks, computer servers, and a loud cooling unit, that's all that was in there, nothing else.

"I'm just going to wait for the last few stragglers to get in here," Chip said, flashing me another saccharin smile as he updated the throng. Riddhi, Ryan, Elle, and Tanner made their way into the garage and settled into the last remaining spaces. I looked over at them and mouthed the words "Sorry, I think I fucked up." Only Tanner seemed to notice. He kindly waved away my apology as though it were unneeded, then pocketed a fancy screwdriver from a nearby set. It was a petty jab at the Stonecyphers, but I liked that he did it.

"Good, now that everyone is here, I'm going to go ahead and start." Chip waited for the crowd's muttering to die down and then continued. "As all of you can see our neighbor Owen is quite mistaken about what is taking place in this garage. Obviously, neither Alexandra nor I are serial killers. This space does not contain a medieval torture rack, or freezers full of dead bodies, or any of the other macabre horrors that he claimed."

Chip paused for a moment allowing people to look around and nod in the affirmative. He wanted to let it sink in, let the crowd process their surroundings, let them realize that what they were seeing confirmed his words and negated mine.

"That said," Chip went on, "if I do my best to be charitable—which is always a goal of mine and Alexandra's—I can see how Owen became suspicious of our activities. I can see it because the truth is Alexandra and I *have* been up to something in this garage. It's nothing illegal, mind you, at least not according to state or federal law, but it is something that violates the Home Owners Association agreement, and as anyone that lives around here can tell you, crossing the HOA is not a trifling matter."

Amused agreement came from the crowd, especially those that live in the area. Even Riddhi, Ryan, Elle, and Tanner gave begrudging nods of confirmation.

"Specifically," Chip continued, "we've been running a business. Actually, it's debatable whether or not it's a business. Boris and Natasha—God rest their souls—we all actually had a lively disagreement on that matter. You see they were in on this with us, we planned it together, the whole—"

"Chip, you're drifting," Alexandra interrupted. She spoke loud enough for everyone to hear. "You need to explain what exactly we were up to before you go into anything else. Tell them what all this hardware is for."

"Right, yes, of course." Chip cleared his throat. "All of this stuff you see, all of the servers and the metal racks and the cooling unit, all of it is for mining crypto-currency, Ethereum to be precise. It was Natasha's idea actually. She pitched it to me at a party a while back and things progressed from there. I have to say I was skeptical at first, but it's proven quite profitable in a very short amount of time, so I'm very thankful to her and Boris. And before you get ahead of yourselves and start thinking that we killed them for their half of the money, I want you to know that we've already given it to their next of kin. We had a contract that laid it all out—who owned what, and who controlled what, and how the assets would be split in the case of something unexpected. That's actually why I thought it qualified as a business and why Alexandra and I ended up with all of the hardware in our garage. It was a compromise. Boris and Natasha agreed to go in on it with us and do everything in secret, and in return we agreed to make the requisite modifications to our house and set everything up here." Chip chuckled to himself, "I mean if Boris and Natasha would have had it their way, they would have just stood the servers up in their garage without making a single change, cooled off all the hardware by leaving the doors and windows wide open, and let the whole world see what we were up to."

Alexandra laughed as if recalling a fond memory from her youth. "Indeed, they would have. God, how I miss those two."

"Me too, my love, me too. Perhaps we should raise a glass to them." Chip lifted his wine in the air. "To live in hearts we leave behind is not to die. We love you, Boris and Natasha."

"Here, here," said the crowd. They raised their glasses high and then to their lips.

Here, fucking, here? Are you kidding me with this shit?

I wanted to yell at everyone, update them on their current stupidity level, show them the GPS coordinates for their heads and how they aligned with the coordinates for their asses. But

I couldn't. The crowd wasn't ready for a tongue-lashing. They didn't want to hear that Chip was peddling crap, not while they were busy eating it from the palm of his hand.

Be smart about this, Owen. I thought. *Guide them gently back in your direction.*

"Bullshit!" I yelled, completely ignoring my own advice. "That's all bullshit."

The crowd scowled. I realized my mistake and clarified.

"Not the toast to Boris and Natasha. That was good. I'm talking about the stuff before the toast, the stuff Chip spewed out. Just take a second and think about it. Think about all the evidence I talked about earlier. How much of it have the Stoneciphers actually disproven? None of—"

"All of it!" Chip interjected his voice strong and composed. "Every last bit. You talked about blood in our house; I explained that that was from cleaning animals after my hunting trips. You talked about our oddly appointed rooms; I explained that those are filled with Great Uncle's things—and even if some of the stuff is ours, it doesn't make us criminals. You talked about our possession of lye in bulk; I explained that Alexandra got a little overenthusiastic with her unusual cooking technique. You talked about a relationship with Boris and Natasha; I explained that you were partially right, we did have a business relationship with them, but it didn't sour. In fact, it was going better than ever when that unspeakable thing happened to them. You talked about us having a rack; I explained that we do indeed have a rack, more than one actually, but that they are server racks not torture racks. You said we had a freezer full of dead bodies in our garage; I showed you that we do not—and, honestly, I'm not even sure where that idea came from, maybe the sound of the cooling unit for the servers? I don't know. Anyway, what else? Oh, yes, you said we had suspicious deliveries come to our house in the middle of the night; I explained that you were right about the deliveries but wrong about the contents of the deliveries. All of these computer servers and racks, that's what we were actually unloading from that van. So, there you have it. All the so-called evidence you presented against us refuted. Unless there's something I forgot."

"The ether," I said, my confidence ebbing. "Alexandra told you to get rid of the ether, I heard her say it."

"We already covered that. Ether is what you call the cryptocurrency generated when you mine ethereum. Alexandra doesn't want to mine it anymore now that Boris and Natasha have passed. It's too painful of a reminder of them. Also, she was concerned about getting caught by the HOA and tarnishing our good name, but I suppose that ship has sailed now. So what else do you have, Owen? Any other incontrovertible proof you want me to address?"

"The blood in the yard," I said, the words coming out of my mouth weak and soft, nearly all my conviction gone.

"Mmm that. Yes, I don't have an explanation for that. I hardly think it's compelling evidence though. It was outside our house so it could have come from anywhere. And to be honest, I'm not so sure there *was* blood. All we have is your word for it."

"Not my word, Izzy's word. And a bunch of you saw it too. It was on my shoe that day we were looking for Riddhi and Ryan's dog, remember?"

It was a feeble point, a point not worth making, but I'd made it anyway. And as I did, I saw the dominant expression in the crowd shift, moving away from anger *at* me and toward embarrassment *for* me.

"Owen, I don't think that was blood," said an unseen but familiar voice. "There were a bunch of us there but none of us said it was blood. I think maybe you need some help."

"Yes, indeed," added Chip, eager to insert himself into the role of composed and forgiving peacemaker. "I think that's a great idea. Perhaps the stresses of parenting a newborn are taking their toll. I know I felt a little crazy when we—"

"Crazy?" I interrupted, raving like a crazy person. "Crazy! I'm not crazy. All of you are crazy, not me. I'm the not-crazy-one, the sans-crazy-one, the uh…"

"Sane one," offered a pitying voice.

"Yes, the sane one," I agreed.

"I tell you what, Owen," Chip interposed. "Why don't we just call it a night? How about that, everyone? Does that sound like a good idea? Give our neighbor and friend a little time to rest. I'll go ahead and open the garage so that way we all don't have to squeeze past Owen and down the hallway." Chip pressed a button on the far wall and the garage door began to lift. "There's certainly no reason to keep it closed anymore, right?" he jested. "The secret of the garage-based business is out of the bag."

A few laughs came from the crowd. Chip's joke wasn't a good one, but they didn't care. They were too thankful. He was handling an awkward situation for them, giving them an easy out, a clear path away from the proximity of the mad man.

Shit, that's how they see me isn't it? A mad man. I'm a mad man — Except for no, I'm not. I'm just tired and inebriated and angry and presenting my case poorly… Then again, a lot of Chip's explanations do make sense. Maybe I was wrong… But no! That fucker absolutely just tried to kill me. That's beyond doubt. Yes. Bring that up, Owen. Now!

"What about the fact that you just tried to kill me, huh? What about that, Chip?" I did my best to speak loudly but not madly. Half the crowd turned in my direction and listened, the other half continued toward their cars, eager to get away. "You and Alexandra just tried to kill me. You can't deny that, can you? You did it right there in the study. She lured me in and then you strangled me from behind."

"Oh, Owen." Chip's voice dripped with faux sympathy. "I really do think your imagination has gotten the best of you."

"Imagination! You lying ass—"

"I don't blame you. I really don't. I remember how tired and out of it I was when our children were newborns, and we even had a night nanny. I simply can't imagine how hard it is without one. I would have been a wreck just like you are now, especially if my spouse worked as much as yours does."

"Izzy's a great mom, don't you dare—"

"Yes, of course she is. I wasn't passing judgment on her. I was merely trying to acknowledge the amount of work you're putting in, the weight of the stress you're under. I think anyone is liable to fray a little in that sort of situation."

I could hear the remaining crowd talking quietly amongst themselves. Most of them spoke admiringly of Chip's composure and grace, the rest expressed concern for my mental health.

Shit, am I losing it? I wondered.

I attempted to ask the question out loud, but my voice failed.

It failed because Chip just strangled you. Get your mind right, man. If you can't believe yourself then how the hell are other people going to believe you?

"Sorry?" Chip, tilted his head. "I couldn't make out that last bit. What did you say?"

"I said stop avoiding the subject. We're not talking about my wife or the rigors of parenting, we're talking about the fact that you just tried to kill me. Are you seriously going to deny that?"

"Yes, I am. Because it's not true."

"You are un-fucking-believable. It literally just happened no more than a half hour ago. Alexandra pinned me down while you tried to strangle me from behind. Fact."

"I never, we never—"

"You absolutely did. Both of you. How else can you explain the marks on my neck, or our disheveled states, or the blood on all of our clothes, huh? How can you explain it?"

"Well, I… I…"

"Yeah, you can't, can you?"

The remnants of the crowd quieted again, compelled by the combination of my argument and Chip's stammering, their confidence in having arrived at the truth of the matter visibly shaken.

"Go ahead, Chip, enlighten us."

"Of course, I'd be happy to—I mean it's just—Umm..."

The crowd's silence turned into a buzz. The tide was shifting back in my direction.

Finally! I got you, you—

"It's okay, Chip." Alexandra interrupted, her voice painfully genuine. "We've told them the truth about everything else. We should tell them the truth about this, too."

Chip took a second to contemplate, grimaced, and then nodded for Alexandra to go on.

Oh shit, I thought. *What's happening now?*

Chapter 61

Alexandra remained quiet for at least twenty seconds. She appeared to be getting herself together, arranging her thoughts, building up the chutzpah to make a difficult divulgence. It struck me as hammy soap opera stuff, but the crowd ate it up.

"This is difficult," she said, breaking the silence, her voice a strange blend of strong and vulnerable. "So, I guess I'm just going to go ahead and say it. The truth is Chip really did just attack Owen."

Yes!

"Actually, it wasn't as much of an attack as it was a defense."

No!

"A defense of me."

Huh?

"Or rather our marriage."

What?

"You see, I wasn't trying to attack Owen, or pin him down, or whatever he claimed. I was trying to seduce him."

The fuck?!

"In fact, I've been trying to get Owen to sleep with me for quite some time."

Shut up.

"My flirting has actually been rather unapologetically overt."

Has not.

"But God bless his heart, he hasn't seemed to pick up on it."

Has it?

"That's why I made a move on him tonight—a move that I thought was unmistakable."

You know, now that I think about it.

"Owen still didn't get it, but Chip did."

It does make some sense.

"Chip knew what he was looking at the moment he saw it."

211

Okay, a lot of sense.

"That's why he came after him."

All right, total sense.

"My husband didn't want to murder Owen, he wanted to fight him."

O'Shea, you're an idiot.

"Chip's not a serial killer, he's just a—"

"Jealous husband," I said, finishing Alexandra's sentence.

Chapter 62

"Alright." I took a slow side step away from the crowd. "Well." Another side step. "That was unexpected." One more.

The exit was close now. I was tempted to slide through it and bail. Avoid all the awkwardness that was coming to a head. But I didn't. I stayed. It's always better to get your mea culpas over with as soon as possible.

"So, I'm gonna go ahead and apologize for my part in—you know—this whole thing." I vaguely waved my hands around the space in front of me. "Going forward, I will definitely be slower to accuse people of being homicidal maniacs."

Chip stared daggers at me. I continued on as if he were smiling.

"And as for the whole strangling me business why don't we just go ahead and forget about it, eh, Chip? You tried to crush my windpipe, I unwittingly became the object of your wife's affection, exposed a bunch of your secrets, publicly accused you of murder, hit you in the ear with my shoe, jumped on your stomach like it was a trampoline—You know what, I don't want to go into the details. Let's just call it a draw. Sound fair?"

Chip clenched his jaw and balled his fists. "Fair?" he fumed. The veins on the back of his hands inflated, his nostrils flared, his face flushed. "Fair!" His wife's public confession had pushed him back into a rage. He looked like a cartoon bull ready to charge. "I'll tell you what's fair, you piece—"

"Peace," Alexandra interrupted, wrapping her arm around her husband's. "Yes, I quite agree we do need peace. Quiet, too. Peace and quiet, that's what everyone needs right now, so why don't we go ahead and call it a night, okay? Thank you all so much for coming. It means a lot. And please remember you really can make a difference on this issue of vaccines. Educate and inform as many people as you can. It's about the children.

Our children. Their health and their safety. I hope that message wasn't completely overshadowed tonight." She paused and took a breath. "Now if you have something left at the coat check, please follow me."

And just like that Alexandra brought a thoroughly graceless night to a somewhat graceful end. People began to depart as though it were the conclusion of any other elegant fundraiser. It was a remarkable piece of hostessing. I couldn't help being impressed. Alexandra even had *me* feeling as though things were somewhat back to normal.

Of course, that feeling didn't last long.

Chapter 63

"Izzy! Babe, I am so glad to see you."

I spotted my wife the moment I stepped outside the Stonecipehers' place. She was midway across the cul-de-sac, storming past our friends and toward me. She looked bad. Her mascara was smeared, her hair was snarled, her left eye was red; her dress was wrinkled and puke-stained and partly unzipped. The phrase "hot mess" seemed apt. None of that mattered though. I was too happy to see her. Somehow during all of the drama she had slipped from my mind and as I looked at her, I realized that I never wanted that to happen again.

"For real, my love, some crazy shit just went down. I have so much to tell—"

"Where is she?" Izzy demanded. She wasn't slowing down as she approached me.

"Who?" I was confused.

"Who! You know who, that uppity bitch that made a move on you."

"Alexandra?"

"Yes, Alexandra! Unless there's another slut she-wolf trying to sleep with you."

"No. No. Just the one."

"Well then, where the fuck is she?"

I pointed toward the Stonecipers' front door. I knew better than to try and stop Izzy. She's great with my female friends. She's even good with women that crush on me. But woe be the woman that actually makes a move on me. Izzy goes from respectable physician, wife, and mother to claws-out-fangs-out-cobra-lioness-hybrid real fast.

"There you are, you big floppy cunt!"

Izzy didn't yell the insult but that didn't matter, everyone that was left still turned toward her. The phrase "big floppy cunt" tends to command attention.

"Now listen, Isobel, let's talk about—"

I'm guessing Alexandra was going to say "this" but I don't know for sure. Izzy's fist prevented her from finishing the sentence.

Chapter 64

There was no prolonged nasty back and forth, no earring removal, no hair pull, no slap—none of the cliché girl-fight stuff. Izzy just waltzed up to Alexandra and threw a haymaker: thumb on top, wrist straight, power from the legs. Bam! Right across the jaw. If Izzy weighed more than a buck fifteen, Alexandra would have been out cold. As it was, she stumbled hard but kept her feet.

As soon as Alexandra processed what had happened, she tried to deliver a punch of her own. Her swing was wild and far from her body. Her hips didn't rotate and her wrist cocked inward. It was an awful attempt at a right hook, and Izzy ducked it easily. Alexandra connected with nothing but the wall. An audible crack followed.

"Ow! Shit!" Alexandra cursed.

Izzy saw if she was okay, by delivering a left jab to her nose.

Blood immediately poured from each of Alexandra's nostrils. It ran in two distinct streams down toward her mouth. "You bitch! Do you know how much that cost?" she yelled while thrashing her fists wildly in retribution.

Izzy covered up and took the hits. Alexandra's form was terrible and her fitness mediocre, so the blows were ineffective and short lived. Twenty seconds in and she was already winded and petering out. That's when Izzy delivered a headbutt, then a shove, then a kick in the ass.

The ass kick couldn't have hurt much, it was right in the meaty part of the cheek, but for whatever reason it enraged Alexandra and infused her with a second wind. She screamed like a barbarian and then lashed out with kicks of her own. All of them were miserable failures brought up short by a form-fitting dress that refused to provide the necessary range of motion. It was pretty funny, actually. Izzy laughed after the first failed attempt. I laughed after the second. Nearly everyone laughed after the fourth.

The humor was completely lost on Alexandra. She didn't find it funny at all. I know because she screamed, "That's not funny at all!" then threw a punch that actually looked like a punch.

Alexandra's sudden competence and coordination took everyone by surprise, Izzy included. Reacting late, an instinctive shrug of the shoulders and turn of the head is all Iz could muster in defense. Fortunately, it proved enough. Alexandra's fist connected with the bony part of Izzy's raised shoulder, and then bounced back as though it had connected with an I-beam. Izzy was unharmed. Alexandra was in serious pain. She cradled her fist and bit her lip while her eyes filled with tears.

"Alright," Izzy said, capitalizing on the moment of calm. "That's good. I've made my point. Now you know not to make moves on other people's husbands."

Her objective accomplished, Izzy took a step toward the door.

I held out my arm to escort her home.

"Yeah, well maybe if you actually paid attention to your husband and child instead of neglecting them for your work it wouldn't be an issue," Alexandra sneered.

"What the fuck did you—"

Smack!

I'd raised my voice to defend Izzy, but got interrupted by the sound of Izzy defending herself. The slap she delivered to Alexandra's face sounded like a whip crack, like Izzy's hand had broken the sonic barrier en route to Alexandra's face.

People's jaws dropped. I'd never seen that happen in real life. I waited for them to close but they didn't, they just hung there while their owners awaited Alexandra's response. I expected it to be tears, or at least a scamper to the bathroom, but it was neither. Instead, it was a smile. But not a normal-person smile, an insane-asylum smile, an I-collect-stranger's-fingernails smile, an I-think-Satan-has-some-good-ideas smile.

"Oh fuck," Izzy muttered to herself as she laid eyes on Alexandra's crazed expression.

Still smiling, Alexandra gripped the fabric on either side of the seam in her dress, ripped an opening up to her hip, and then took off at a full sprint toward Izzy. Iz tried to sidestep the attack matador-style, but it didn't work. Alexandra lifted her up like a skilled linebacker, carried her into the living room, and then drove her into the ground. It was a vicious tackle. It shook lamps and serving trays off of the surrounding tables, and elicited winces and groans from the audience.

Instinctively, I moved to check on my wife.

Chip did the same.

"Stay the fuck out of it," Izzy and Alexandra screamed in unison.

Happy that they were agreeing on something, I did as instructed.

Chip didn't. He continued forward and as a reward for his effort suffered successive blows from both Alexandra and Izzy.

"Ah! Okay, okay!" He whinged, backing up.

Chip gone, the women immediately returned their focus to each other. My stomach churned as I watched. Having dominated the fight early on, Izzy began to struggle as it transitioned into a wrestling match on the floor.

Alexandra used her size advantage to pin Izzy to the ground and then began administering blows. Nearly all of them were delivered with her left hand. Clearly, her right was still messed up from the successive run-ins with the wall and then Izzy's shoulder.

"Iz, her right hand is—"

I didn't need to finish the sentence. Izzy had already spotted the weakness. She had Alexandra's injured hand gripped tightly between both of her own.

Alexandra screeched in pain but refused to relent, her body weight still pinning Izzy to the ground, her left hand still slapping and punching.

"Give up!" Izzy screamed.

"Eat a dick!" Alexandra screamed back.

"Fine then," Izzy declared. Then she pulled Alexandra's broken hand toward her mouth and bit down. Hard. It sounded like gravel under a boot.

Alexandra bellowed and rolled off of Izzy.

"Giff uph." Izzy said again, her words difficult to make out, encumbered by the hand still clinched between her teeth.

"Ow. Yes. Fuck. Ow." Alexandra conceded.

The fight was done. Izzy loosened her jaw, laid down on her back, and caught her breath. A few seconds later she propped herself up on her elbow, caught my eye, and gave me a smile and a wink. I don't know why but I found it super endearing. It made me want to tell her I loved her, so I did. Or at least I started to.

"I love y—Iz Watch out!"

My warning was too late. The lamp was already descending toward Izzy's head, gripped tightly by Alexandra's good hand.

I lunged forward to intervene but it was futile. I was too far away. All I could do was cringe in preparation of the impact—But the impact never came.

Inches away from its intended destination, the lamp suddenly sprang backwards out of Alexandra's hand, yanked in the opposite direction by a cord that was plugged in at an odd angle and stretched to its limit.

"Fughhh," Alexandra groaned, flopping back down, giving up at last.

Izzy picked up her opponent's injured hand, flicked it, then stood up and walked out the door with me.

Chapter 65

"Damn, babe," I gushed, "you weren't fucking around."

"No, *Alexandra's* not fucking around." Izzy grinned. "I just made sure of that."

We both laughed as we made our way across the cul-de-sac, my arm around my wife's shoulders, hers around my waist. We both knew that the ordeal wasn't over, that it would take months to sort out all the stuff that just went down, but in that moment we didn't care. It was nice.

"Isobel Yang-Hee Bang?"

"Yeah?" Izzy replied, puzzled by the formal voice and the use of her full name.

We turned around to see where the query had come from. It was the cops.

Chapter 66

The uniformed officers immediately cuffed Izzy and read her Miranda rights. I barely processed any of it. I was too busy arguing. It could have gotten bad; I could have ended up handcuffed beside her. Fortunately, Tanner arrived in time to prevent that from happening.

"What's this about?" he interjected, sliding himself into the small space between myself and the nearest officer.

Duh, she just got into a fistfight with the neighbor, I thought but didn't say. Instead, I attempted to comfort my wife as the other officer lowered her into the back seat of the squad car. "Don't worry, Izzy," I said, loud but calm. "I'll be right behind you. We'll get this all sorted. Everything will be okay. I love you so much!"

The moment the police car door slammed shut I took off toward our house, charged inside, and headed to the basket where we keep the keys. I didn't find them within the first quarter second so I dumped everything out onto the ground.

"Owen, what the fuck?"

Sota looked alarmed and confused. He stared down at me as I rummaged frantically through the upturned contents of the basket.

"Sota, what are you doing—" I cut myself off, ashamed by the fact that I'd forgotten he was babysitting. "Shit. How is Lola? Is she okay?"

"What? Yes, of course, she's fine. What are you—"

"Good. Okay. I'm sorry, but I gotta run. I'll explain later."

I rushed past Sota and hopped in my car. I needed to be quick. I couldn't leave Izzy alone. I had to be there with her. Or at least as close as possible. I wanted to be immediately behind the squad car as it took her to the station. I wanted my car's headlights shining into the backseat with her, comforting her, letting her know that she wasn't alone.

"Let me in!" Tanner said, knocking on the passenger side window.

I leaned over, unlocked the door, and pulled the handle. It couldn't hurt to have a lawyer come with me.

"Are you good to drive?" Tanner asked. It wasn't a reproof, it was an honest and direct question. He was looking out for me.

"Yes."

"Good, let's go. Watch out for people, there's still a crowd out there."

"Right."

I reversed briskly but not recklessly. It was easy. Riddhi, Elle, and Ryan had already backed up the crowd to help me out. I had treated them like shit, but they were still looking out for me. Even in my frenzied state, the kindness registered.

"Thank you, and sorry." I yelled out the driver's side window. It's all I had time to say. It was insufficient, but my friends didn't seem to mind. They waved their arms in a way that encouraged me to get going and not worry about them. I did as they suggested and within a minute, we had caught up to the squad car, our headlights shining into the back seat.

The sight of Izzy's silhouette made me feel slightly better. Tanner noticed and used the opportunity to venture some communication.

"Listen, Owen, I know you're pissed but you have to keep a grip on yourself. You can't help Izzy if you get thrown in jail, and that is exactly what will happen if you blow up at the police station."

I breathed deeply through my nose and nodded in agreement. Tanner's word's annoyed me, but I knew he was correct.

"Good. Alright, so as soon we arrive we're both going to walk in there quickly and calmly, and then you're going to let me do the talking."

I took another breath and gave another nod.

"Perfect," Tanner replied. He had more to say, but he could tell I needed a minute.

It ended up taking three.

"Alright, so what sort of charges are we looking at?" I asked, finally calm enough to proceed with a rational conversation. "Battery? Is that a misdemeanor or a felony?"

"Well, assuming that's why they're bringing her in, it could be either one. Simple battery is a petty misdemeanor, aggravated battery can be a full misdemeanor or a felony."

"Which do you think it will be?"

"It could go either way depending—"

"Hold on," I interrupted. "Why did you say, *assuming that's why they brought her in*? What else could they be bringing her in for?"

"You're right. That's most likely why they brought her in."

"But maybe not? What else could it be? Don't dance around the point, Tanner. Shoot straight, I can handle it."

"Okay, listen, I'm probably off base here, but I was surprised at how quickly the cops arrived. That fight between Alexandra and Izzy took what, two or three minutes?"

"Yeah. I mean it seemed a lot longer, but yeah, that's probably all it was."

"Right, plus maybe another minute or two for you guys to walk outside? That adds up to a maximum of five minutes."

"So?"

"So, that's fast. The average police response time here is over ten minutes, easy."

"Okay, well maybe they happened to be close by."

"Yeah. Maybe." His face took on a contemplative expression. "And I suppose somebody could have called the moment the fight broke out."

"Right."

"Or…"

"Or what?"

"Or maybe they were already coming to get her."

"What? That's crazy. Why would they be coming to arrest Izzy?"

Tanner stayed quiet.

"Dude, don't do that, just say what you're thinking."

Tanner paused for a beat then spoke carefully. "Were you with Izzy the night of the murders?"

Chapter 67

I veered onto the rumble strips then pulled the car back onto the road.

"Whoa. You good?" Tanner asked, concerned by my brief lapse in driving ability.

"Good?" I answered, my voice higher than normal. "Of course I'm not fucking good, you just suggested that my wife might be a murder suspect."

"Yeah, that's fair. I just meant, are you okay with finishing the drive to the station?"

"No," I answered honestly. "But I'm not going to pull over so we can swap spots. We'd fall behind the police car."

"Okay, yeah." Tanner agreed. "Just let me know if you change your mind."

I nodded grimly, my thoughts already elsewhere.

Where was Izzy the night Boris and Natasha died? We were together, right? We must have been. We always are. I mean we're apart when one of us is off with Lola, but that's it. She couldn't have snuck away and done anything while I was downstairs or in the nursery, could she? No way. And even if she could've, she didn't. Come on, Owen, you know your wife isn't a murderer.

Angry with myself for entertaining the idea of Izzy as a cold-blooded killer, I set my jaw and redoubled my focus on driving. I stayed that way, honed in like a laser, for an entire sixteenth of a mile. Then my thoughts ran away again.

That cop did say Izzy's middle name though, my brain nagged. *What the hell was that about? People don't just know strangers' middle names. Do warrants have middle names on them? I think they do. Then that would mean that he was coming to arrest her already. Fuck. But no. I mean maybe not. Maybe he just happened to know it because someone in the crowd told him? No, that's stupid, they wouldn't know it either. But he might have known it because everyone in the cul-de-sac has their name up on some board at the police station. Yeah, that seems likely. It's a huge case, it's probably all hands on deck over there. All the local police probably know all of our names, they've probably been grilled into their heads.*

I started to feel better, like I was getting on a roll.

Mmm Hmm, that all makes total sense. And the cops' quick arrival, that was probably because someone called them when I took over the stage and started laying out my case against the Stoneciphers. People would have been crazy not to call at that time. Either I was right and the Stoneciphers were murderers, or I was wrong and I was a lunatic. Whichever one it was, a call to the police was totally warranted.

"No, not that space, it's reserved for police vehicles," Tanner said, extricating me from my thoughts. I was pulling in beside the squad car.

"Fuck it." I parked anyway.

"Remember what I said about keeping it together?"

"Yes, fine, you're right." I shifted into reverse, backed into the legal spot behind us, then hopped out of the car.

"Walk, don't run," Tanner advised. "Cops don't like it when the suspect's angry spouse runs after them."

I grunted my assent. It was good Tanner had come along—for legal reasons but also for keeping-me-sane-and-out-of-trouble reasons.

We entered the station just as Izzy was getting escorted through the door to the back. I quickly yelled out some comforting words. Tanner told her to stay quiet then turned his attention to the policeman at the front desk. He spoke to the officer in a commanding tone using legal jargon that neither I nor the officer understood. It didn't work. The officer just stared at him like a confused dummy, so Tanner changed tack. He increased the volume of his voice and began waxing lyrical about the shameful denial of his client's sixth amendment rights. The officer shrunk from the attention it drew. Eyes big, ears down, he slid out from behind his desk and showed us to the back.

"Good lawyering," I muttered to Tanner as we followed the officer.

"You haven't seen anything yet," he replied.

Chapter 68

"This is a betrayal of the constitution."

"I'll have your badge for this."

"She agreed to finger prints, that's her thumb. The thumb's not a finger."

"What an unconscionable injustice."

"Do you like harassing working mothers? Huh? Do ya?"

Sitting in the police station, I heard every single one of those phrases leave Tanner's mouth. And I wasn't even allowed inside for Izzy's interrogation. I can only imagine the hell he unleashed in there. It certainly made Izzy feel better. We were too far away from each other to talk, but the distance didn't prevent me from noticing that her condition had visibly improved from when she'd been put in the backseat of the cruiser. She even gave me a smile as the police chaperoned her back to the holding cell.

"Excuse the histrionics." Tanner said, returning to his normal demeanor as he approached me. "Sometimes being a good lawyer requires a little theater."

"Don't apologize, I loved it. The cops were reeling. Also, I learned that the thumb is not a finger."

"Fun fact, right?"

"Yup," I nodded. I'd mentioned the thumb bit to try and lighten my own mood. It didn't work. I couldn't help myself from immediately returning to the unsparingly serious matter of Izzy's arrest. "So, what's the deal? What are the charges? Are they letting her out now?"

"No, they're keeping her overnight—maybe for the full forty-eight hours—but they don't have anything. I think they're trying to intimidate her with the battery charge so that she'll give up something on the murders."

"But she doesn't know anything about the murders!"

"I know she doesn't, and I think Detective Nikolasdottir is starting to realize that as well, but as long as they have the opportunity to put pressure on her, they're going to try."

"That's crap. I—"

"Come on, let's talk about this in the car." Tanner interrupted, shuffling me along toward the exit.

"No way. I'm staying here until Izzy gets let out."

"Listen, friend, that's sweet, I can tell that you're a caring husband, but I promise it's pointless. They're going to hold her for as long as they're going to hold her. You being here won't make a difference. Not to the police, not to Izzy. So, let's just head back home. It'll be more comfortable and we can talk in private there."

"Is that code for, we-need-to-leave-otherwise-you'll-get-pissed-off-and-make-a-scene-and-get-yourself-arrested."

"Yeah," Tanner shrugged. "I thought that was obvious."

He patted me on the back and we headed out. I handed him the keys on the way to the car. Given my mental state, the fact that I'd gotten us to the police station in one piece was fortunate. I saw no reason to push our luck on the return leg.

"So, what makes you so confident that they're using the battery charge as leverage?" I asked as we turned out of the parking lot and onto the road. "Maybe the battery charge *is* the main thing? Did they say something in the interrogation that makes you think otherwise?"

"Yes, numerous things." Tanner replied. "In fact, they barely even mentioned the fight with Alexandra."

"Shit, seriously?"

"Seriously. And when they did bring it up, it was more in the form of a threat than anything else, an insinuation that if she didn't provide information on the murders, then they would throw the book at her for the fight."

"That's terrible. How did Izzy react?"

"Like a pro. I mean you could tell she was a bit rattled, but she kept it together and kept her mouth shut."

"Yeah, she's a badass."

"Agreed." Tanner nodded his head in simple confirmation, then flipped on the blinker and took the exit. "Honestly," he continued, "I think she found it easy to keep it together after I explained that the police would never actually bring the battery charge."

"And why won't they do that?"

"The Stoneciphers."

I knew the spirit of what Tanner meant, but I wanted him to elaborate so I said, "Elaborate."

"Pshh, I could elaborate all day. They're the goddamn Stoneciphers. Like I was saying earlier, I've only lived here a little while, but I've already learned that they have a crazy amount of pull in this town, and in this case that means that the battery charge will never get brought against Izzy because that would mean they'd have to bring a battery charge against Alexandra as well."

"Even though Izzy threw the first punch?"

"Definitely. I mean they might have been able to get around it if Alexandra had just defended herself, but she didn't. She attacked Izzy after Izzy tried to bring the whole thing to an end."

"Good point."

"And there were what? Fifty people there that witnessed it, so there's no way for them to spin some other story."

"Right," I said, understanding the logic. "And since there's no way they're going to charge Alexandra, there's no way they're going to charge Izzy."

"Exactly."

"Good." I exhaled with relief as it suddenly dawned on me just how bad things could have gone. Izzy could have been sent to prison; she could have lost her medical license. Eleven years of schooling, poof, buh-bye. I liked that she wanted to kick another woman's ass for making a move on me, but I didn't like it *that* much.

"So, that's it then." I went on, as Tanner pulled into the cul-de-sac. "We're good. Izzy just stays quiet for the next forty-eight hours and we're out of the woods."

For a moment I felt immense relief. Then Tanner laughed.

"Dude, what are you talking about? You guys are so not out of the woods. You're still up to your neck in the fuckin' woods. You need to come over to my place. We have a lot to get sorted."

Chapter 69

I did as Tanner suggested and headed over to his place. I didn't even check on Lola before I went. It made me feel like a bad parent, but I knew that if I went in, I wouldn't want to leave. And I had to leave. There was too much to figure out.

So, in lieu of actually checking on my daughter, I took a beat and focused on the crackle of the baby monitor as it came through my tiny bluetooth earpiece. Everything sounded normal.

See, she's fine, I thought. *And even if she's not, your friends have got it.*

Then I thought: *Oh shit, my friends. I gotta text everybody and let them know what's up.*

I reached into my pocket.

"No need, I already sent the group a message," Tanner said, holding up his phone.

"Everybody? Elle, Riddhi, Ryan, Sota?"

"Yup."

"And Lola's okay?"

"Yes, Lola's okay." Tanner put his hands on my upper arms, squeezed firmly, and looked me in the eye. "Listen, Owen, I know that a whole lot of crazy shit is going down, and I understand that your mind is going a million miles a minute, but I need you to sit down with me and concentrate. I promise it's the best thing you can do right now. As your lawyer I need a full picture of what's going on, which means I need you to tell me everything you can think of."

"Yeah," I said, corralling my thoughts. "Okay. Let's make some coffee, coffee helps me think."

"Done. Grab a seat at the kitchen counter while I brew a pot."

I did as instructed.

Tanner came back a few minutes later with two large mugs and multiple stacks of sticky notes. He set everything down then spoke in a friendly but serious tone.

"Alright, so here's the deal: In my experience clients tend to do a garbage job of relaying information. They fixate on the facts that fit the narrative that they've constructed in their minds and then completely ignore everything else."

"Mmm," I said, in the tone of a tut-tut.

Tanner raised his eyebrows knowingly.

"What?"

His eyebrows went higher.

"What? Why the hell are you—Oh."

A light bulb went off in my head. Not a nice one, an icky and unwelcome one, a bowling alley blacklight pointing out the dinginess of my teeth and the pee pee dribble on my jeans.

"Yeah," Tanner agreed. "Oh."

"So, you think that's what I did? You think I decided that the Stoneciphers were evil before I got started and then forced all the facts to fit that story."

"I think it's a possibility."

"But you think they're bad too, right?"

"Yeah, I do, but that doesn't mean they're killers."

"True," I said with an exhale. "So, what then? How do we try and figure out what's going on? How do we exonerate Izzy and me?"

"Just write." Tanner replied, sliding the sticky pads toward me. "Write everything you can think of. One thought per note then we'll start making sense of it all."

"Yeah, I can do that."

An hour later we ran out of stickies. Tanner's sliding glass doors were completely covered in bright paper squares, a mess of facts, opinions, and guesses scrawled out and sprawled out. As I sat there and took it all in, one thing became perfectly clear: It was the goddamn Stoneciphers.

Chapter 70

"It's the goddamn Stonecithers." I said, giving voice to my anti-epiphany.

"Yeah," Tanner replied, he put his hand in his hair and ruffled it up, a gesture of exhaustion and wry amusement. "I have to say the evidence does point in that direction."

Tanner and I both got up and started rearranging stickies on the glass, batching related info together then organizing it into timelines. With each bright paper square we moved, the case against the Stonecithers grew stronger.

I knew it. I fuckin' knew it! Caffeine and self-congratulations pulsed through my veins. *Their excuses were total bullshit. There has to be a way to prove that.*

I stood back from the sliding doors in order to better process the groupings and chronologies laid out on the glass. It was tough. I was beat and so was Tanner. Our adrenaline was keeping us up, but it wasn't keeping us sharp.

"The timeline fits." I gestured at a row of stickies that indicated the Stonecithers' known movements then took a sip from my mug. My belly lurched. The coffee was mixing with the booze from earlier in the night. They were not getting along.

"It does," Tanner concurred. "Or at least nothing up there precludes them from being the killers."

"Do you think—"

A thump and then a crackle came through the bluetooth in my ear. I jumped a bit then pushed the earpiece in deeper to aid in my hearing.

"What's—"

I cut Tanner off with a raised finger. He looked confused so I tilted my head in his direction and pointed toward the earpiece. He mouthed the word "oh" and then nodded.

I listened intently, waiting for Lola to start crying, but she didn't. The faint sound of her baby snores became audible again the moment the crackle stopped. I relaxed and lowered my shut-up finger.

"What happened?" Tanner asked.

"Not sure, a loud noise came from Lola's room."

"But everything is good now?"

"Yeah, the old iPad we use as a monitor probably just fell or something."

"I thought it was bracketed to the crib?"

"Oh, yeah." My stomach lurched again. Terrible thoughts of Lola being taken flashed through my head. "I better go check on her," I added, trying and failing to sound casual.

"Yes, of course." Tanner replied, hurrying toward the front door.

As he opened it for me the sound of another door—Lola's nursery door—came through the earpiece.

Fuck. What's that? Is that someone going into my baby's room? They're gonna die. I'm gonna kill 'em.

I transitioned into a panicked sprint.

A voice came through the monitor.

Chapter 71

"You trying to wake the neighborhood, little lady?"

I slid to a stop in the middle of the cul-de-sac. I was barefoot so it hurt like hell, but I didn't mind. I was too relieved to mind. The voice coming over the intercom wasn't that of a Stonecipher or any other evil intruder. It was Sota's, the babysitter, the person whose voice it was supposed to be. His SoCal accent was unmistakable. He even did the thing where he collapses "trying to" into a half a word—"tryna."

"Never mind." Sota continued, speaking to someone else now, probably Elle and Riddhi. "She's not awake, this just fell."

I continued to listen as he tiptoed across the room, picked something up, and then tiptoed back out. The door creaked a bit as he closed it. I could almost feel him holding his breath, hoping the noise wouldn't wake Lola. It didn't. Her faint baby snores became audible again the moment the door came to a rest.

I exhaled in relief, turned, and walked back toward Tanner's. He was still standing by the entrance to his house.

"False alarm?" he asked, as I made my way up his front steps.

"Yeah. Sota's there. Everything is fine. I guess I'm just a little paranoid from—" I stopped mid-sentence and bent over at the waist. It was an attempt to relieve the sudden bout of pain coming from my stomach. The coffee and liquor were really coming to blows in there.

"Oh!" I stood up straight and clenched my butt cheeks. The pain had disappeared, replaced by the sudden and urgent need to sit on the toilet.

"You okay?"

"Nope. Emergency poop. Where's your bathroom?"

Tanner pointed to a door a few yards from where we'd been working.

"Uh uh, this is gonna be bad. I need a buffer zone. What else you got?" A wave of pressure pushed on my butthole. It felt troubling. Watery. "Hurry man, this is gonna happen."

Tanner laughed. "One in the basement at the bottom of the stairs, four upstai—"

I plowed passed him and rushed down the steps. I kept my legs as straight as possible during the descent. Any bend in the knees was bound to result in some turds in the trousers.

Inside the bathroom, I flipped on the light and the fan with one swift movement, then lifted the seat, undid my belt, pulled down my pants, and sat. Ugly stuff instantly shot out of me. It hit the water before my ass hit the seat.

"Ahh."

Yes, I actually said *ahh*. The feeling of relief was that good. And as I sat there relieving my tummy of its troubles, the relief spread from my abdomen to my cranium.

Things are going to be okay, I thought. *Everybody is going to be fine. Everybody but the Stoneciphers that is. Those fuckers are going down. You might have blown it the first time around, but not this time. This time you're going to get it right. This time you're going to consult with your friends before you make any moves. Plus, you have Tanner now. Elle and Riddhi are great, but Tanner does this shit professionally, he's going to help a ton. So, stop freaking yourself out, Owen. Stop jumping at every noise. Stop sprinting to the nursery every time the baby monitor falls off the table. Not even the baby monitor, actually. Just some random thing. The baby monitor can't even fall, it's bracketed to the freakin' crib—*

Hold up.

IT'S BRACKETED TO THE FREAKIN' CRIB.

"OH, FUCK!"

Chapter 72

I covered my mouth as if that could somehow reverse the "oh fuck" that had just come out of it. It didn't. Tanner for sure heard something. He called down to check on me.

"Everything good down there?"

His tone was casual, but I heard it as maniacal.

"Yu-up," I answered.

My voice cracked like I was fourteen. I worried it gave me away, so I held my breath and thought: *please don't notice, please don't notice,* until he replied.

"Good deal. Just give me a shout if you need anything."

"Will do!" I called back.

Keep it together, man. He doesn't know you know. But do you know? Shut up. Yes, of course you do. How else could he know that Lola's monitor is bracketed to the crib? He had to have been in there, and you never let him in, which means he went in on his —

I squeezed my shoulder blades in an attempt to suppress the shiver running down my vertebral column.

Alright. Okay. Maybe you're jumping the gun. Maybe you mentioned it and forgot.

I shook my head. There was no point in lying to myself. That wouldn't help anybody.

No, he was definitely in Lola's room without you. Probably in other parts of your house as well.

"Fuck, that's creepy," I muttered.

But was that all it was? Was he just being creepy to be creepy? I doubt it. He was probably — the trowel!

Images of the small gardening shovel I'd found in Lola's room flashed into my head, the one I'd used to pick up poop and then exhaustedly dumped into the trash.

That's a trowel, too. That's what the police were looking for. You were thinking of the masonry type, but they were looking for the gardening type. And that asshole planted it in there. He must have. That's why Lola's window was open.

My eyes widened and my head shook as comprehension poured down on me.

It was pure luck you found it, pure luck you threw it away. Imagine if you hadn't.

"Shit, that would have been bad."

Okay, but what else you got? Is there any other evidence that points to Tanner, or is it just the one slip of the tongue and the trowel in the nursery?

I rested my elbows on my thighs and my chin on my left palm. I had time to think. Tanner didn't know that I was done depositing my tummy troubles. A bad belly can leave you laid up in the bathroom for ages. I had a good ten, maybe twenty minutes before he got suspicious.

The blood on my shoes! I thought, another insight striking. *That ties to his place just as much as it does the Stonceiphers'. I picked it up from walking between their two houses. It could have easily come from him instead of them. Oh, and there was that noise that same day. That came from Tanner's direction. Maybe that was something... Or someone. Ahh!*

Another shiver ran through my spine. I didn't fight it this time. I let it run its course, atlas to coccyx.

Alright, calm yourself. You have about fifteen minutes before Tanner gets suspicious. You need to use that time to do some snooping. You need hard evidence. Nothing you have right now will hold up in court.

"Good idea. Go look around," I said quietly, encouraging myself.

But is it? Is it really? You think it's a good idea to go sneaking around the house of a suspected murderer all by yourself? At least with the Stonciphers you were snooping in the middle of the day. Plus, the girls knew you were there, so if something went wrong....

Wait. They also know I'm here. The girls know and Ryan knows and Sota knows. So, I'm good. There's no way Tanner will try something.

The thought was reassuring. Not completely, but enough. I held onto it as I wiped my butt, washed my hands, and crept out of the bathroom to search the place.

Chapter 73

I could feel my heartbeat everywhere: eyeballs, earballs, teste balls. It was unlike anything I'd ever experienced, ten times greater than what I'd felt while searching the Stoneciphers' place.

Maybe that means you're onto something.

"Eek."

The word snuck out of my mouth. It was equal parts excitement and fear. I concentrated on the excitement. It helped. My heartbeat kept pounding, but it made me focused, not frantic.

If I was hiding murder-y stuff, where would I put it? Garage? Attic? Basement? Yeah, the basement is as good of a guess as any, and you're already there. Might as well start where you're at. And be smart about it, methodical, work your way diligently across the space.

I walked to the far wall of the far room and proceeded from there. It was dark, but the moon was nearly full and the basement was a walkout with plenty of windows, so the space was navigable. At least most of it. The room with the water heater and furnace was a different story. That sucker was creepy. Dark, damp, cobwebbed. It seemed a century older than the rest of the house.

Gross, I thought. *But, promising.*

I reached into my pocket and pulled out my phone to use as a flashlight. It was dead. Not even a last gasp screen-flash.

No way.

I slapped it against my leg as though that would fix it. No luck.

Fuck me. What are the odds?

I paused, and thought, and shrugged.

Pretty good actually. It's four hours past its normal charging time.

I made my way into the room.

Whatever. It'll be fine. It's not that dark.

I held my hands out in front of me, feeling my way around until my eyes adjusted.

Good thing I already texted the—

I stopped.

Shit. I didn't text the gang. Tanner did. Or claimed to.

It was an unwelcome realization. All at once the darkness of the room pressed in on me. Sweat bloomed from my pores and turned cold on my skin. My body squeezed tight, hands under armpits, knees together, the posture of a stranded traveler amidst a winter rain.

This is not good.

I shook my head in confirmation of my own thought.

Better get going.

I removed my hands from the warmth of my pits, waggled off the chill, and picked up the pace of my search. My eyes had adjusted. The room was still dark but not impenetrably so. Now that I could see, it looked less promising. It took me all of ten seconds to confirm that there was nothing in there.

Next.

I moved across the hall. It was equally disappointing. A routine guestroom: bed, nightstand, empty dresser.

Next.

A workout room, a nice one with weights, benches, a squat rack, and mirrors. It even had a little drain in the middle in case you got super sweaty. Nothing incriminating.

Next.

A storage closet. A full one. Cluttered.

This will take forever to search thr—

The sound of footsteps came from overhead lopping off the end of my thought. It was a nice house, and a new one, so the noise was faint, but it was there.

Shit-shit-shit.

I hustled back to the bathroom, slid inside, and closed the door behind me. Tanner's voice came down the steps seconds later.

"Are you alright down there, Owen?"

I replied with a grunt as I stepped out of the bathroom and flipped off the light, pretending I'd just wrapped up.

"That bad, huh?" he queried.

"It sure wasn't good." I said, holding my belly while ascending the steps.

"I'm sorry, man. I have some Pepto if you need—"

"Uh-oh." I stopped mid stride and grabbed my stomach tighter.

"More on the way?"

"Yup. It's gonna be bad."

"Don't worry about it. Take your time."

"Thanks," I said, hustling back toward the bathroom.

I closed the door behind me, scurried over to the toilet, pulled down my pants, and sat. I didn't actually have to poo, but going through the motions seemed like the best way to sell the lie. I kept up the charade until I heard Tanner leave. As soon as he did, I got up, went to the sink to wash my hands, decided not to because Tanner might hear the water, made an icky face while pointlessly wiping my dry hands on my pants, and then crept back out to recommence the search.

My first thought was to go back and comb through the storage closet, but I decided against it. That place looked like a junk drawer and homicidal maniacs don't stuff away their most prized possessions haphazardly.

Nah, they keep their sadistic mementos somewhere nice, somewhere special, somewhere close, somewhere like... the bedroom!

Chapter 74

The trip up the basement steps was harrowing. The ascent to the second floor even more so. Torn between the urge to rush and the need to be stealthy, I proceeded at a medium pace that satisfied neither impulse. It was tortuous and nerve racking and ultimately a success. Tanner didn't hear anything. I know because I paused at the top of the second flight, listened for movement, and heard zero. Crickets and my own pulse. That's it. That's all there was.

I exhaled in relief.

Alright, now hurry up.

I walked down the hallway and looked into one room after another. They were all clean and fully furnished with their own bathrooms. It made it impossible to tell which was the master bedroom.

Balls.

I took a beat and problem-solved.

It's okay, just check the closets.

It seemed an efficient way to figure out which room was his.

The first was empty. The second was half full but it was all winter stuff, a storage space for off-season clothes. The third was it. The real closet. Tanner's closet. It was obvious the moment I opened the door.

Here it is. The moment of truth.

My perspiration level went up to nine, my racing mind to ten, my heartbeat to eleven, each thump a big middle-finger to the traditional ten-point scale.

Mastering the fear and adrenaline, I stepped into the closet and took it all in. It was meticulously organized. Neatly pressed suits on one wall, business casual clothes on another. It was deep, too. I walked to what I thought was the back only to realize that it extended another five yards to the right making an L shape.

Sweet Mother Mary, how big is this thing?

Big. That was the answer.

The back corner had even more stuff than the front. It wasn't cluttered though. Every shirt, every pant, every loafer and sneaker was neatly placed half an inch away from the ones adjacent.

"Yuck."

It seemed like the appropriate word. Austere and sterile can be just as icky as dirty and cluttered.

Whatever.

Yuckiness doesn't matter.

Keep going.

I plowed on with the search. I couldn't touch anything because Tanner was bound to notice even a small alteration to the organizational layout. Fortunately, it didn't matter. The closet was so fastidiously arranged that I could examine everything without touching anything. All I had to do was look. And I did look. And there was nothing.

What the hell?!

I started to doubt myself.

Maybe I'm wrong. Wrong about Tanner. Wrong about the Stoneciphers. Wrong about everything.

I gave a defeated groan, then immediately admonished myself.

Don't whine. Fix it. There's still a ton of this house to check. You've barely even scratched the service. Shit, you haven't even finished with the second-floor closets. Why don't you do that before you start doubting your mental fitness.

Reinvigorated, I walked into the last remaining upstairs bedroom and opened the closet door. The top shelf was filled with pristine gardening tools neatly arranged by size, the next with mannequin heads and wigs, the rest with clothes, none of which were Tanner's.

My eyes widened at the sight of it.

They widened even more when a rope suddenly closed around my neck.

I struggled to no avail, blacking out in under a minute.

Chapter 75

Three sharp points dug into my left temple. They drew pain but no blood.

I opened my eyes.

Tanner was already staring into them.

"There he is!" He sounded excited, like the birthday boy had arrived at the party. I'm assuming he looked excited as well. I couldn't tell for certain. My vision was too blurred.

I squeezed my eyes shut and reopened them in a bid to regain twenty-twenty. It worked, and I regretted it immediately. I really did not like what I saw.

I was in the basement workout room tied to a bench. A plastic tarp was spread out underneath with a hole cut out for the drain in the floor. Tanner was smiling and holding a three-tined gardening fork up against the side of my skull. An assortment of additional gardening tools was laid out neatly on the ground to my right alongside the screwdriver he'd purloined from the Stonecyphers' garage. I didn't know the names for most of the tools, but I knew I didn't like them. They looked evil, like soil was never their intended target, like human flesh was always their aim.

"Hey, buddy!" I acted upbeat.

Tanner laughed. Just once. It sounded like a bark. "*Hey, buddy!* he says. That's an interesting response. Most people start pleading right away." He dragged the fork slowly down the side of my face. "Some scream. I expected you to scream."

"About what?"

Another bark. "*About what*? That's good. Funny. You're a funny guy, Owen."

"Thanks, bud. That's kind of you to say."

"I'm really going to miss that sense of humor."

"Don't worry, it's not going anywhere."

"No?" Tanner dug the sharp tines of the fork into my cheek. One of them punctured my skin. A drop of blood ran down to my chin.

"No, I don't think so," I replied, ignoring the pain. "I know some people lose their sense of humor when they become parents. I don't think I'll be one of them though. I actually think I've gotten funnier since we had Lola. It's a good way to cope with the exhaustion."

Tanner squinted an eye and tilted his head like a perplexed dog. "Are you trying to gaslight me, Owen?"

"What's gaslight mean?"

"Oh, come now. You know what it means."

"Like the lamp with the flame?"

Tanner gave an annoyed exhale. "I don't like this game." He moved his gaze away from my face down to the row of gardening implements. "Perhaps a different tool will change your tune."

"Maybe," I said, my tone earnest and optimistic.

Tanner was trying to scare me out of my everything-is-hunky-dory schtick. I took that to mean it was working.

"So, which one should it be," he queried.

"Whatever. Dealer's choice."

"Perhaps the dibber? Or maybe the twist cultivator."

"Cool. I'm good either way." I had no idea what those things were, so it was kind of true.

"No," Tanner raised his index finger and wagged it side-to-side. "No, I don't want to jump straight to dessert. I want to enjoy the whole meal."

"Smart. A balanced diet is key."

"I'll start with the weeder." He picked up a long skinny tool. It looked like a metal snake tongue.

"So, tell me a little bit about this closet upstairs," I went on, ignoring his selection.

"Which one?"

"Tanner, are you being coy with me? Don't be silly. We're just two friends talking."

"Very well, I presume you're referring to the closet I caught you looking in."

"Yeah, that one. I mean I wouldn't say you *caught me.*" I made air quotes with my voice. "I was just being a little nosy. But anyway, yes, that's the one I'm talking about."

"What do you want to know?"

"Just looking to have you walk me through it a bit. Tell me what I was looking at up there."

"What did you see?"

"A bunch of stuff. Wigs, some clothes that I don't think were yours, these gardening tools." I nodded to the implements on my right. "Pretty much everything."

"Mmm. And what did you make of that?"

"I don't know. That's why I'm asking."

"Come on, Owen. You must have some idea, some sort of educated guess."

"No, not really."

"Now, I know that's not true. You always have guesses. You had too many guesses about the Stoneciphers."

"Fair point. Maybe that's why I'm trying not to guess now."

"Mmm Hmm," Tanner replied, skeptical.

I followed him with my eyes as he walked slowly behind me. He tested the sharpness of the tool as he went, tapping his thumb against the two points.

"Do you think a manicure might inspire some guesses?"

I felt his hand wrap around my index finger.

"I don't know, maybe. I've never had one before. Izzy's tried to get me to go, but it never seemed all that appealing. But if you're paying, I'll give it a try."

"No, I wasn't going to take you out for one. I was going to do it right here."

"Okay. Coo-ahhhhhh!"

The metal snake-tongue dug in under my nail. Slowly at first, then fast until the nail popped like a soda tab. The tip of my finger pulsated. My eyes watered. I blinked away the tears and talked through the agony.

"Cool." I swallowed hard. Saliva and pain. "Cool, I was saying cool before I interrupted myself there." I took a beat, cleared my throat, and made my voice as cavalier as possible. "So, do all manicures hurt that bad? Like I said, this is my first, so I have no frame of reference."

"No," Tanner replied. "Some feel more like this."

Tanner dug the tool in once again. This time he started at the base of the pinkie nail and pried it off. It hurt even worse. I told him as much.

"That one was less enjoyable. If I ever get another manicure, I'll ask for the first type. What was that called?"

Tanner didn't answer. Instead, he walked back in front of me, took a towel out of his pocket, wiped the gore from his weeding tool, and looked down at me. I met his gaze and attempted nonchalance. I failed. My eyes were filled with tears, my brow with perspiration, and my hands with blood. My pit stains went down to my hips and my voice cracked like I'd re-hit puberty.

Still, Tanner respected the effort.

"Alright, Owen. I like that you're doing something different, so I'll play along for a bit. That was called denailing. It was the preferred manicure technique of the Spanish Inquisition."

"Gotcha. Gotcha. Pretty extreme though. They must have had real bad cuticles."

"That's cute."

"Thanks, I try." I swallowed again, and wiped my face on my shoulder. "And what about that closet of yours? You didn't walk me through it yet."

Tanner gave a wry smile, then shrugged. "Yeah, okay. I'll tell you about it. It can't hurt anything."

I nodded encouragingly.

"That's my special closet," he continued. "It's where I keep my favorite things."

"Favorite, huh? I mean I knew you liked gardening, but I didn't know it was your favorite."

"Gardening is fine, but it's the tools' other function that I really enjoy."

"Oh, manicures."

Tanner laughed again. From the belly this time. "Yes, exactly."

"And what about the clothes? They didn't seem like your style."

"You're right, they're not. Actually they're no one's style. Well, no one's and everyone's. At least all of my victims."

I flinched involuntarily at the word victims. Sure, I was already tied up and missing fingernails, but the explicit mention of people that Tanner had already killed still freaked me out.

"Ah, there's the look of terror I'm used to seeing. You don't like hearing about my victims."

"No," I regained my composure and improvised poorly. "Um, you know, I just don't like the word victim."

"No?"

"Yeah, no. You know the whole *victim* thing." I did air quotes with my voice again. "It's overplayed these days."

"Sure it is," Tanner grinned, seeing through my bluff. "Then you won't mind if I tell you about some more of mine."

"By all means."

"I could tell you about the guy that I impaled with garden spikes. He swore a lot. Or the woman whose intestines I…"

Tanner went off on a monologue. It was horrifying and gross and I was happy he was doing it. So long as he was talking about people that he had tortured in the past, he wasn't actively torturing me in the present. Also, it gave me some time to work on my restraints. The blood had loosened the ropes a bit, but I still couldn't get them over my thumbs.

"...of course, they can't all be that fun. Sometimes, I have to rush my work. Like with the Russians..."

I brought my full attention back to Tanner, drawn in by the mention of Boris and Natasha.

"...that was improvised and sloppy and quick."

"Why?" I asked.

"Ah, I see that one piques your curiosity. That makes sense I suppose, considering you found the bodies."

I stayed quiet, encouraging Tanner to go on. He obliged.

"The truth is I had no intention of murdering those two. They forced me to."

Bullshit.

"Fair enough," Tanner amended, reading my expression. "They didn't literally force me to, but their intrusiveness had to be dealt with. They were always at that front window, staring out at the cul-de-sac, spying. They were bound to notice something."

"And did they?"

"Actually, no. I thought they did. I thought they noticed Autumn."

"Autumn like the season? I'm sure they did, it's a quarter of the yea—"

"Don't be obtuse, Owen. You're smarter than that."

"Oh. Shit. Autumn was a woman. Someone you killed."

"Yes. She was quite beautiful too. Amazing hair. Silky and thick with shades of mahogany. And her legs—mmm—her legs were exquisite."

"Hold on, are you talking about the woman that came back to your house the night before I found Boris's and Natasha's bodies?"

"Yes, that's the one."

"But that's impossible Iz—" I feigned a cough, interrupting myself. I'd begun to say Izzy but wanted to change it to I. There was no way I was going to give Tanner a reason to go after anyone else, especially not my wife. "Excuse me." I apologized, wrapping up my cough. "All that strangling is taking its toll."

"Understandable. Please, go on with what you were saying."

"Right, yeah. I was saying that's impossible because I saw the brunette with the legs leave your house in the morning."

"Did you?" Tanner smirked.

Oh fuck. He knows. He knows Izzy was the one that saw her.

"Or is that just what you think you saw?"

Oh, thank Mother Mary. He doesn't know... Wait. What's he on about?

"I'm confused." I admitted.

Tanner looked disappointed in me. "Come now, Owen. I really expected you to do better than this."

I thought back to what Izzy had said. She hadn't been impressed with the woman's legs.

No, it was more than that. Remember, she said they looked manly. There is no way that brunette's legs could have been mistaken for manly.

"That was you that left in the morning," I said, the truth snapping into place. "You dressed up as her. That's why you have all those different clothes and wigs. So you can pretend to be your victims if you need to."

"Very good."

"That's why you shave your legs too isn't it? The ankle taping excuse is bullshit."

"Excellent. I didn't think you'd connect that bit."

I nodded in acknowledgment of the compliment while continuing to talk out the epiphany. "I understand how you get the wigs; you just scope out your victim's hairstyle beforehand, but how do you know what clothes they're going to wear?"

"Yes, that's tough. I've had to make some adjustments in that regard." Tanner was enjoying himself, delighting in the opportunity to talk about his craft. "I used to try and stalk them, figure out their go-to outfits for dates and clubbing and all that, so that I could purchase those clothes in my size ahead of time. That was too difficult though. It was massively time consuming and I missed more than I hit."

"Interesting." I said, feigning captivation, urging more confession, more time to work on my restraints. "So, what solution did you come up with?"

"A simple one. Elegant."

I leaned in, like I was eager for his words to hit my ears.

"I just find victims that are roughly my size."

"Huh." I wasn't impressed, but I didn't say anything. I just kept the convo going. "Yeah, I get it. That way you can just wear their clothes."

"Precisely."

"It must be hard though, finding women that are your size."

"A bit. But I am trim, and not too tall, so it can be done. That said, I did eventually have to open up my victim pool."

"Open it up how?"

"To men as well as women."

"Wait so you're not actually a switch hitter?"

"Huh?"

"Bisexual. You're not actually bisexual?"

"Oh, I see. No, I'm not actually bisexual."

"You just pretend to be so you can murder more people."

"Precisely. It works, too. I haven't *struck out* in ages."

"Look at you, extending the baseball metaphor. That was good."

"Thank you," Tanner smiled. "Actually, the bisexual facade is quite new. I decided to do that when the Stoneciphers offered me the job here. A new town, a new sexual orientation, it was too good of an opportunity to pass up."

"Totally," I said.

Fucking Stoneciphers, I thought. *It's their fault even when it's not their fault.*

"Maybe I'll reinvent myself again the next time I move." Tanner tapped the metal snake tongue against his chin, contemplating the future.

"Why are you moving again?"

"Well, the situation here is far too messy. I mean it will get better after I kill you and blame it on the Stoneciphers, but still. There's just going to be too much attention on the cul-de-sac."

"Sure, too much heat. You're right on that point. In fact, I'm not sure the neighborhood can handle any more bad stuff. The police will just come in and dig up dirt on everyone. Nobody will escape unscathed."

"Nice try, Owen."

"What?"

"Trying to appeal to my self-interest to get out of this situation."

"No, not at all"

Tanner shot me a knowing look.

"Yeah, okay," I conceded. "Maybe a little bit. But that doesn't change the fact that I've got a point."

"Oh, bless your heart. You are trying so hard."

"No, I'm just—"

"Obviously, I can't let you go. That would definitely lead to my arrest. Whereas if I kill you and make it look like the Stoneciphers did it, then I'll get away scot-free."

"That's not realistic. How the hell are you going to frame the Stoneciphers? They're the most powerful family in this town."

"Owen, don't you see?"

"Uh uh."

"Well you should, because you basically framed them for me."

"Huh?"

"Yes, of course. Although I suppose the Stoneciphers and Izzy helped as well. Think about it, an entire party of people just watched you slander the Stoneciphers. Then they watched your wife and Alexandra have a fistfight because Alexandra tried to lure you into infidelity. Honestly, it's too good. I couldn't have designed a better motive. I even managed to grab a screwdriver from the Stonecipher's garage while I was there."

"Fuck." He was right.

"Yes, fuck indeed. At least for you. For me it's more of a hurray!"

A look of delight on his face, Tanner leaned over, put down the weeder, and picked up something new. It was one of the few tools for which I knew the name: gardening shears.

Chapter 76

Tanner walked toward me, testing the shears out on the way.

Snip.

Snip.

Snip.

"Wait. Hold up. What about... What about, uh..." My mind raced, desperate to think of something to delay the use of the clippers. "The trowel! Yeah, what about the trowel?"

"You want the trowel?" Tanner was taken aback. "I really don't think you do. That's my finishing tool, there's no coming back from that one. Anyway, I have to use the Stoneciphers' screwdriver today. It won't be as fun, but it will tie the frame job up nicely."

"What? No, I'm not talking about now. I'm talking about the trowel you planted in Lola's room."

"Oh, I put that there as an insurance policy. I do it to a neighbor wherever I live. It gives me someone to frame if I get in a bind. I got it in your place just in time too, I had to silence the Russians a day or two later."

"Smart."

"Yeah, didn't do me much good though. I told the police right where to look and those fools still couldn't find it."

"That's because I'd already found it and thrown it away."

"Ah, that explains that." Tanner nodded, then continued toward me.

"Wait, don't you want to know how I found it?"

"No, I'm tired of talking. I want to play."

"Well, what about the..." My mind sprinted even faster, grasping for another question, a more engaging one. I looked frantically around the room for inspiration. Dumbbells, pull-up bar, treadmill, none of them inspired an idea. I exhaled in defeat and looked toward the heavens. The smoke alarm looked back.

It reminded me of the one I had to take down from our vaulted foyer. "What about the window in our entryway, the one up high, was that you? We found it open right after we moved in. It freaked us out."

"Owen, your efforts are getting sad. Clearly, that wasn't me. You and Izzy have lived here far longer than I have."

"Right, yeah, but what about—" another piece of evidence flashed into my head "—the noises. Yeah, what about the noises I've heard from your garage."

"I don't do anything in my garage."

"Are you sure because—"

"Yes, I'm sure." Tanner paused, something dawning on him. "We *are* under the garage right now though, so maybe you did hear something. That's good to know. I might have to add more soundproofing. Thank you for that."

"Yeah, no problem. Glad I could help. So does that mean you do all your killing in here because—"

"It's time to be quiet now, Owen."

Tanner continued toward me. I kept talking, desperate to delay the impending torture.

"Right, yeah, I would stop, but you know I'm enjoying our chat so much, it's just..."

"Shh."

"...so easy to talk to you. And you know speaking of this room that we're in, it's a great work out room. I mean really nice, it's like...."

"Quiet."

"...legit better than any gym I've been to. Maybe we can start working out together and—"

"SHUT THE FUCK UP!"

Tanner's scream was visceral. It hit me like a crack of thunder, shockwaves reverberating in my chest.

My lips tightened.

My eyes widened.

Tanner grinned, big and maniacal.

"Good. Now where were we?" His voice had returned to its normal volume. "Ah, yes." He closed the shears swiftly in the air.

Snip.

Snip.

Snip.

He stepped behind me.

My adrenal glands amped up, a torrent of fight hormones flooding my body. With the epinephrine came an idea. It wasn't a great one, but it was something.

"Please don't cut off any of my fingers," I pleaded.

But it wasn't a plea, it was a lure. A lure inspired by a newly learned fact.

"Very well." Tanner replied. He grabbed my left hand and pulled out my fattest digit. "The thumb it is."

Yes! I thought. *The thumb it is.*

Happy, I waited for the squeeze of the blades.

Chapter 77

The gardening shears were outrageously sharp. They went through my thumb like prunes through intestines—quick, smooth, done. Had it taken more than one squeeze I probably would have passed out. As it was, my adrenaline conquered my pain and I kept it together.

The instant my thumb said goodbye to my hand, I yanked through the restraints. With only four digits remaining and ample blood for lubrication, it proved easy. Both hands free, I grabbed the nearest tool and swung it wildly in Tanner's direction. The tines of the gardening fork hit him in the hip and bounced off. The handle vibrated in my hand. Undeterred, I swung again. Tanner was ready this time, he stepped back avoiding the blow, and then lunged forward with his shears like a fencer with a foil. The shears hit me in the belly, but they were closed so they didn't break the skin. It hurt, but it didn't slow me down. I swung the fork again. It hit bone again. This time it was the ball of Tanner's shoulder, and this time the tool popped out of my hand upon contact.

Fuck!

Recognizing the opportunity, Tanner threw his shears into the corner and picked up the fork.

I reached toward the row of gardening implements, and grabbed the nearest thing. It was my thumb.

Not helpful.

I shoved my bad thumb into my pocket using my good thumb, grabbed the nearest tool with my other hand, and swung back around. Halfway through the journey the trowel flew from my grip. It wasn't on purpose. I was still acclimating to my absent digit. Fortunately, the sharp little shovel still managed to reach its intended target, flying swiftly through the air and implanting itself in the meat of Tanner's thigh.

"Yes!"

Tanner looked down at his leg and screamed. When he looked back up, his expression was even more deranged than it had been. Jaw clenched tight, he pulled the trowel from his leg. Blood shot out of the wound like water from a cheap squirt gun. He paid it no attention, he just kept on staring at me. It was the most unnerving thing yet.

"Uh oh."

"Yeah, uh oh," he confirmed.

Tanner came at me with the trowel in one hand and the gardening fork in the other.

Unarmed, I flipped the weight bench in front of my charging assailant, turned, and ran. Tanner fell hard over the bench. It bought me enough time to get out of the room, and almost enough to get out of the basement. Not quite though. Tanner caught me by the collar as I stepped over the threshold of the sliding door and into the backyard. My forward momentum combined with the backward yank resulted in me landing hard on my back. The oxygen in my lungs left in a gush.

Tanner looked down at me struggling to breathe and waved happily with the fork.

I flipped him off.

He shook his head in disapproval, bent over, and swung the gardening fork into my leg. The three tines implanted themselves in my quad, the same spot where I'd hit him with the trowel.

The pain was acute, but I didn't scream. I couldn't. My lungs still refused to fill. Luckily you don't need oxygen to punch and that's exactly what I did. One swift jab upwards. I think I got him in his balls and part of his taint. I can't say for sure. I didn't hang around to find out. Instead, I got up and made another attempt at running.

It went poorly.

The absence of oxygen in my lungs and the presence of a gardening tool in my leg resulted in a less than impressive pace. I'd gone no further than twenty yards when Tanner jumped onto my back and wrapped his arm around my throat...

***

And now we're back to where we started. The beginning. Or maybe it's the end. My end. Or the story's. Or both. Either way we're up to speed. We know what happened from then until now: I persevered through the chokehold, carried Tanner out of the backyard into the cul-de-sac, and launched backward into the streetlight to try and shake him loose. When that didn't work, I started to lose consciousness, a stream of trivial stuff ran through my head, I heard a crackle and the sound of my dead mother's voice asking, "How did this happen?" I replied, *It's a long story,* then I told that story, and now here we are—Tanner's arm around my neck, the voice of my mother in my ear.

Chapter 78

"What a mess!" my mom exclaimed.

Yeah, no shit, I replied.

"It's going to take forever to clean this up."

I think it's too late for that.

"You've got poop everywhere."

I do?

"Up your back…"

Did I shit myself?

"…down your legs…"

I thought you didn't do that until after you died.

"…in your hair…"

Maybe I am dead.

"Yuck…"

Mom! Don't insult me when I'm dying.

"Who knew such a little lady could produce such a huge amount of poo…"

Well, it had been a while since my last bowel… Wait. What?

"Oh, it's okay, girl, don't cry…"

Girl?

"Riddhi's got you…"

Riddhi?

"I'm not really mad…"

Oh my God.

"I know it's not your fault, Lola…"

I'm not hearing my mom from heaven.

"We'll just get Ryan to clean this up…"

I'm hearing Riddhi through the bluetooth.

"That's what husbands are for."

Which means I'm still alive!

Lola laughed.

The sound of my daughter's happiness hit my heart like sunshine and my head like smelling salts. All at once I was back in the moment.

Tanner's arm was still around my throat but it was looser. Oxygen was not coming easy, yet it was coming, a trickle with each ragged inhale.

As I came to, I fought back.

I threw an elbow into Tanner's ribs. Then another. And another.

He winced, but didn't relent.

I tried a head butt. That failed too.

Desperate, I removed my good hand from the arm that was strangling me and slid it into my pocket. I could feel something in there, but I couldn't remember what. I prayed for a useful tool. Nope. It was my thumb, and the napkin I'd vomited into earlier in the night.

Gross.

Fuck it.

I grabbed both in my fist and swung them wildly over my opposite shoulder toward Tanner's head.

They got him in the eye.

He screamed.

I swung again.

They went into his mouth and slipped from my hand.

He gagged and loosened his grip.

I attempted another head butt. This time there was a solid connection. Snap, right to the bridge of his nose. Tanner was too distracted to avoid it, his attention dominated by the severed thumb and pukey napkin obstructing his airway. His grip slackened.

I broke free and stood up.

A choice flashed through my head: *run or kick him while he's struggling?*

I was moving toward my house before I'd made a conscious decision.

"Help!" I yelled as I went. The word came out hoarse and weak. I tried again: "Help!" Even worse. Weaker. Hoarser.

I chanced a glance over my shoulder. Tanner was struggling to his feet, his nose bloody, his breathing labored.

I can take him, I thought. Then I looked at myself and realized I couldn't. I was in even worse shape than he was.

"Fuck."

I tried to pick up the pace, but I didn't have another gear in me.

I tried to scream, but my voice still failed me.

I could hear Tanner gaining ground. His footfalls nearer. His grunting louder.

I thought of my wife and daughter. I spoke to them even though they couldn't hear me: "I love you, ladies."

The words felt warm.

Comforted, I braced for the end.

Then came the crack of a rifle.

Chapter 79

Responding to the gunshot I dove on the ground, face first hands out like a baseball player stealing second. It was painful, especially when the ground dragged the fork out of my leg, but it was worth it. It got me out of the line of fire before the next shot.

Crack! The sound of the rifle startled me again.

What the fuck is happening?

Trying to make sense of the situation, I rolled over and looked back. Tanner was still coming toward me, but his progress was slow.

He's moving like a fucking zombie, I thought.

It was an accurate assessment of the situation. The man had two bullets in his back. He was dead on his feet. Still, I remained vigilant. I knew better than to relax.

You relax and they get you, I thought. *They get you with their last breath.*

My focus locked on Tanner, I crab-walked backward as I waited for him to fall.

He kept shuffling toward me.

I kept moving away. Up the curb, over the sidewalk, over the lawn, up the steps—Bonk!

The back of my head bumped into our front door. It was the end of the road. There was nowhere left to scuttle and Tanner was still coming.

A second later he was upon me.

He lifted the sharpened trowel over his head—

Crack!

Blood, bone, and brain spattered my face. My thumb sprang from Tanner's mouth and landed on my chest.

I closed my eyes and wiped away the gore. I reopened them just in time to see Tanner collapse. He went down like a marionette after a snip of its strings. The top half of his body landed on the lower half of mine, his torso on my legs, his head in my lap. I looked down at him. His skull was a mess, inside parts on the outside, outside on the inside. I raised my gaze to prevent myself from puking, and immediately spotted the Stoneciphers. Chip, Alexandra, Great Uncle Highpockets, all three of them stared at me from their front porch, Chip holding an antique rifle by the barrel.

Unable to shout, I had to improvise a sign of my appreciation.

I grabbed my severed digit off of my chest, gave the Stoneciphers a double thumbs up using just one hand, and passed out.

Chapter 80

I couldn't feel my thumb, but it was reattached. My eyes told me so.

"So, you're sure?" I asked Izzy for the third time.

"Yes, I'm sure. You'll get some feeling back in the next few months, possibly all of it. Two-thirds of replantation patients regain good-to-perfect hand function."

I nodded, feeling reassured.

"Don't worry, babe." She squeezed my arm. "So long as you're diligent with the physical therapy you'll be fine."

"Oh, I'll be diligent with the physical therapy," I winked. "I need full thumb functionality in order to properly honk those boobies of yours."

Izzy rolled her eyes, leaned over, and gave me a kiss.

Our lips were still together when Riddhi and Elle walked in. It was the first time they'd seen me since I was loaded into the ambulance. They entered cautiously, like I was a game of Jenga and the room a minefield.

"Oh my God, I'm fine," I said, waving them inward. "Get your asses in here."

"Are you sure?"

"Yes, Riddhi, I'm sure."

"Okay, good, because I'm gonna beat the shit out of you, and I'd rather have you healthy when I do it."

"Naturally, otherwise you'd feel bad for beating up an invalid."

"Exactly."

"Just one quick question."

"Yup."

"Why are you beating the shit out of me?"

"Because of your massive stupidity. You know how many horrible decisions you made in the last twenty-four hours."

"Mmm, yeah, quite a few."

"Quite a few. That's the understatement of the goddamn century. You fucked up more times than I can count."

"Yeah, but math isn't—"

"Nope, not the time to make fun of my math skills, you stupid ballbag. You almost got yourself killed!"

I turned to Izzy and Elle for support. They provided none. Instead, they offered Riddhi looks that encouraged her to keep going. So, keep going Riddhi did. She reamed me out for five minutes straight. It was brutal and loud and uncompromising and I loved it. It was nice to see how much my friends and family cared. Plus when she was done, and I'd been properly reprimanded, the setting was ripe for me to ask some difficult questions of my own.

"You're totally right," I conceded. "I should have fully trusted you guys, and communicated better. And I shouldn't have gotten so pissed off and acted so rash."

"But..."

"No buts. I was wrong in all of those ways and I'm sorry." I made eye contact with each of them in turn. "For real, I'm sorry."

They all accepted my apology and we did a group hug.

"Good," I said as the embrace broke up. "And now that I've apologized, it's time for you two," I pointed at Riddhi and Elle, "to tell me about the shady stuff I saw you doing. Riddhi, why the hell were you talking to a cop in the middle of the night? And Elle why are you sneaking off to your shed to smoke weed?"

Elle looked uncharacteristically sheepish, Riddhi amused.

"That wasn't a cop," Riddhi smiled. "It was Ryan."

"No, it wasn't," I protested. "It was a cop, he had the whole uniform, shirt, hat, aviator sun—Oh my God it was a sex thing."

"Yeah, it was!"

"That good, huh?"

"Absolutely. Best roleplay yet."

"Well, you two did seriously commit—a legit uniform and a Crown Vic and everything."

"You have to go all out, it's the best way to get lost in the fantasy. You know you all should—"

"I was smoking cigarettes!" Elle interjected. She covered her mouth after she spoke as if the blurt was involuntary. A few seconds later she removed her hands from her face and said it again, quiet this time: "I was smoking cigarettes."

A parade of condemnation followed:

"Elle, no."

"Ew."

"Gross."

"Do you wanna get cancer?"

"It's so bad for your hair."

"Do you hate living?"

"Good thing *your* finger didn't get chopped off, because it wouldn't reattach."

"Was it peer pressure? Did someone peer pressure you? I'll kill 'em."

It went on like that for a while, wildly over the top, but fun. In the end Elle vowed to quit. We all shared a cigarette to celebrate.

Some Weeks Later

Epilogue

"A small soy latte for Elle, and a large red eye for Owen."

Riddhi set the drinks down on the table. I thanked her, grabbed the cup, maneuvered it around Lola, and took a drink. Elle was impressed.

"Look at this guy, picking his coffee up like a champion."

"Don't get too excited, it's the other one that's fucked up."

I raised my reconstructed hand from under the table and attempted to give my mended thumb a wiggle. Nothing happened.

"Shit," Elle frowned. "Sorry."

"No worries. It's only been a few weeks."

"Yeah, you can't expect to recover that fast," Riddhi said, staying positive. "And you know it might not be working yet, but it looks really good. Almost like your own thumb."

"It is his own thumb," Elle laughed.

"Shut up. You said it was a transplantation."

"No, I said it was a replantation."

"Well, what the fuck does that mean?"

"It means they reattached his own thumb to his own hand."

"So that's your own thumb?" Riddhi asked, turning toward me for confirmation.

"Yeah," I smiled.

"So, it's the same thumb that was stuck in Tanner's throat?"

"Yup."

"That's gross."

"Oh, for sure. But better than no thumb at all."

"True. Life would suck without a thumb." Riddhi frowned thoughtfully while nodding in acknowledgement of her own wisdom. "It's a good thing Chip blasted it out of Tanner's mouth, huh?"

"Yeah," I laughed. "It is good. Good and surprising."

"Very surprising," Elle echoed. "I did not expect them to be the good guys."

"Me neither."

"Oh, they're not good guys," Riddhi corrected, her cavalier tone belying the gravity of her claim.

Elle and I stared, taken aback.

"What do you mean they're not good guys? They saved Owen's life."

"Yeah," Riddhi shrugged. "So what. Bad guys can do good things."

"Sure but—"

"But nothing. They're bad. I know it. I can feel it in my bones."

Elle rolled her eyes, "Bone feelings aren't evidence, Riddhi."

"I know."

"So do you have any evidence?"

"No."

"So, it's just a feeling?"

"Yes."

Elle made a dismissive noise then looked toward me so we could shake our heads together.

I met her eyes but didn't share her expression.

"Seriously? Owen, come on, you don't still suspect the Stonecipher's."

"Not of killing the Russians, no."

"Nor of killing any of Tanner's other victims."

"Nor of killing any of Tanner's other victims," I agreed.

Elle exhaled in relief, pleased that sanity was prevailing. "Excellent, so only one person in the group is—"

"But there is *something* about them."

"Dear God."

"What? I'm just saying I don't buy all their excuses."

Elle put her face in her hands.

"Come on," I countered. "Some of their claims were crazy. Cooking lye and crypto mining and all that shit."

"All that shit was checked out by the police. It's indisputable. I mean I've been leery of the Stoneciphers my whole life, but at some point you have to change your mind if the evidence proves you were wrong."

"Okay, sure, but what about the bricking up of their garage windows, or the Peabodys' peeing on their place, or Chip strangling me?"

"Come on, we've covered this. They sealed up their garage to conceal their server farm, and the Peabodys' probably hate them because of a business dealing, or a local high-society squabble, or something else that's fairly mundane."

"And the strangling?"

"Owen, Alexandra was trying to have sex with you! I'm not saying that makes what Chip did okay, but it is an understandable human reaction. That's the sort of shit people do when they catch their spouses engaged in infidelity. Also, I think his saving your life by shooting Tanner in the skull more than made up for his mistake."

"Maybe."

"What do you mean 'maybe'? You'd be dead without him."

"Sure, but maybe he wasn't shooting Tanner to save my life, maybe he was shooting Tanner to save his own."

"What are you talking about?"

"I'm talking about the fact that Tanner was planning on blaming them for my murder. Maybe that's why they shot him. Maybe it was nothing more than self-preservation."

"No, that doesn't align with the facts."

"Why? Tanner told me he was going to try and pin it on them."

"Yes, he told *you*. Not them, *you*. And he said it while you guys were alone in his house, so unless the Stoneciphers have supersonic hearing or NSA level surveillance there is absolutely no way they could have known what he said."

"Mmm."

"Sorry, what was that? I missed it."

"It was 'mmm.' As in *mmm* you have a point."

"Thank you. I accept your concession with grace and class."

I laughed, "Elle, if you talk about yourself doing something with grace and class then you're not doing it with grace or class."

"That's true. I was actually just gloating. Let me do it again: Riddhi, I also accept your concession with grace and class."

"Oh, I'm not conceding."

"What!"

"I said I'm not conceding."

"But I just proved that the Stoneciphers couldn't have murdered Tanner out of self-preservation."

"Meh."

"*Meh.* What do you mean, *meh*?"

"I don't know. They're sneaky fuckers. And they're super rich."

"So?"

"So who knows what they're capable of."

"Well, I know what they're not capable of: breaking the laws of physics. They can't hear things through multiple walls."

"I don't know."

"*I don't know!* You can't say 'I don't know' about breaking the laws of physics."

"I don't know," I smirked. "I think she just did."

"Oh my God," Elle closed her eyes and massaged her temples. "You two are the absolute worst."

Laughing at Elle's exasperation, I leaned back, took a sip of coffee, and smiled. It was a nice moment. The subject matter was still crazy but the interaction was us being us. It was a return to the ordinary that felt extraordinary. I paused and soaked it up, all of it: my friends, my family, my life. I've always known I was lucky, but at that moment I felt it more powerfully than ever.

Then my gaze shifted up toward the Stoneciphers' place and the good vibes scattered. Uncertainty and foreboding took their place.

I don't know, I thought, my eyes fixed, my skin cold. *I really don't know.*

About the Author

C. McGee lives in North Carolina with his wife, Beth, and their daughter, Jo. His previous novels, *Feral Chickens* and *Exteriors and Interiors,* are also available from Roundfire Books. More of his writing can be found on his website *borderlineatbest.com.*

ROUNDFIRE
BOOKS

FICTION

Put simply, we publish great stories. Whether it's literary or
popular, a gentle tale or a pulsating thriller, the connecting
theme in all Roundfi re fi ction titles is that once you pick them
up you won't want to put them down.
If you have enjoyed this book, why not tell other readers by
posting a review on your preferred book site.

Recent bestsellers from Roundfire are:

The Bookseller's Sonnets
Andi Rosenthal

The Bookseller's Sonnets intertwines three love stories with a tale of religious identity and mystery spanning five hundred years and three countries.

Paperback: 978-1-84694-342-3 ebook: 978-184694-626-4

Birds of the Nile
An Egyptian Adventure

N.E. David

Ex-diplomat Michael Blake wanted a quiet birding trip up the Nile – he wasn't expecting a revolution.

Paperback: 978-1-78279-158-4 ebook: 978-1-78279-157-7

Blood Profit$
The Lithium Conspiracy

J. Victor Tomaszek, James N. Patrick, Sr.

The blood of the many for the profits of the few... *Blood Profit$* will take you into the cigar-smoke-filled room where American policy and laws are really made.

Paperback: 978-1-78279-483-7 ebook: 978-1-78279-277-2

The Burden
A Family Saga

N.E. David

Frank will do anything to keep his mother and father apart. But he's carrying baggage – and it might just weigh him down ...

Paperback: 978-1-78279-936-8 ebook: 978-1-78279-937-5

The Cause

Roderick Vincent

The second American Revolution will be a fire lit from an internal spark.

Paperback: 978-1-78279-763-0 ebook: 978-1-78279-762-3

Don't Drink and Fly

The Story of Bernice O'Hanlon: Part One

Cathie Devitt

Bernice is a witch living in Glasgow. She loses her way in her life and wanders off the beaten track looking for the garden of enlightenment.

Paperback: 978-1-78279-016-7 ebook: 978-1-78279-015-0

Gag

Melissa Unger

One rainy afternoon in a Brooklyn diner, Peter Howland punctures an egg with his fork. Repulsed, Peter pushes the plate away and never eats again.

Paperback: 978-1-78279-564-3 ebook: 978-1-78279-563-6

The Master Yeshua

The Undiscovered Gospel of Joseph

Joyce Luck

Jesus is not who you think he is. The year is 75 CE. Joseph ben Jude is frail and ailing, but he has a prophecy to fulfil ...

Paperback: 978-1-78279-974-0 ebook: 978-1-78279-975-7

On the Far Side, There's a Boy
Paula Coston
Martine Haslett, a thirty-something 1980s woman, plays hard on the fringes of the London drag club scene until one night which prompts her to sign up to a charity. She writes to a young Sri Lankan boy, with consequences far and long.
Paperback: 978-1-78279-574-2 ebook: 978-1-78279-573-5

Tuareg
Alberto Vazquez-Figueroa
With over 5 million copies sold worldwide, *Tuareg* is a classic adventure story from best-selling author Alberto Vazquez-Figueroa, about honour, revenge and a clash of cultures.
Paperback: 978-1-84694-192-4

Readers of ebooks can buy or view any of these bestsellers by clicking on the live link in the title. Most titles are published in paperback and as an ebook. Paperbacks are available in traditional bookshops. Both print and ebook formats are available online.

Find more titles and sign up to our readers' newslett er at http://www.johnhuntpublishing.com/fiction

Follow us on Facebook at https://www.facebook.com/ JHPfiction and Twitter at https://twitter.com/JHPFiction